TAYLOR'S END

Naomi H Brown

Puddin' Pants Press

ISBN: 978-0-6482768-9-0 (Print)

ISBN: 978-0-6482768-2-1 (eBook)

Cover design by roosterrepublicpress.com

One

For weeks now, the sleepy rural community of Taylor's End had watched the sky, waiting for the crisp sun-filled days to give way to winter's vicious bite. The arthritic elderly, plagued by the cruel disease that crippled them, were grateful for the reprieve. Although they had been around long enough to understand that clear skies and mild temperatures at the end of the first month of winter were a decidedly bad sign of things to come.

Old-timers who had lived through the dreadful winter of '62 predicted a repeat of that utterly merciless season sixty-odd years earlier. They were not alone in their predictions. Many locals were bracing themselves for what they feared would be a particularly fierce winter when it finally came. Hopefully, when the cold front rolled in, folks would be adequately prepared. Full-page advertisements plastered the community newspaper. They warned the residents to stormproof their homes in preparation for this week's winter snowstorms.

Out in the east paddock, which ran along the now-defunct blacktop that had served as one of the main roads into town until the construction of the new highway a few years ago, Tom McCormack grumbled to himself as he tinkered with his bitch of a tractor. It had spluttered to a lurching stop the previous afternoon. The timing couldn't have been worse, if he believed the blasted weather reports. And although Tom didn't give two shits for the weather reporter on the six o'clock news, he reluctantly agreed with the twit's forecast of an approaching storm that would rival the Great Ice Age.

A greasy nut slipped out of his hand and fell among the dried tufts of grass at his feet. He cursed the ancient machine—not quite as old as himself, but not far from it—and spat a thick green wad of phlegm onto the ground behind him. At the rate he was going, winter would have come and gone, his livestock starved and dead, their skeletal remains littering the paddocks before he managed to repair the temperamental machine.

He was starting to wonder if it would be necessary to admit defeat and make a call to the guys at Fodder & Farm Machinery. After forking out most of his savings for a truckload of winter feed, the prospect of finding money to pay for a mechanic to come out to the farm and attempt to revive the tractor was particularly unappealing. No, he'd stick it out for a while longer. If he hadn't managed to get the tractor to turn over in another couple of hours, then he'd make the call.

Cussing under his breath, Tom stooped to search for the nut that had fallen from his hand. Movement on the road caught his attention. He shielded his eyes against the glare of the midmorning sun with his gnarled hand to take a better look. It was at least two hundred yards to the fence and the road beyond, and Tom's eyesight wasn't the best, but he'd be damned if some fool girl wasn't walking along the blacktop, just strolling along like she hadn't a care in the world. Never mind that the farm was over ten miles from Taylor's End, or that she was wearing a flimsy slip of a dress that barely reached midway down her thighs. He squinted, watching as she walked toward town. She had a scarlet coat draped over one arm, and Tom wondered why she didn't put it on. Although the sun was shining, and it was a good ten degrees warmer than ordinary, it was still too cold to wander around with bare limbs. The silly girl would catch pneumonia if she weren't abducted by some sicko pervert first.

It made absolutely no sense to him. What was she doing all the way out here anyway? These days, most people passing through Taylor's End on their way to someplace else used the highway, especially since those GPS gadgets had been updated to include the new road. It shaved at least ten minutes off the average trip thanks to improved conditions. So what exactly was she doing?

It occurred to him that she might have gotten a flat tire or, even worse, been involved in an accident. People unfamiliar with the road had often miscalculated the bends, taking the turns too fast and finding themselves in someone's paddock, surrounded by a herd of curious cattle.

"Hey!" he called out, walking toward the road. "Hello there. Is everything all right?" For a moment, he thought she didn't notice him and was going to walk right on by. He raised his arms and waved them above his head to get her attention. Still no reaction. "Is everything all right?" he asked again. That got her attention.

She paused midstride and turned in his direction. He waved again and hurried across the paddock to the fence that ran parallel to the narrow blacktop. The girl seemed reluctant to approach. Tom beckoned to her, and she picked her way down the slope toward the paddock.

"Hi. Is there a problem?" Tom asked. She joined him, maintaining a polite distance as she looked him over curiously. A strong breeze had picked up, whipping her long, dark hair into a mess of tangles. She brushed a lock of hair from her face.

"A problem?" she asked, seemingly perplexed by the question.

"Yeah, a problem. Did your car break down or something? I could go back to the house and call a tow truck for you if that helps."

She wrapped her slender hands around the top string of wire while she listened to Tom's offer, her head tilted slightly. "I don't have a car."

Tom frowned. He had been too busy examining her slightly disheveled appearance to notice at first. "You might want to let go of the fence. That's barbed wire you're holding." The girl glanced down, a puzzled expression on her delicate features. She released her grip and turned her hands palm upward to examine the damage. Jewel-like beads of crimson blood welled across her palms. "I hope you're up to date with your tetanus shots. Those barbs are as rusty as all hell," he said.

For the first time during their brief encounter, the glazed, spaced-out expression had left her face, and it seemed like she was present and focused on what he was saying. Tom didn't know much about drugs, just what he saw on television, and that was mostly sensationalist bullshit, but he wondered if the girl, who was only in her early twenties at most, was under the influence of something.

"I didn't even realize," she admitted with an embarrassed laugh. "Do you think that they will get infected?"

Tom nodded. "I reckon it's highly likely. As I said, that wire is well rusted, and the animals often reach across it, scraping themselves. And if you haven't washed up for a while, that's gonna make infection even more likely." She sighed and wiped her bloody palms on the front of her dress. Despite the black fabric and his poor vision, Tom could make out the ugly smears. They weren't the only dirty marks on the dress, and he wondered when she had last had a shower and a clean change of clothes.

"I've got a first aid kit over at the house if you want to follow me back there. I can treat those wounds before you continue on your way." It was not a genuine offer. He didn't have time to mess about helping some drugged-out stranger, and yet he'd opened his fool mouth and made the offer anyway.

"Thanks," she said. "That's sweet of you. If it's not too much trouble, I would appreciate the help. I'm not too keen on getting an infection." Tom nodded and spread apart two strands of wire so she could climb through. He noticed goosebumps covering her pale skin, and more than a few discolored bruises marked her arms and legs. Wherever she had come from, she'd had a hard time of it, by the look of her.

She followed him across the paddock. They paused at the tractor long enough for Tom to collect his toolbox before lugging it up the gently sloping hill to the farmhouse. They crossed the dirt drive, and his old cattle dog, Rosie, came out from her doghouse. She raced to the end of her chain, barking furiously at the stranger. Tom was surprised by the dog's aggressive turn. It was rare for Rosie to act in such a violent and protective manner. She pulled at the chain, bouncing back and forth. Her lips curled back from her snapping teeth.

"Settle down, Rosie. That's no way to act around a guest," the old man admonished his canine companion. "Try not to take any notice of her. She doesn't normally act this way. I honestly don't know what's got her so riled up."

The girl gave the dog a wide berth. Her eyes never left the animal, which provoked the dog even more. Tom ushered the bleeding girl inside and led her down the dimly lit hall, dusty pictures of better days hanging from the faded, wallpapered walls. They passed through a wide arched entry to the eat-in kitchen. "You'll have to excuse the mess," he apologized sheepishly. "It's just me and the grandson lives here, and we don't always clean up as best we should."

"That's OK. Truthfully, it's not nearly as bad as you might think. I doubt a bit of dust and a few dirty dishes ever killed anyone." She looked around the tired room with its dated cabinetry. The laminate was chipped and peeling in places. Dirty dishes crowded the sink, and a carton of juice sat abandoned on the counter. It was evident that a woman hadn't been inside the house for a very long time.

"Sit down at the table while I go fetch the first aid kit from the bathroom," said Tom. "I'll only be a minute."

The girl pulled out a chair and sat down, dropping her small shoulder bag on the table in front of her. It felt good to be off her feet, even if it was only for a few minutes. She had been walking all morning. Although she wasn't certain, she would have sworn it had been twenty-four hours since she'd last slept.

Tom returned with the first aid kit and placed it on the table beside the girl's purse. It was leather and finely made, and there was shiny gold hardware suggesting some designer label he'd never heard of.

"You said you don't have a car. Were you hitchhiking or something?" he asked. "I have to tell you you'll struggle to get a ride on that road. Since they built the new highway, it's mostly only local traffic that uses it, and even then, there aren't that many vehicles. Mostly the handful of folks who live out here really."

She watched as Tom opened the first aid kit and rummaged around inside, searching for antiseptic wipes and adhesive bandages. "Yeah, I noticed that. I got a lift last night, which helped, but they dropped me off a fair way out of town. I've been walking ever since."

Tom shook his head as he tore open the packaging of an antiseptic wipe. "It's not safe hitching lifts with strangers. You never know what sort of psycho could pick you up."

She smiled in amusement at his concern. "You're right. It can be dangerous, although the worst thing to happen so far seems to have been sticking myself on your rusty fence."

Tom asked her to hold her palms up so he could sterilize the wounds. She opened her fingers out, resting the backs of her hands on the tabletop. He wiped the tiny puncture wounds as gently as he could, hoping he wasn't causing her too much discomfort. Even with his ministrations, she'd be damn lucky if they didn't get infected. How on God's green earth hadn't she noticed the sharp metal barbs penetrating her skin?

In a mocking tone, completely unlike the lighter girlish voice she'd used earlier, she said, *"God's green earth?* You don't *actually* believe that crap, do you?"

Her eyes bore into him, dark and unflinching, and Tom suddenly questioned the wisdom of admitting the stranger into his home. "Well?" she pressed when he didn't answer. Tom shook his head, perplexed by the sudden change in the girl's demeanor and the icy atmosphere in the room. He pulled his hand back from hers.

She sprang forward and snatched his wrist in an instant, dragging him forward across the table. When their faces were only inches apart, she hissed, "Answer me, pig!"

He peered at her in horror, at her eyes black with rage. The bones in his wrist ground against each other painfully as she tightened her grip. It was inconceivable that a waif of a girl could overpower him so easily. Although he was getting on in years, Tom couldn't believe someone who was one hundred pounds fully clothed could dominate him with such little effort.

Confused and afraid, he stammered, "It was just a figure of speech. I didn't mean anything by it." Her eyes narrowed to hateful slits. They made him think of the darkest horrors of war, atrocities so violent and devoid of humanity that he'd spent the best part of a lifetime trying to forget them.

She sensed his vulnerability, and the barest hint of a smirk twisted up the corners of her mouth. "It must weigh heavily on you, the knowledge of who you truly are, and how easily you committed heinous acts against your fellow man."

Tom renewed his efforts to free himself from the girl's iron grip, but it was futile. Her hold on him was unshakable. "I don't know what you are referring to, but you need to let go of me right now and get the hell out of my house," he managed to say, with more command than he felt.

She threw her head back and laughed. The sound was sharp and brittle, like shards of glass grinding against each other. It sent chills through him, and he felt his stomach roil.

"What do you know of *hell*, old man?" she taunted, squeezing his wrist harder still, her nails digging into his fragile skin. "You might think you've been there, but those dead women in the jungle were like a leisurely picnic on a warm summer's day. Maybe I should stick around and show you just a tiny taste of hell. What do you think?"

A bone cracked in Tom's wrist. He cried out pathetically, ashamed of his weakness. "No! My grandson will be home soon. You need to leave. Please . . ." he begged, hoping the threat of someone showing up at any time would deter her from further violence.

"Mmmm. I *like* the sound of that. Someone a bit younger, more of a challenge. Do you think he'll have more fight in him than you do?" She leaned forward over the table, their faces so close that he could feel her breath on his cheek. Tom desperately wanted to avert his gaze, but his eyes were locked on hers. As he peered helplessly across at the stranger, he understood she was something more than a girl wandering the roads alone.

"Jesus, help me," he implored.

His plea, although almost inaudible, enraged the girl, and with a hateful snarl, she propelled him across the room with a vicious thrust. "Jesus won't help you. Nobody will." She pushed up from the table and stepped over the first aid kit that had been knocked to the floor. Its contents spilled across the linoleum tiles.

Tom lay in a crumpled heap on the floor beside the doorway. The wind was knocked out of him, and a trickle of blood dribbled from the corner of his mouth where he had bitten through his lip. He forced his eyes open long enough to see the girl bypass him and walk off down the hall. The front door opened, banging against the wall, followed by the sound of footsteps on the porch. Rosie barked briefly before yelping once. Then there was silence.

Tom's chest heaved as he forced air into his lungs, and he allowed his eyelids to close for a moment. Only a moment, though. He'd get up soon. He just needed to rest for a bit and catch his breath. Everything hurt, and the prospect of dragging himself to his feet was more than he could manage right now.

Two

A few hours later, the girl arrived at the outskirts of town. She paused for a minute to examine the large sign positioned in a manicured green space with picnic tables and colorful winter garden beds. The sign welcomed her to the cheerful community of Taylor's End. She couldn't quite recall the reason for passing by this way. The last twelve hours or so were foggy and unclear. Snippets of half-memories floated just beyond her recollection, taunting her with the promise of elucidation. She squeezed her eyes shut, willing herself to remember, yet the harder she tried, the more elusive the fragmented memories became.

Frustrated, she opened her eyes and continued into town. These memory lapses had been plaguing her for months now. Frightening chunks of time passed without her knowing what she'd done or where she'd been. Occasionally, an image would flash through her mind, so grim and foreboding that she would shy away from its implications, preferring to continue in ignorance.

When she'd first found herself wandering some lonely backroad with no idea of where she was, she'd dug her cell phone from the bottom of her purse, planning to call home, only to discover her voicemail full of hysterical messages from her family and closest friends. The short recordings prevented too much detail from being revealed, but she could piece together enough to know something had happened back home, and it wasn't good.

"Ella, please come home. Your father and I will help you in any way that we can. Please. Just call and tell us where you are," her mother's anguished voice had implored. The final message had been from her parents' lawyer, advising her to get in contact as soon as possible.

If a lawyer was trying to track her down, it had to be bad. The police were looking for her, and without knowing the extent of her crime, there was no way she'd return home. Withdrawing all the money from her bank card, she'd then destroyed all her identification and kept on moving. Fear of discovery pushed her onward, with no true destination in mind.

Now, after months of crossing the country, the nomadic lifestyle was almost second nature. She was sometimes forced to live rough. Other times her purse was filled with enough cash to provide a comfortable journey. The sedate existence before her memory blanks felt like a dream world that she could never revisit. Despite this, she would kill for a good feed and a comfy bed to sleep in. It had been a while since she'd had a decent meal or accommodation.

It took another twenty minutes to reach the main street. It was lunchtime, and the delicious aroma of deep-fried food had

Ella salivating as she continued down the tree-lined sidewalk. She stopped to study her reflection in one of the spotless windows of a shopfront and was disheartened by what she saw. Her boots were dusty, and her long dark hair was a mess of tangles thanks to the chill wind that had stirred up in the last half hour. She slipped on her coat to escape the cold, concealing some of the bruises and scrapes covering her slender body.

As she examined her shabby appearance in the glass window pane, she saw a bunch of teenagers sauntering toward her. Clutching the edges of her coat together across her narrow chest, she slowly turned to face the group of boys. They were almost comical in their matching uniform of baggy jeans and oversize hoodies, topped off with angled baseball caps. They had spent far too much time watching rap videos and taking fashion cues from their idols.

Too bad no one had bothered to tell them how ridiculous a bunch of countryfied, corn-fed white boys looked trying to emulate the African-American musicians they worshipped. She thought of The Offspring's song "Pretty Fly (For a White Guy)." These boys looked a lot like the try-hard from the music video. Stifling a giggle, she cocked an eyebrow at them questioningly.

They crowded around her, eyeing her up and down appreciatively. An older boy with a neck tattoo and penetrating blue eyes said, "Damn girl, you sure are a fine piece of ass, even all covered up in that grubby-looking coat. Why don't you open it up and give us a peek at the goods inside?"

Feeling vulnerable, she took a step back and pulled the coat tighter around her body. "How about no, you pathetic, half-baked wannabe?" she retorted, not wanting to show even a hint of weakness.

If they thought there was the slightest chance of getting under her skin, she wouldn't stand a chance. They couldn't do much more than make lewd comments while it was broad daylight in the middle of downtown, but that might change if she decided to stick around for more than a day or two. The last thing she needed was for a restless gang of youths to start trouble for her.

One of the boys turned his head and chortled, quickly fumbling around in his pocket for a cigarette. His big-talking friend scowled at him before back-peddling. "Whoa. Take it easy, sweetheart. I was only messing with you." He held his hands up in surrender. "No need to get your titties in a twist."

Ella gaped at him, wondering if the wannabe gangster *believed* the bullshit he dribbled. Part of her wanted to tear shreds off him for being such a misogynistic pig, but she held her tongue, if only to avoid trouble. She had a niggling feeling that it could end badly otherwise.

"Look, I don't want any drama, so please let me pass." She stepped forward, desperately hoping one of the boys would move aside. For a second, they continued to block her path, but then the stocky one with a buzz cut shuffled closer to one of his buddies so she could squeeze past. She caught his eye and nodded her thanks before continuing along the sidewalk. Despite feeling their stares as she walked away, Ella refused to look back.

"What an uppity fuckin' bitch," the boy with the tattooed neck grumbled. "Who'd wanna tap a bitch like that anyway? I bet she's no fun."

The others agreed half-heartedly, their eyes still following the stranger as she wandered off down the sidewalk.

"Hey, Connor, you got any weed left?"

The boy with the shaved head looked around at his friends and slowly nodded. "Yeah, I've got a little something," he admitted. They knew he usually had something to smoke. It was probably the main reason why they let him tag along when he had nothing better to do. They would kick his ass if they discovered he was carrying and hadn't shared it with them. One of the boys grinned and slapped him on the back. "Let's go smoke that shit." He followed them as they headed away from the main street.

Ella paused outside the post office, an imposing red brick building that was over one hundred and fifty years old, according to the brass plaque proudly displayed near the entrance. She stopped an elderly woman making her way down the steps, a stack of parcels in her pencil-thin arms. By the look of things, someone had gone crazy on the home shopping channels.

"Excuse me?" Ella asked. "Could you point me in the right direction of a good place to eat? I just got into town, and I'd kill for a decent meal." She smiled, displaying teeth perfected by years of orthodontic work. Inexplicably, the attempt at friendliness didn't quite hit the mark. The woman, who must have been pushing eighty, eyed her suspiciously and juggling the stack of parcels, reached up and fingered the small gold cross hanging on a chain around her neck.

"I can see that you are not from around here," the old woman said, in that imperious tone that only the elderly could ever truly pull off. "There is a diner on the corner of the next block that seems quite popular. I can't say I have ever eaten there myself. But people rave about the Russian's homestyle cooking. Now, I'm in a hurry, so you will have to excuse me." She frowned, shaking her head in displeasure, and continued down the steps.

Taken aback by the old woman's curt response, Ella watched her scurry across the street. Whatever happened to country hospitality? If her interactions so far were anything to go on, Taylor's End wasn't exactly the most welcoming of communities. It was a disappointing prospect. Wandering across the country solo was a lonely enterprise. If she was completely honest with herself, the lack of companionship and sense of isolation were beginning to get her down.

Something dark and threatening lurked just beyond recognition. The holes in her memory only added to her feelings of being an interloper. The bitter longing for a familiar face gnawed at her like the hunger pangs cramping her stomach. She closed in on the diner and the mouthwatering aromas emanating from within.

Shaking off the sudden melancholy that had settled over her, Ella paused outside the diner long enough to square her shoulders and read the bold yellow sign painted across its glass window. People seated on stools that ran the length of the large window peered out at her curiously from between the bright yellow letters. Realizing she was staring like a half-wit, she pushed open the glass door. A small bell jangled overhead.

A few people stared at her entrance, but most were too invested in their meals to pay any attention. Ella made her way over to the counter. She half-listened to snippets of gossip swapped between mouthfuls of the day's special while she waited for service. After a few minutes, a large plain-looking woman, her greying hair pulled back in a loose bun, came up to her and smiled warmly. Her teeth were big and square, not unlike the rest of her. When she smiled, Ella smiled back. Ella already liked the place, and she hadn't even tried the food yet.

"Sorry about the wait, hon, but it's always hectic in here at lunchtime. It should start to quiet down as soon as the lunch crowd heads back to work. What can I get for you today?" Ella read the menu board, considering her options. "Today's special is beef stroganoff served with a creamy mash. We also have pumpkin soup, if you want something lighter."

Ella shook her head vigorously. "No soup, thanks. I haven't eaten for a day or two, so I'll need something more substantial —although I'm sure the soup is yummy."

The big woman took a pen and pad from the pocket of her apron and gawked at her. "Are you kidding me? In that case, you need to hurry up and decide what you want so I can get some food into you. It's not right going hungry like that."

"I think I'll get the cheeseburger and fries with a chocolate thickshake. I know it's not very healthy, but ..."

The woman scribbled down her order and ripped the sheet from the pad. "Hon, by the look of it, you could use the calories. I reckon a strong breeze would easily blow you over."

"Not quite, but I understand what you're saying. It's hard to eat regularly when I'm always on the road."

The woman shook her head in dismay. "That's no way to live. Take a seat. I'll have your food out to you in a flash."

Ella plunked onto a stool vacated by a harried-looking man in a crumpled business suit. She was glad to be off her feet. While she waited for her food, she considered the woman who had taken her order. She was almost certain she could detect a Russian accent when the waitress spoke. Ella debated whether it would be rude to ask when she returned with her thickshake and a plate piled high with fries.

"Here you go. Dig in. Do you want ketchup?"

Ella jammed a fry into her mouth and nodded. "Yes please." She sipped at the thickshake, sucking the viscous drink up through the straw with considerable effort.

The big woman returned with the ketchup bottle, placing it on the counter beside Ella's plate. She took a cloth and wiped up some crumbs, taking the time to clean up after the lunch crowd, now quieting down.

"So are you just passing through, or do you plan on sticking around on a more permanent basis? I don't mean to sound nosy, but it's a small town, and we could sure use a new face or two around the place. Folks get the idea that life's going to be sweeter in a bigger town someplace else, so they pack up their things and move on out, leaving Taylor's End that little bit smaller each time. It would be nice to have it work the other way for a change."

Ella took a bite of the burger, surprised by the woman's frank admission. "You must genuinely care about this town," Ella replied. "Truthfully, I don't have any solid plans. I kind of flitter from place to place. If I like it here, I could always stick around for a while," she said, shrugging.

"I'm Anna, by the way. I probably should have introduced myself before giving you the hard sell on country living."

"You were flat out earlier. I'm Ella, and this might be the best burger I have ever eaten." Anna smiled at the compliment. "I don't suppose you know of anywhere cheap to stay?"

Anna sighed and rested her ample backside against the bench behind her. She glanced around the diner as she considered the question. The lunch crowd had thinned out. There were only five customers left in the diner, including the girl seated at the counter in front of her. "Only the Motor Inn comes to mind, but it might get a bit pricey if you plan on staying more than a couple of nights. You could check the bulletin board on the wall over there." She pointed across the diner to a large board covered with various business cards and notices. "People sometimes advertise rooms to let. Do you want anything else? A coffee? Some pie? Or would you like the check?"

"Pie is tempting, but I'd better not. I need to watch my money, at least until I can pick up some work."

After paying for her meal, Ella crossed the diner, weaving between tables. She paused in front of the bulletin board. It was crammed with sheets of paper printed with upcoming community events. There were hastily scribbled For Sale signs written by people desperate to part with unwanted goods. Even the local church had posted flyers welcoming newcomers to the Sunday service. "Damn it," she cursed under her breath. People were advertising for practically everything except rooms to let.

Then she spotted a dog-eared business card partially obscured by a bright printout touting Lizzy's Babysitting Services. She plucked the tack from the board and removed the card: *Webster's Boarding House—Affordable Rooms & Home Cooked Meals Guaranteed. Corner of Bourke & Faithful Streets, Taylor's End.* Considering her complete lack of alternatives, Ella thought it sounded reasonable enough.

"I wouldn't bother if I were you," a male voice advised. Ella turned to see a young man not much older than her seated at a table, nursing a cup of coffee.

"I'm sorry, were you talking to me?" she asked.

He smiled and nodded. "Sure was. You don't want to stay at Webster's. The place is a real dump. And the guy that owns it is a total jerk."

Ella took a step toward his table and returned his grin. "I'm not in a position to be too picky. I only got into town today, and I need a place to crash."

The guy sipped at his coffee and motioned for her to join him at the table. "I'm Christian." He reached out, and she met him halfway, his hand closing around hers in a warm and secure grip. She couldn't recall the last time she had even had a normal conversation with a guy her age, much less had any physical contact with them. Her slightly grubby and disheveled appearance made her acutely self-conscious, and she drew her hand away. "Do you want to have a coffee?" he asked. "I've still got twenty minutes before I'm due back at work."

"I don't drink coffee," she blurted before she could think of a better answer. She blushed, and silently berated herself for being so socially inept. She hadn't always been this awkward. Lack of practice had seriously impaired her ability to flirt.

"Although I'm inclined to distrust anyone who doesn't drink coffee, I'm willing to give you a second chance. Would a piece of pie entice you to join me?"

She liked his slightly lopsided smile, and despite having only just finished lunch, Ella couldn't refuse a free slice of pie. "OK. You've won me over with the promise of pie."

She pulled out a chair and sat opposite him. He motioned for a waitress, and a gangly young woman with brittle bleached hair made her way over to the table. "What else can I get you, Christian?" she asked in a syrupy voice, ignoring Ella.

"Two slices of pie with some of that fluffy canned cream would be great, Cindy."

"Sure thing. Do you need a refill on the coffee?"

Christian checked the cup's contents, glanced across at Ella, and shook his head almost regretfully. "Nah, I'm good." Cindy gave Ella a sideways glance.

"I don't think she likes me," Ella said.

Christian shrugged. "Probably not. Don't take it personally. She hates any girl I talk to. Poor Cindy has had a crush on me since she started working here a few years ago."

"Have you considered eating somewhere else? Assuming you're not interested in her, that is."

Christian grimaced. "Wait until you try the pie, then tell me to eat someplace else. Plus, Anna is like an aunt to me."

There was an uncomfortable silence between them while they waited for their order. Ella picked at her nails self-consciously, wishing she had some clean clothes and a hairbrush to detangle her matted hair. She was starting to question Christian's reason for inviting her to join him. He might not be interested in the bottle blonde working the tables, but that didn't explain why he wanted to talk to some grubby homeless girl without any direction or purpose. Ella had nearly succeeded in talking herself into standing up and walking away when the waitress approached the table with two generous helpings of pie.

"Here you go." She placed the plates in front of them and reluctantly retreated. Ella picked up her spoon and scooped up some pie. Christian watched expectantly as she popped it into her mouth.

"Well?" he asked. "Was I right? Isn't it the best damn pie you've ever tasted?"

Ella nodded appreciatively while she chewed. "It's delicious," she admitted with a smile once she swallowed. They both ate the dessert with relish, their joint enjoyment dissolving the earlier awkwardness.

"Are you sure you wanna stay at that shithole boarding house?" Christian asked.

Ella lowered her spoon and looked across at him. "Yeah, I'm going to stay at that shithole boarding house. Unless you know someplace else where I can go?"

"I wish I did," he replied regretfully.

Ella licked cream from the back of her spoon, and Christian swallowed. Damn. She didn't even realize what she was doing. He shifted in his seat. Over at the cash register, Cindy glared at them, the stranger's provocative display not lost on her either.

"I'll be fine," Ella said. "I can take care of myself. All I need are clean sheets and a hot shower. Anything on top of that is a bonus."

Christian shook his head. While he didn't doubt her ability to handle herself, she'd probably never met a redneck loser like Jim Webster before. "OK, just watch yourself."

Ella pushed her chair back and stood up. "Thanks for the pie. It was delicious. But I'm utterly wrecked, and I need to find a place to sleep."

"Will I see you again?" he asked.

Ella placed her purse over her shoulder and considered the question. He stirred something inside her. For the first time in months, she was willing to risk getting to know someone. "Sure. You know where I'll be staying." And with that, she turned and left.

Christian watched as she slipped out the door and disappeared down the street. He realized too late that he didn't even know her name. Shit. Checking his cell phone, he jumped up and threw some money on the table. He waved to Cindy. "Keep the change. I'm gonna be late." He dashed out the door with his helmet in hand. If there weren't any cops around, he might reach the hospital before he was due back from his lunch break.

Three

I t took Ella nearly half an hour to locate Webster's Boarding House. After leaving the diner, she had to stop and ask for directions a couple times. More than once, she wondered if she'd taken a wrong turn. Two blocks back from Main Street, the neighborhood went from quaint country to dilapidated hick. The county must have given up on the northeast side of town long ago. Worn dirt tracks replaced the neat concrete sidewalks elsewhere.

Ella had to watch where she walked to avoid stepping in the countless piles of dog shit scattered everywhere. Empty beer bottles lay discarded in the gutter, and the odd chip packet caught the breeze and skittered across the ground. Weeds grew high along crooked fences. In overgrown driveways, rusted-out cars, jacked up on cinderblocks, outnumbered roadworthy vehicles three to one. She was starting to understand why Christian had tried to warn her about the boarding house. It was unlikely that a reputable establishment would do business in such a shabby area.

She passed a house with a pair of toddlers running around out front, unsupervised. They ran over to the fence when they spotted her, abandoning the battered plastic dolls they had been playing with. Snot ran freely from their noses, and neither child looked like it had been bathed in days. They wrapped their small fingers through the chain-link fence and stared up at her.

Ella glanced down at the grotty pair. Their unwashed hair and stained clothing reminded her of her own neglected appearance. "Hey, lady, where you going?" the older child asked. His whiny voice annoyed her, and she turned away from them without answering the question. She was too tired to engage in a pointless conversation with a couple of kids that weren't even potty trained yet.

Less than five minutes later, she found Webster's Boarding House. It stood on the corner of Faithful and Bourke Streets like a huge diseased tooth. She gazed at it from across the road and seriously contemplated turning around and marching back into town. Instead, exhaustion and the cold wind whipping at her face convinced her to cross the street.

Stepping between a pair of run-down vehicles parked on the median strip, she opened the front gate, cringing as the rusted hinges squealed in protest. From the outside, the building looked like a total dump. It had most likely been a proud and eye-catching dwelling in its heyday. But years of neglect had taken its toll. The paint had faded and peeled away from the two-story home in many places, allowing rot to take hold. The inside was bound to be as shabby as the exterior.

A young pit bull came racing along the side of the property and launched itself at the chain-link gate, all snarls and snapping jaws. Great globs of saliva flew from the dog's mouth as it barked and gnashed at the wire in front of it. Ella jumped back, startled. "Easy, boy. I won't hurt you," she cooed. It was futile. Her voice was anything but soothing. It seemed to agitate the dog further.

A window at the front of the house was hoisted up, and a voice boomed from within. "Leave the fuckin' dog alone, or it'll chew ya goddamn face off!"

Ella retreated along the path, unnerved by the menacing outburst. She was reaching for the gate when the front door flew open, and a man stepped out onto the porch. "Are you some bible basher? Because I've told your lot to keep the hell off my property." He growled at her, sounding an awful lot like his dog.

Turning around to face him, Ella shook her head. "I'm not a bible basher. I found your business card on the bulletin board at a diner in town. I'm looking for a place to stay. Do you have any rooms available?" Part of her wanted him to say no. Then the decision would be made for her, and she would be forced to find someplace else to stay.

"Why didn't you say that straight up?" he complained.

He stood on the porch above her. His arms crossed over his protruding belly as he scowled down at her. He was a large hulking man. The knowing gleam in his eye made her believe that he was accustomed to using his size to intimidate people. It worked. She was sorely tempted to turn on her heel and leave. Desperation made her stand her ground.

"It wasn't like you gave me a chance," Ella said. "You started hollering before I even reached the porch."

He shrugged and dropped his hands to his sides. "Like I said, I thought you were a bible basher or some idiot peddling overpriced junk."

He beckoned for her to follow him inside. "You're in luck. It might not enjoy a five-star rating, but we manage to keep the place at full occupancy most of the time. However, we do have one room available. I'm not sure you'll find the accommodations to your liking."

"If you have a room, I'll take it," she replied as she climbed the porch steps and followed him into the boarding house.

"Suit yourself, just as long as you understand that we ain't no Holiday Inn."

"Yeah, I think I got that."

It was dark and dusty inside the boarding house, the heavy drapes letting in little natural light. The unpleasant odor of old cooking oil fouled the air, and Ella wondered if they ever opened the windows long enough to circulate some fresh air.

The man led her into a small room at the front of the house that served as his office. He squeezed behind a desk littered with overdue bills and crumpled receipts and sank into a worn chair. The upholstery was stained with years of ass sweat and food spills. He did not offer Ella a seat, so she perched on the edge of a chair piled with hot-rod magazines.

"I haven't seen you around town before," he said.

Ella couldn't tell if it was a question or a statement, and she didn't much care. Engaging in small talk with the man was the last thing she wanted to do. The sour stink of sweat mixed with a pungent yeasty smell filled the small office, and she just wanted to hurry up and register for the room so she could get away from him.

Ella shifted in her seat, and a handful of glossy magazines toppled to the floor. Jim glared at her, and she hastily bent over to scoop them up.

"Leave the damn things on the floor," he snapped, eyeing the hem of her dress. Ella placed the magazines back on the pile and adjusted the hem of her dress, tugging it down as far as it would go. She was glad there was a desk between them.

"Sorry about that."

"It doesn't matter. How long are you planning on sticking around? It's a boarding house, not a motel. The minimum stay is a week. You got a problem with that?" A dull gold band encircled his ring finger, proof that some poor woman had shackled herself to the odorous man. Ella wondered what it must be like being married to him.

"I'm not sure how long I'll be staying," she said, "but a week should be fine."

He sifted through the mess of papers on the desk and eventually uncovered a red vinyl-bound ledger. Flipping through the pages, he located the most recent entry and scribbled the date on the blank line underneath. "Got some ID on you?"

Ella slowly shook her head. She'd had a driver's license once, but she disposed of it some time ago. She had nothing in her possession to prove who she was: no license, no Social Security number, no phone, not even a library card. She was a ghost.

"You don't have any ID?" he asked incredulously.

She shook her head. "Is that a problem?"

He ran a hand over his stubbled chin and sighed. "I don't suppose so. If you pay in cash and in advance, it shouldn't be an issue. Are you an illegal or something?"

"I'm not an illegal immigrant. I just lost my wallet a while ago, and I haven't had a chance to get any of my cards replaced. You know how it is."

Jim studied her from across the desk. "Do you think you can manage a name for the ledger at least?"

Ella suppressed the urge to roll her eyes. The guy was an obnoxious jerk. "Ella."

"Ella what? You have a last name, don't you?"

Ella stared at him blankly. Why did so much of her life feel like a black hole? With every day that passed, a piece of her identity seemed to fade away. "It's Ella . . ."

"Yeah, I got that part already, sweetheart." He drummed the desk with his fingers. There was a game on, and he was wasting valuable time screwing around, waiting for her to answer the goddamn question.

Ella glanced at the faded print of Marilyn Monroe hanging on the wall behind Jim. She was naked and stretched out against a red velvet backdrop. "Ella Monroe," she said.

"Monroe? As in Marilyn?" he said, cocking a thumb over his shoulder at the picture.

"Yes. Monroe, as in Marilyn. M-O-N-R-O-E."

"Thanks," he replied drily. "And you said you didn't know how long you'll be staying?"

"Not at the moment. If it's all right with you, I'll pay for a week and see how it goes. If I like it here, I might stick around longer."

"You're on the move a lot by the sound of it."

Ella shrugged. "I get around."

Jim ran his tongue across his bottom lip and eyed her up and down. Clearing his throat, he announced, "It's a week's board and the same as a deposit in advance. The deposit's refundable at checkout. Did I mention we take cash only?"

"You didn't, but cash works for me. How much do I owe you?"

"Two hundred and eighty dollars. That includes the deposit."

Ella fished around in her purse and pulled out a handful of crumpled bills, smoothing out the creases as she counted them out onto the desk. When she finished counting, she handed them to Jim. He flicked through the bills to check she wasn't trying to shortchange him. When he was satisfied it was all there, he removed a small cashbox from one of the desk drawers. He placed the money inside and secured the box before putting it back in the drawer. He tossed the ledger across the desk and motioned for her to sign it. She took the pen he flicked in her direction and scribbled her signature.

"OK then. Now that that's done, I'll show you to your room."

"Great." Ella rose and followed him out of the office, waiting while he pulled the door shut and locked it.

"That's the guest lounge across there," he said. "The television remote should be in the wicker basket on the coffee table, but if it's not, I'd suggest checking behind the lounge cushions. The kitchen is through that door to the right of the stairs. Put your name on any food that's yours. Otherwise, it's fair game. Somebody will probably steal it anyway."

"How many other people live here?" she asked.

He started up the stairs, the wooden boards creaking under his weight. "I live in an apartment on the ground floor with my wife and two boys. The older one has a room in the basement since he thinks he's too good to share with his folks anymore.

There are three other boarders here on the second floor." He led her across the landing and pointed down the hall. "The bathroom is the last door on the right. Providing toiletries is your responsibility, but you look like you're traveling kind of light."

Ella glanced down at her purse, which wouldn't hold much more than a wallet, some lip balm, and a hairbrush. Since she'd tossed the wallet in a trash bin at a Burger King somewhere in Nevada, she didn't have much after paying for the room. "I guess I'll have to walk down to the supermarket later and get some supplies."

Jim gave the girl an odd look. "I'll get the wife to bring you a towel and a bar of soap if we have any spares. That way, you can at least have a shower. There are some specks of something on your chest." He pointed at her décolletage, and Ella was quick to button her coat. "Looks like dried sauce or something. Anyway, your room is up in the attic." He pointed to a steep flight of stairs leading up to the attic. They were narrow and so dark she couldn't see the top until he flipped a switch on the wall and a dusty bulb lit the way. "It don't look like much from down here, but it's probably the best room we have as long as the stairs don't bother you."

"Stairs don't bother me," Ella assured him.

"Good. Would you believe we've had the same tenant in that room for over twenty years? Ms. Reid moved in straight after her divorce and never moved out. God knows I tried to get rid of her over the years. I inherited her from the previous owner, my wife's old man, and she wouldn't budge. Sometimes, I think she stuck around just to piss me off."

"Wasn't she a good tenant?"

"She never stopped nagging me to fix this or fix that. My wife even offered to relocate Ms. Reid to one of the rooms on the second floor to save her having to tackle the attic stairs, but she politely declined the offer every time. I still can't believe she's finally gone."

"Did she die up there?" Ella asked.

Jim laughed and shook his head. "No frigging way. The old coot went and got the Alzheimer's disease, started forgetting shit, stopped eating and showering. In the end, she had to be taken away to one of those assisted-living facilities."

"That's too bad."

"It didn't happen soon enough, if you ask me. Anyway, up you go. Ladies first and all that." Jim waved her up the stairs with a lewd smirk, and Ella cringed. What a creep. She gave him a withering look before climbing the stairs, acutely aware of his lustful stares as he followed behind her.

Ella reached the top of the stairs and stood with her back pressed against the wall, putting as much distance between her and Jim as physically possible. He reached the tiny landing, huffing and puffing. The stink of him was overbearing in the tight space. He eyed her for a long moment, and she was sure he was going to proposition her, but the dirty look she directed at him must have given him second thoughts, because he slipped the key into the lock and opened the door.

"My wife painted the room after Ms. Reid left, said it needed freshening up. We got a new mattress too, so the old lady smell should be gone now."

Ella squeezed past him, fleeing into the relative safety of the room. The room surprised her, and it must have shown on her face. "It looks great. I'm sure it will be comfortable." She yanked the key out of the door before slamming it shut, relieved to have a barrier between her and the sleazy landlord. She made a mental note to watch out for him. He wasn't someone she wanted to be alone with if she could avoid it. She turned the lock before surveying the room.

It was surprisingly pleasant, not rundown and tatty like she had expected. It was spacious and well lit thanks to the fresh white paint on the walls and a large window that filled the room with sunlight. An old-fashioned brass bed, neatly made up with a pastel patchwork quilt, was pushed against one wall. A chest of drawers, fashionably distressed in the shabby-chic style, stood on the opposite. A mirror on top of the drawers and a few carefully placed knickknacks made the place homier.

Ella walked over to the window and dropped her bag onto the wooden school desk beneath the window. The view was nothing special, mostly just rooftops and untidy backyards, but what did she expect for a hundred and forty bucks a week? She shrugged out of her coat and slung it over the chair. A shower would have been wonderful, but until someone brought her a towel and some soap, she couldn't do much about it. Instead, she collapsed onto the bed, wrapping herself in the quilt. Her eyes slipped shut, and she was asleep almost instantly.

Four

J im stood outside the room, his hand hovering over the doorknob. The girl's swift dismissal enraged him. How dare she slam the fuckin' door in his face? The urge to beat on the door until the uppity little bitch let him in was almost more than he could bear. The look of disdain she'd given him at the top of the stairs was infuriating. If she only knew who she was dealing with, she wouldn't be so quick to dismiss him. No fuckin' way. He had half a mind to use the master key and storm into the room and teach her something about respect.

He rubbed his crotch. The boner he'd sprung while watching Ella climb the stairs was already beginning to wilt. Ten years earlier he would have had to toss off to get rid of the damn thing before it gave him blue balls. Now, if he didn't act on it immediately, his dick deflated like a punctured balloon. It was getting old that did it. He was over forty now, and everything was going downhill fast.

He'd been built like a brick shithouse when he was younger, all thick muscle, bulging through his shirts even when he was relaxed. Slowly that muscle had turned to fat, especially around his gut. The beer had a lot to answer for. Since getting into the habit of putting away a six-pack or two each day, his body had started to pack it on.

A soft cock, a soft body, and completely powerless to change. How could Jim ever give up the only thing in his life that made his shitty existence bearable? If it weren't for the anesthetizing effects of the alcohol, he would have gone postal long ago.

Life hadn't quite turned out as expected for Jim Webster. Fresh out of high school, life had been rife with promise. He'd been young, fit, and good-looking. He'd had a group of like-minded friends, and they'd known how to have fun. They'd gone to work—in his case as an auto mechanic for a local establishment that had an excellent reputation around town—partied on the weekends and then started the process all over again the following week. Life was sweet.

Then his high school sweetheart had fucked everything and gone and got pregnant. Determined to be the gentleman, Jim had proposed to Sophie shortly after he'd learned he was going to be a father. It was the right thing to do, and he still loved her. He knew how Sophie felt about abortion, so a termination was never an option. If she refused to scrape out the fetus, he'd have to do the right thing and put a ring on it. After all, she was his sweetheart. They'd been together for over four years. What sort of chump abandoned his girl when things started getting rough? Initially, it had all gone reasonably smoothly. Married life hadn't been so bad. The only real, definable change had been the wedding band on his finger. Sometimes, on a night down at the Blue Two Tavern with his buddies, that gold band circling his finger acted as a deterrent when he was trying to flirt with a girl, but usually the skanky bitches drinking at the blue-collar bar couldn't give a shit if a dude was wearing a wedding ring.

It wasn't until he knocked up Sophie with baby number two that he started to feel the pressure. A wife and one brat to feed was one thing. Two stinky, whining kids were something else altogether. Coming home after a hard day toiling in the workshop was a complete downer. How could a man relax when the second he stepped inside the house, he was bombarded by a couple of brats, yanking at his overalls, demanding his attention?

Then there was his wife. She was only in her early twenties, but having the babies had spread her hips, and her tits hung low and heavy from breastfeeding. It was damn near impossible to get excited by a woman who had let herself go in favor of running around after a pair of annoying kids. No wonder he'd started drinking more heavily after getting hitched. Who wouldn't?

As the years rolled by and he felt more and more trapped in his domestic life, he struggled to contain the anger and frustration growing inside him. The cycle never changed. Slugging it away at work, day after never-fuckin'-ending day. Head down to the tavern for a beer or two, then home to face the wife and kids.

Home for him consisted of walking through the door to a mess of gaudy plastic toys littering the floor, waiting for unsuspecting feet to trip over them. The boys constantly fought, yelling and crying while Sophie sat around watching her soaps. They were left to run amok in an apartment so small that there wasn't a single space he could call his own.

To this day, Jim remembered the precise moment when all the frustrations of marriage and family and unfulfilled dreams came to a head. It was a Thursday night, and he was enjoying a few beers at the tavern. His buddy Jerry had somehow managed to hook up with a pair of tarts so easy they weren't even wearing panties. He'd seen it himself when the redhead flashed him after he bought a round of drinks. The momentary glimpse of her ginger pussy had sent a thrill of excitement through him, and he'd had every intention of finding out exactly what she tasted like. Except Sophie had already called the tavern twice, begging him to come home because Connor had a fever, and she needed him to stop in at the gas station and get some Tylenol. Fuckin' bitch was determined to kill his buzz.

With a heavy heart and heavy balls, Jim left Jerry with the bimbos and made his way home. Shit, he'd thought as he pulled away from the gas station, there was probably nothing even wrong with the boy. He whined and cried all the time, doing whatever he could to gain his mother's attention.

When he walked through the door, Sophie didn't even acknowledge him. She was too engrossed in one of those pathetic shows of hers to get off her lazy ass and say hello, much less thank him for leaving the bar early. She called the tavern repeatedly, hounding him with her nagging requests and defiling the sanctity of the one place he went where he could still feel like his own man. There was not a single fucking word of thanks. No apology for dragging him away from the bourbons and babes—not that she had a clue about the other women—no, "Hello hon, how was your day?" Just the sound of her stupid fucking laughter as she cackled at that idiot television show.

After closing the front door behind him, he went to tell her he had picked up the Tylenol for Connor. She shushed him. She didn't even turn away from the television. Instead, she kept on watching the mindless drivel, preferring the two-bit actors overselling the preposterous plots to greeting her hard-working husband. "What the fuck did you say?" he bellowed indignantly. Sophie finally tore her eyes away from the show and looked back at him fearfully. It hadn't been the swearing that alarmed her. He swore all the time, even in front of the children. Instead, it was the way he said it. There was a vicious undertone that set alarm bells ringing in her head.

She quickly stood up and smoothed the front of her floral print dress self-consciously. "I'm sorry, honey. I got a bit caught up in the story."

Jim strode across the cramped living room and swung his arm in a powerful arc, his open hand connecting with her face. The blow sent her sprawling across the floor. Her lip split from the impact, and she stifled a shocked sob. Once the ringing in her head eased, she got to her feet, swaying unsteadily as she cupped her hands to her chin to catch the blood dripping onto the carpet.

Jim reached out and took her face in his hand, pinching her cheeks as he examined the damage. He peered into her teary eyes and smiled grimly. "Don't you ever tell me to shush again. Do you understand?"

Sophie, still half dazed from the attack, nodded up at him. He released her, and she scurried away, locking herself in the bathroom to sob and tend to her wounds.

That first taste of violence against his spouse was an enlightening experience for Jim Webster. There was life *before* slapping Sophie—the monotonous drudgery filled with frustration and disappointment and the bitterness of dreams unfulfilled. And then there was life *after* the slap. All his shortcomings remained the same. Lashing out at his wife couldn't change that, no matter how desperately he wished it could. But it did provide a certain degree of relief, reducing the unbearable tension that built as the day-to-day grind wore him down.

It was not an isolated incident. The Webster household would change forever after that first night. There would be no more pretending they were high school sweethearts living the American dream. The bruises and bloody noses, and split lips told a different story.

Initially, it only happened when she truly deserved it—a punishment for those occasions when she failed to fulfill her duties, which was practically every other day when Jim thought about it. She obviously wasn't the sharpest tool in the shed. Despite numerous warnings, dinner was constantly late. Why couldn't she ever manage to serve dinner on time? Not an hour before, so his meal was stone cold and congealed on the plate. Not an hour after he came home from work, exhausted and hungry. Sophie knew the time he finished. Was it that difficult to have some meat and veggies on the plate shortly after he stepped through the door?

Sometimes he wondered if she secretly enjoyed it when he brought her into line. Otherwise, why the fuck would she keep pissing him off at every opportunity? Dinner was either late or too early. *Smack.* The house looked like a shit heap, the floor strewed with too many toys to count. *A punch to the gut.* She tried to shrug him off when he wanted some action, and he would backhand her until she became more agreeable. Admittedly, once he started reining her in with some physical discipline, whatever affection they had once shared was well and truly extinguished. And while a small part of him mourned the loss, he undoubtedly felt more powerful giving her the occasional thrashing.

Not only did the beatings help Sophie understand her place in the family hierarchy, but they also provided Jim with a sense of sexual arousal that inevitably led to a satiating of his needs in the bedroom. Whenever he had a go at his wife with his fists or the thick leather belt he wore, his cock grew long and hard. A split lip or puffy eye was no deterrent. Frequently, any discipline he dished out ended with a trip to the bedroom. And after he brought her into line, the sex was always out of this world. It was rougher and dirtier, and the climax so explosive he slept like a lamb afterward.

Most of Jim's rage was directed at his wife during the early years of their marriage. The boys had a way of disappearing into the background whenever things turned nasty. He suspected Sophie had pulled them aside at some point and told them to clear out if daddy got angry and started yelling.

Once Connor was six and his brother only a few years younger, Jim finally grew tired of waiting for their no-good mother to rein in the sniveling brats when they started acting up. After showing the boys what happened when they defied him, he turned his attention to Sophie. To her credit, she didn't make a sound until he removed his thick leather belt and flogged her from one side of the room to the other. The vicious bite of the belt buckle made the stupid bitch scream so loud that the neighbors heard. One of the nosy goddamned do-gooders called the cops on him.

The flashing lights on the cruiser as it pulled up announced the arrival of the police moments before they pounded on the front door. Jim quickly threaded his belt back through his pants, growling at his wife to keep her mouth shut, or there'd be worse to come. Then he reluctantly opened the front door.

One look at Sophie's battered body was all they needed to cuff him and lock him up for the night. Sophie was bundled up and taken to the emergency room with the boys. The trio was patched up and given pain relief before being released. Jim was released the following morning after Sophie refused to press charges. He felt smug and emboldened by the lack of repercussions beyond a night spent in the lockup.

Any accusations regarding his children were pure hearsay. And if Sophie wouldn't press charges, the cops were powerless to do more. The stupid cow wouldn't dream of speaking up against him. Jim knew she was shit scared and would never risk the blowback if she talked about the beatings. A few nasty threats involving the boys ensured her ongoing silence.

Jim stalked downstairs to the family's private living quarters, which took up the rear two-thirds of the ground floor. Squeezing a family into a cramped two-bedroom apartment wasn't easy, but Sophie had done her best to make it look nice —not that Jim cared for the frilly shit that adorned the place; all he needed was the flat screen and his armchair. Everything else was superfluous.

He made his way straight to the kitchen and grabbed a beer from the fridge. In the few short minutes he'd spent with her, that damned girl had worked her way under his skin. She managed to frustrate, humiliate, arouse, and perplex him all at once. Annoyed and edgy, Jim cracked open the beer and took a long swig. The bitter liquid sent a wicked chill down his throat, its anesthetizing effects cocooning him in a feeling of calm that allowed him to relax enough to plant his ass in the armchair and switch on the TV. He belched loudly and surfed the channels. ESPN couldn't hold his attention on this occasion.

He got up out of the chair and rummaged around in the back of the entertainment unit for his stash of old porno DVDs. They were poorly concealed in an old shoebox that was dented and covered in dust. It had been so long since he'd watched them that he had to think for a moment how to use the DVD player. Once he figured it out, he made himself comfortable and chugged the remaining beer. His eyes fixated on the silicone-enhanced blonde pumping away at some buff stud with a crew cut. It was just the thing to get him in the mood for when Sophie returned from the quilting group she attended twice a week.

An hour or so later, Sophie quietly entered the apartment, which never quite felt like home no matter what personal touches she added. She didn't need a degree in psychology to understand that her feelings had more to do with her dysfunctional relationships with her family than the physical house itself. Nevertheless, she was in an upbeat mood, having just completed a particularly challenging square on the quilt she was creating for next year's county fair. It was a complicated design that she would have never considered attempting without the constant encouragement of her sewing mentor, Mrs. Matthews. The older woman struggled to convince her to take on the project, but eventually, Sophie was excited by the prospect of tackling something of this magnitude. With Mrs. Matthews's guidance, she finished the first square of the quilt. She felt buoyed by this early success and giddy with the sense of achievement it induced.

Making as little noise as possible as she entered the apartment, Sophie eased the door closed behind her. She placed the wicker sewing basket down on the hall table near the light switch by the door and continued through to the kitchen. The seedy and sadly predictable combination of lame music and overacted groans coming from the television alerted her to Jim's presence. Her mood plummeted.

Earlier in the day, Jim had mentioned his plans to go down to the hardware store and get some caulking to reseal the windows before winter arrived. Sophie had hoped he'd be out working on the house when she got home. Now she would have to tiptoe around like a sad little mouse while she prepared the evening meals. Realizing that her husband was in the apartment, she closed in on herself, silencing her very spirit along with her body to allow her to move about unnoticed. It was a skill honed by years of abuse, and it had saved her more than once.

The kettle was almost empty. Sophie unplugged it and took it to the sink to fill it. She flicked the switch to set it to boil. While the kettle grumbled and groaned, she reached into the cupboard to the right of the stove for the box of teabags. Still distracted by her sewing victory, she bumped the jar of coffee jammed in beside it.

Sophie watched in horror as the jar tumbled from the shelf. She reached out to grab it before it could smash on the tiles, but her reflexes were rubbish. Her hand snatched at empty air, and the jar of coffee shattered on the tiles, sending shards of glass and coffee grounds across the floor. Sophie wasted no time getting the dustpan and broom out from beneath the sink and knelt to sweep up the mess before Jim noticed.

Too late.

"What the fuck is going on in here?" Jim bellowed. Sophie whipped her head around, startled. Jim stood at the threshold between the kitchen and dining room, scowling down at her.

She swallowed, recognizing the sadistic gleam in his eye that was an inevitable precursor of the violence to come. "I'm sorry, Jim," she stammered. "I was getting a teabag, and I accidentally knocked the coffee off the shelf." She looked guiltily down at the mess of glass and coffee grounds on the floor, not daring to meet her husband's gaze.

She braced herself for a harsh slap to the face or a nasty boot to the stomach, but neither happened.

"You can get your clumsy ass down to the store later and buy another jar to replace it. I ain't going without my coffee tomorrow morning." The sheer relief on her face didn't escape him, and he couldn't help but sneer at her. "But first, you can come join me in the bedroom."

Sophie frowned, confused by her husband's uncharacteristic reaction. Any other time he would have beaten the crap out of her. "What?" she asked, unsure she had heard him correctly.

"I said, make sure you go down to the store later and replace the fucking coffee. But first, get your ass into the bedroom. I'm horny as fuck."

"I beg your pardon?" Sophie scoffed, hoping she'd misheard him.

"Don't fuck me around, Sophie. I'm not in the mood for your games."

"No games," she was quick to assure him. "I just wasn't sure what you meant."

"I meant, get your ass in the bedroom. I'm horny, and I wanna fuck. Is there anything about that you don't understand?"

Sophie caught his dangerous tone, and despite having zero desire to have sex, she knew better than to resist. She chewed on her lower lip, her hands tight fists at her sides, nails digging into her palms.

More than anything, she wanted to run, grab her handbag, and bolt out the door, away from the boarding house and her psychotic husband. But that could never happen. There was nowhere she could go where Jim wouldn't find her. He wouldn't track her down because he cared. He'd do it so he could drag her back, kicking and screaming in terror of the beating that she knew would follow. Jim had warned her what would happen. Whenever she contemplated the possibility of leaving, the man seemed to know her thoughts, cruelly reminding her of the repercussions if she attempted to walk away.

"What the fuck are you waiting for?" he growled, snatching her arm and pulling her toward the bedroom. Having no choice but to follow, Sophie joined her husband in the bedroom. He pawed at her clothes with little care or consideration. She removed her jumper and the shirt beneath to avoid having him rip them off in a temper. Standing at the foot of the bed in her bra and pants, Sophie kept her eyes focused on an old scorch mark on the carpet while Jim roughly kneaded her breasts.

It was difficult maintaining a neutral expression as he groped at her, her nipple caught between fingers that pinched and twisted her unkindly. Experience had taught her to show as little emotion as possible. Any display of weakness seemed to fuel his need to dominate and demean.

She reluctantly tore her eyes away from the threadbare carpet to assess her husband while he was preoccupied with her body. Often his dick went limp before anything much could happen, and he would slap her around a bit to disguise his shame. There would be no half-hearted attempts at intercourse today. The bulge in his pants was unmistakable. He was primed and ready to go.

Jim unbuttoned his jeans, pulling his engorged cock free while motioning for Sophie to remove her pants. She sat on the edge of the bed, pulled off her boots, and shimmied out of her slacks. Down to her underwear, she waited for Jim to climb onto her in his usual fashion. Instead, he grabbed her arm and rolled her over, exposing her backside. She felt his cock poking into the back of her leg as he ripped her knickers off and tossed them aside.

Something wasn't right.

She tried to pull away, but he held her in place. "No, Jim, get off me," she cried in alarm. "Let me go! Please just let me go." She felt his breath on her back. He spread her ass cheeks and forced himself inside her. Pain ripped through her as he pushed deep into her body. Sophie screamed. She couldn't stop herself.

Jim grunted and groaned like a repulsive barnyard animal. He pumped away, his fingers digging into her hips while he sodomized her. As he approached climax, he rammed into her harder and faster. He exploded inside her with one final thrust, collapsing on top of her afterward in a sweaty heap. Sophie remained frozen in place, too stunned to move until he eventually withdrew and pushed her aside. "Go get me something to drink, would you? That was damn thirsty work."

Sophie wiped the tears from her face and retrieved her knickers from the floor. She gingerly pulled them on. She could have gladly smashed his face in with the baseball bat he kept beside the bed. For an instant, she tossed up the odds of reaching it before he did: he was sweaty and out of breath. She could barely walk, her insides bruised and throbbing. Most likely, it was a fifty-fifty split.

"Hurry the fuck up, woman!" he snapped. The moment passed. Sophie stepped into her pants. Sitting down wouldn't be an option for the next day or two. "We've got a new guest," Jim informed her as he lit a cigarette. He inhaled deeply before continuing. "Some young girl from outta town. She's paid up for a week, but she might stay on longer. You'll have to take a towel up to her. She looked like she was traveling kinda light. I don't think she has any toiletries or nothing."

Of course. Now Sophie understood why he'd been so wound up. It wasn't the porn that did it. Their new guest had had a powerful effect on him, and Sophie had been the one to bear the brunt of it. "I'll sort it out," she replied through gritted teeth.

"Don't forget to go down and buy another jar of coffee." He lay back on the bed, all sweaty and disgusting, puffing at a cigarette, oblivious to the ash falling onto the coverlet. With any luck, he'd nod off and burn the house down while she was out at the supermarket.

Five

Not long after Ella arrived at the boarding house, a police cruiser roared up Main Street, lights flashing and sirens wailing. It barely slowed enough to make a right on Oakleigh Street. The passenger, a uniformed man in his late thirties, held onto the door handle for support and glared across at the overly eager officer behind the wheel.

"Jesus frigging Christ! Slow down before you get us both killed. If the reports are correct, there's no need to rush. We've already got people at the scene, and it sounds like the poor shmuck isn't going anywhere."

"Sorry, Chief." The young officer eased his foot off the accelerator, and the cruiser slowed a fraction. Bremner sighed. It was the first and last time he allowed Officer Smith behind the wheel. The kid had been begging to drive for weeks, and in a moment of weakness, he'd agreed to let him have a go. Big mistake. They took another turn as they headed toward the new highway, which wasn't so new anymore. The road had been completed over six years ago, but locals still referred to it as the "new highway."

The tires squealed as they made the turn, and Bremner cracked. "Slow the heck down or pull over and let me drive. I won't tell you again."

Smith nodded, chastened. "Got it, boss. I'm just keen to get there and check it out. DeAngelo made it sound like something pretty messed up happened. Do you think the dude ate a bullet?"

"Smith, you haven't seen a body before, have you?"

"Nope. This will be my first. I've been waiting, but people aren't exactly in a hurry to die around here."

"I'm happy about that. It means I must be doing my job right," Bremner responded drily.

Smith flushed, embarrassed by his insensitivity. Since graduating and being assigned to the Taylor's End Police Department, Smith was quick to volunteer for overtime and dealt with the petty disputes and nuisance calls nobody else on the force wanted to touch. Hoping Bremner would notice and take him under his wing. Now, after months of hard work, they were finally on patrol together, and he was coming across as a lead-footed asshole. "I didn't mean it like that."

"I know. I vaguely remember what it's like to be fresh on the force and eager to experience more than breaking up the usual Friday night bar brawls and issuing speeding tickets."

Smith turned onto the entrance ramp to the highway, and Bremner relaxed a little. It was a relatively straight drive out to the rest stop from there. He pushed aside thoughts about Smith and his youthful exuberance and focused on what awaited them. DeAngelo's description had been brief. All they knew was that they were dealing with a fatality. The officer had refrained from giving too much information over the radio, which worried Bremner. It worried him a lot.

If they were dealing with a suicide, which was an unfortunate but unavoidable aspect of the job, DeAngelo would have said as much. From time to time, folks decided to end their lives. In that one terrible moment, death seemed preferable to pushing through whatever darkness swamped them. It was always an ugly and unbearably sad situation for any of his people to deal with. The wasted life—and worse, the devastated loved ones they were left to deal with—weighed heavily on any officer unfortunate enough to be called out to a suicide.

But DeAngelo hadn't mentioned suicide, nor had he suggested death by natural causes. Although it was a leap, Bremner had a terrible feeling they were speeding toward something dark and unspeakable. Something that would change the very heart of the sleepy rural town he had taken an oath to keep safe. Maybe it was the sudden change in the weather. A mass of dark and ominous clouds gathered on the horizon, bringing with them a sense of drama. But that couldn't account for the tight-knotted feeling in the pit of his stomach.

They drove the rest of the way in silence. Bremner tried to ignore his mounting concern over what was waiting for them at the rest stop. Smith focused on winning back the chief's approval by driving only ten miles an hour over the designated limit.

When they reached the rest stop, Smith waited for a truck to rush by before turning onto the gravel drive. He took the turn too fast, and the cruiser slid around on the loose surface. Gravel sprayed out from beneath the tires. Bremner cursed, pointing to a picnic table. "Park over there."

"Sorry about that. I guess I should have slowed down."

"Yep, guess you should have. Tell me something, Smith. Do you even have your driver's license?" Bremner opened the door and climbed out of the cruiser, relieved to be outside in the crisp air.

"I've had my license for over three years, sir. I'm not used to driving an SUV is all."

Bremner wasn't buying it. When they got back to the station, he'd be checking Smith's driving history. If the kid had been driving for three years, Bremner would eat his goddamn hat.

They crossed the open gravel parking area and headed over to the stand of silver birches that sheltered the rest stop from the highway. A late-model Ford sedan was parked alongside the trees. There had been no visual of the car from the road, and it could have easily gone unnoticed for days. Most people preferred to continue to the town, where they could get coffee and gas and maybe look around the local stores instead of staring at open fields with the lingering stench of the composting toilets fouling the air.

DeAngelo met them midway between the gravel drive and the stand of trees. "Chief," he said solemnly.

Bremner nodded. "What have we got here? You were kinda cagey over the radio."

DeAngelo glanced over his shoulder at the silver Ford, a frown creasing his heavy brows. "Fucked up is what we've got. I don't know what else to tell you. It ain't pretty in there. I only did a cursory check of the vehicle because I figured I'd better not disturb anything until you've had a chance to check it out for yourself." Bremner examined DeAngelo closely. The older officer was pallid, and the skin around his eyes was more pinched than usual. It took Bremner a moment to realize what was wrong: DeAngelo was seriously shaken up.

"Do me a favor and go tape off the entry and exit to the rest stop. I'll go take a look inside the car," Bremner said. DeAngelo nodded and hurried away.

Bremner pulled some disposable gloves from his trouser pocket and squeezed his hands inside as he walked over to the car. Smith followed behind, hanging back where he wouldn't be in the way. As they drew closer to the vehicle, Bremner was confident he could rule out death by natural causes.

Blood splattered the interior of the car. Gore, dried to a muddy red, coated the windows. Bremner cupped his hands near the glass and squinted. He could barely make out the shape of a body within.

He stood with one hand hovering near the door handle. Whatever atrocity had happened to the poor soul inside, Bremner understood that its discovery so close to town would cast a shadow over Taylor's End for years to come. No small town could endure a violent murder without succumbing to fear, paranoia, and wild accusations that could destroy reputations. Despite its flaws, Bremner had grown to love the community he'd served for over a decade. A crime of this nature was an affront to everything he worked hard to maintain.

"Everything all right, Chief?"

Bremner nodded. "Yeah. I was thinking about the repercussions this situation will have on the town. Smith, I hope you're wearing your big boy pants, because I have a feeling the shit is about to hit the fan. Now, I'm gonna open the door and see what we're dealing with. Are you ready?"

"I'm ready," Smith answered, with bravado that was at odds with his strained expression.

Bremner gripped the handle and pulled open the door. The stench of an abattoir killing floor wafted out, driving both men back. Bremner put a hand over his nose, swallowing hard to control his gag reflex. Behind him, he heard Smith gasp and stumble away, his boots scuffing in the gravel, followed moments later by loud retching. He didn't blame the rookie. It took all his willpower to keep from barfing himself.

The scene inside the car was like nothing he'd ever encountered before. He'd attended some truly horrific car accidents over the years, the occupants dismembered, crushed, or smeared along the road, but those injuries were the result of poor judgment, fatigue, or bad weather. Sometimes shitty luck played a part, but the situation facing them now was entirely different. Another human being had inflicted the carnage inside the Ford. Bremner couldn't begin to imagine the type of person capable of such a heinous act.

The man in the car lay slumped against the driver's seat, his face a contorted mask of agony. His mouth hung open as if death had interrupted his scream. His eyes, now cloudy in death, stared sightlessly at the roof of the car. He was partially undressed, his cheap polyester shirt hanging open. The fly on his trousers was unzipped. Presumably, in the lead-up to being butchered, the poor sap had been expecting a carnal tryst. Instead of some sweaty bump-and-grind, the man received massive trauma to his chest and abdomen. Someone had torn him open from sternum to crotch. The edges of the wound were ragged and untidy. His guts spilled out in a reeking pile between his feet.The nature of the weapon was unclear. Bremner had never seen anything like it. In his youth, he had accompanied his father on hunting trips, helping him dress the kills before proudly returning to the family home to show off their hunting prowess. Although it had been years since he'd shot a deer, the memory of gutting the animals, still warm with life, was impossible to forget. It was performed with precision and care. And it was done after death.

The dead man in the car appeared to have been torn open in a violent frenzy while he was still very much alive. Overwhelmed by the brutal vision inside the nondescript vehicle, Bremner turned away. He strode over to Smith, who was still doubled over throwing up the last remnants of his lunch. Bremner clapped him on the back and peered out across the gently undulating land on the other side of the fence. He studiously avoided looking at the officer's puddle of steaming vomit. "Are you all right, Smith?"

Smith nodded and slowly stood up, taking a hankie from one of his pockets and dabbing at his mouth. Grimacing, he apologized, "I'm sorry, Chief. I saw his guts hanging out, and that was it. I thought we were responding to a heart attack or something. What if I can't get that image out of my head? If I see that dead guy every time I close my eyes, I think I'll go freakin' crazy."

Bremner guided him away from the vomit and over to a picnic table. "Sit down and rest for a bit. I'll go grab you some water from the cruiser. I wish I could tell you that you'll forget what you saw, but I can't. It will get better, but something like that is going to stick with you forever."

"You don't seem too disturbed by it."

"Smith, that was the sickest shit I have ever seen. Over a decade on the job has conditioned me to react in a certain way. Don't feel bad for throwing up; we've all been there before. I'll get that water for you. You'll feel better after a drink."

Bremner left him and returned to the cruiser. While there, he notified the coroner.

DeAngelo joined him after sealing off the rest stop with tape. "Did you look inside the car? What are we dealing with here?"

"We're dealing with some seriously fucked-up shit," Bremner admitted.

DeAngelo gawped at his boss. The chief rarely cussed. That he was dropping the f-bomb was worrying. "I suppose I should go check it out, then."

"Yeah. Be careful not to touch anything, though. We still have to process the scene." He tossed DeAngelo a bottle of water. "Give this to Smith, would you? He's not coping so well."

It was well after dark by the time the body was removed from the car and taken away to be examined by the coroner. Bremner watched as it was loaded into the back of a van and driven away. He rubbed his eyes, willing himself to stay alert. It had been an exhausting afternoon, and he was beginning to feel fatigue settling over him. All he wanted to do was go home and collapse on the couch with a stiff drink. Instead, he faced an evening back at the station buried in the sad aftermath of Chester Jurgenson's messy demise.

He was headed for the cruiser when Smith came jogging over. "Chief, dispatch has a message for you."

Bremner suppressed a sigh. "What now?"

Smith consulted his notebook to confirm the details before relaying. "Tom McCormack has been taken to the hospital. Sonja thought you would want to know."

"Did she mention what was wrong with him?"

"Something about a home invasion, I think."

"You probably should have led with the home invasion part. It's been a rough day, so I'll let it go, but try to remember for next time." Bremner wasn't in the mood to lecture the kid about procedure.

"Yes, Chief."

"Come on. I'll drop you off at the station on my way to the hospital."

When he arrived at the hospital, Jeb McCormack was out front, standing off to the side of the covered main entrance, smoking a cigarette. Bremner joined the young man, standing upwind of the smoke coiling up into the night air. "Hey, buddy."

"Hi, Nick. Thanks for coming. I know you've got your hands full with that rest stop murder, but I was hoping you could talk some sense into the old man."

Apparently, somebody at the station had leaked the news. If Jeb knew about the murder, it was safe to assume that everybody in town was aware of the situation. "I was told there was a home invasion. Is that true?"

Jeb stubbed out his cigarette and aggressively blew out a puff of smoke. "Yeah, it's true, all right. Some asshole smashed up the kitchen and beat the shit out of him."

"What happened? Did Tom recognize his attacker?"

Jeb ran a hand through his close-cropped hair and shook his head. "Tom hasn't said a word about the assault. I got home from work a bit after four and found him slumped over on the kitchen floor. There was dried blood all over his face. It was a real mess. The doctor thinks he's got a broken wrist, so he's in getting X-rays now."

Bremner couldn't even begin to imagine which rotten snot rag had driven all the way out to the farm just to beat up an old man. Nobody in their right mind would be stupid enough to think there was anything worth stealing out at the McCormack place. The farmhouse was a good decade overdue for a coat of paint and a remodel. Jeb worked weekends just to help make ends meet.

A few years back, Bremner had helped steer Jeb onto the right path after he fell in with the wrong crowd as a teenager and boosted a car belonging to one of the town's country club wives. Luckily, the gin-swigging owner was too sloshed to notice that her car was missing from the parking lot. Thanks to Jeb's complete ineptitude as a criminal, Bremner managed to pull him over five minutes into the kid's half-baked joyride. When he burst into tears before Bremner had even asked him to step out of the car, the chief decided to cut him a break. Bremner was able to return the vehicle without anyone ever realizing that it had a few extra miles on the odometer.

From there, he gently steered Jeb away from the group he'd been hanging with and called in a favor or two to get the boy a job with a local plumber, a member of his Friday night poker games.

Despite their age difference, Jeb and Nick had developed a solid bond. Since Jeb's dad had long since run off to find a better life and his mom had died from cancer when he was eleven, Nick found himself playing uncle to a kid he had no blood ties to. He didn't mind. Without a wife or any family here in Taylor's End, it was kind of nice to have Jeb and his grandpa in his life.

Jeb reached out and gripped Nick's arm. "That's not all they did. The bastards killed Rosie."

"They killed your dog?"

"Yeah. We had her since she was just a little pup. Who goes and kills an innocent dog? Her neck was broke. Oh God," he said, choking back a sob. "Do you think she suffered?" Jeb asked.

"If her neck was broken, I think it would have been instant. I doubt she felt any pain." He hated to see the anguish on Jeb's face. He could only imagine how the kid felt.

As he comforted the younger man, Bremner pondered the strength it would take to break a dog's neck. Rosie had been a good-sized animal—medium height, medium build. Not only would it take considerable force to snap its neck, but you'd also have to be stone-cold to commit such an abhorrent act. Possibly the same sort of person that would gut a man at a lonely rest stop. It was a reach. He was stretching for connections that may not be there, but two violent crimes committed nine or ten miles apart in the same town? While he didn't yet know if the rest stop murder had occurred on the same day as Tom's attack, Bremner thought it was too much of a coincidence to be a coincidence.

"I'm sorry to hear about Rosie. It's a real shame. How about we go check if Tom's back from getting X-rays and see if we can find out who attacked him?"

"Yeah, maybe you can convince him to talk. I sure as hell couldn't."

Bremner led Jeb in through the automatic glass doors. The heated interior was a welcome relief after being in the biting wind for more than half the day. They walked over to the reception desk and waited for the nurse to finish typing up her admission notes for a couple with a squawking, feverish baby. When she noticed Bremner, she quickly apologized for making him wait.

"I need to know if Tom McCormack's back from being X-rayed," he said, rather curtly. Any other time he would have accepted the nurse's apology gracefully, but it had been a difficult day and the night was getting away from him, so he wasn't in the mood for screwing around.

"Let me check for you, sir. I'll just be a moment." She picked up the phone and punched a number into the dial pad with the end of her pen. After a few short words with someone on the other end of the line, the nurse placed the receiver back in the cradle and returned her attention to Bremner. "He's in room 24B. If you continue down the hall and take a right after the elevator, you'll see Ward B. The nurse on duty will be able to answer any questions you have."

"Thanks," Bremner said. He headed down the hallway with Jeb at his side, their shoes squeaking loudly on the polished linoleum floor. They found 24B and entered the brightly lit room. A nurse was tending the wounds on Tom's face, gently wiping away the dried and crusted blood around his nose and lips. Bremner introduced himself, and the nurse, an older woman with a no-nonsense expression, frowned at the intrusion.

"I understand the timing might not be ideal, but I need to have a word with Tom. I'll try to make it quick, I promise."

Bremner smiled coyly. Bullying or manipulating this woman would get him nowhere. Any strong-arm tactics would be met with stubborn resistance.

The nurse clucked and dropped a bloody swab into the stainless-steel tray beside the bed. "Are you OK to talk for a few minutes, Mr. McCormack?" she asked gently. Tom nodded somewhat reluctantly.

"You have five minutes to ask your questions. Not a second longer. When I get back, you'll need to leave. The patient still has to have his arm set."

"His arm is broken?" Jeb asked in dismay. Noticing his distress, the nurse softened.

"In two places, but we'll fix it. He might have to take it easy for a month or so, but he should recover without too much trouble."

After she left the room, Bremner walked over to the bed, taken aback by how old and worn-out Tom looked under the unforgiving glare of the fluorescent lights. He flipped open his pocket notebook and jotted down a few things before asking, "How are you feeling, Tom?"

"I've been better, although I'm still alive, so I shouldn't complain."

"Tom, I'm sorry to hear you've been through such an awful experience. I need you to tell me what happened so we can catch your attacker. Anyone that can beat an old man and kill a dog needs to be locked up before they can hurt anyone else."

Tears spilled down the old man's cheeks, running along the wrinkles in his skin. He looked across at Jeb for confirmation.

"Sorry, Grandpa. I didn't tell you before because I was scared you might get too upset."

"Tom? What do you remember about the attack? Did you recognize your attacker? Can you describe them?"

Tom turned his face away from Bremner, staring out the window at the bleak, black night. "I don't know them, and I don't remember anything."

"So you didn't recognize them, or you don't remember anything? Which is it?"

"Grandpa, if you know anything, you have to tell Nick, even if they threatened you. If you help identify them, they'll go to jail, and you'll be safe."

"Jeb's right. I can help only if you tell me what you know."

"I don't remember anything. I took a fairly decent knock to the head. I guess it messed with the old marbles." He avoided making eye contact with Bremner.

Before Bremner could probe the old man further, the nurse returned with the doctor in tow. "Sorry gentlemen, it's time for you to leave. Mr. McCormack needs his arm set, and we have to take care of it now. Any further questions can wait until tomorrow." The doctor glanced across at the nurse and gave her a nod of approval. She ushered Jeb and Bremner out of the room and gently closed the door behind them.

"What do you think?" Jeb asked as they headed down the hall.

Bremner chose his words carefully, not wanting to alarm the younger man. "I think your grandpa has had a traumatic experience and he's still in shock. I'll come back tomorrow and see if he remembers anything else."

"Should I be worried?" They were out in the parking lot now, and the first spits of rain were spluttering in the wind.

Bremner was honest. "I don't know what we're dealing with yet. With the situation out at the rest stop and now Tom? I would advise caution. Lock the doors, be alert. At least until we catch the bastard responsible. Do you need help burying Rosie? I'll come out in the morning and give you a hand if you need me to."

"Nah, I'll manage. Thanks for coming to see the old boy."

"Is there somewhere else you can stay for the night? I'd like to send someone out first thing tomorrow morning to have a look around."

"Sure, I'll see if I can crash at Christian's."

They waved goodbye and parted company, each heading to their respective vehicles. Bremner climbed behind the wheel of the cruiser, his brain a whir of disturbing possibilities. It would be easy to get carried away and entertain all sorts of preposterous theories, which, while running on little more than fumes at this stage, might seem completely reasonable no matter how absurd they truly were. He rubbed his eyes before starting the engine, forcing himself to focus on the hot shower and stiff drink that waited for him at home after he wrapped things up at the station.

Six

On a wide tree-lined street on Glenview Estate, the neighborhood of choice for the well-heeled families of Taylor's End, Michelle Tanner sat at her dressing table with a curling iron. She wound a lock of long honey-blond hair around the tong and examined her reflection in the mirror, waiting for the curl to form. Her skin was smooth and without blemishes, her brows full and immaculately groomed. She was easily one of the prettiest girls at school, and she'd been taking advantage of her great genetics since kindergarten. People naturally gravitated toward her. It wasn't because of an infectious personality or incredible intellect. She possessed neither. She was an average student, and that was with the benefit of a regular tutor, and her personality was nothing special.

She finished curling her hair and switched off the heated tong. She flipped her head to loosen the ringlets into the softer, cascading curls that were her signature style. The weather had done a complete one-eighty earlier in the day, and she was unconvinced the style would hold, so she gave her hair a spritz of hairspray.

Tonight, she was going out with Dan Cumberland for the first time. They'd flirted for weeks, circling each other with the wary eagerness of oversexed teenagers. On Tuesday, during lunch break, he had convinced her to give him her phone number. They began messaging and it wasn't long before Dan got dirty. He repeatedly begged her to send him a photo of her tits or, better still, a full-body shot.

It hadn't happened. While she might not be as smart as some, Michelle sure as hell knew better than to send some dumb jock she barely knew a nude selfie. She figured it was prudent to avoid the possibility of images of her vagina being leaked onto the web by some pathetic ex-boyfriend unable to move on with his life. Besides, if her father ever caught her sharing nude pictures of herself, it would shatter him.

She left that sort of thing for the cheap trailer trash girls, who were so desperate for approval that they would give away their dignity for even the slightest show of attention from a guy.

She walked over to her built-in wardrobe and rifled through the racks of clothes, searching for a top to wear. It needed to be cute, but not like she was trying too hard to impress Dan. While she was weighing up her options, there was a short, sharp knock at her bedroom door. The door opened before she could answer, and her mother entered the room, her eyebrows drawn together in disapproval. "I don't think it is appropriate to wear a skimpy bra like that," her mother said.

Michelle glanced down at her ample cleavage, barely contained by a flimsy lace bra that she'd deliberately chosen for that very reason. "For starters, it's *lingerie,* not underwear, and secondly, I can't begin to imagine why you would think it's inappropriate for your daughter to wear a bra. Would you prefer I didn't wear one at all?" Michelle goaded, unable to help herself. Her mother had become such a bore since she'd found God. Everything was a sin.

Most days, Michelle wanted to grab her by the shoulders and shake the Jesus out of her. She wanted to scream at him to give her mom back. The lighthearted woman who used to smile and joke and would listen to her daughter without passing judgment on her every action had been replaced with a disapproving shrew. Resigned to her mom being against everything, Michelle chose to stir the pot even more. If her mom insisted on being a ball-breaking bitch, Michelle would have some fun with it one way or another.

"I would prefer it if you chose something slightly more modest. Think of the message you are sending to all the boys."

Michelle's eyebrows rose. "Exactly what sort of message am I sending by wearing a bra? Would you be happier if I wore nothing under my sweater? I bet the boys would just love that."

Michelle's mother sucked air between her clenched teeth and folded her arms across her chest. "Please don't talk that way, Michelle. I'm concerned that people will get the wrong impression. Surely you can see where I'm coming from?'

Michelle applied a coat of gloss to her lips before tossing the tube into her purse. She glared at her mom in the mirror before sauntering over to the wardrobe once more. She snatched a powder-blue cashmere sweater from its hanger and pulled it on over her head, careful not to disturb her hair. It covered everything but hugged her generous assets. "Happy, Mom? I'm all covered up now."

"I honestly don't know how to talk to you anymore, Michelle. Everything I say is wrong." Great. Now her mom was throwing herself a pity party. When her bitchy, judgmental sermons failed to have an impact, she invariably fell back on her old favorite—poor, long-suffering Mom.

Michelle checked her cell. It was almost ten to nine. "Mom, I don't have time for this right now. Dan's picking me up in ten minutes."

Accepting defeat, her mother said, "I suppose you'll need some money." Michelle shrugged. She had precisely five dollars in her purse, but she wasn't about to beg for handouts.

"If you don't mind," she said. She slipped into her shearling jacket and collected her purse from the dressing table.

"Ask your father for some money on your way out, but no more than twenty dollars."

Michelle gave herself a final inspection in the mirror, and, satisfied with what she saw, she pushed past her mom and went downstairs to find her father.

Her father was in the living room, watching the twenty-four-hour news channel and going over a stack of papers he had brought home from the office.

"Daddy, that is no way to spend your Friday night. You're supposed to be relaxing. Why don't you pour yourself a scotch and have some fun for a change?"

John Tanner smiled up at his daughter tiredly. "If I get this work finished tonight, I'll be able to enjoy the rest of the weekend. I promise."

"OK, Daddy. Try not to stay up too late. You look exhausted."

Her father sighed and removed his glasses so he could rub his eyes. "Another hour, two at the most, and it should be sorted. Wait, shouldn't I be the one telling you not to stay up late? I feel like the roles are being strangely reversed here."

Michelle gave him a cheeky grin and shrugged. "Despite what Mom thinks, I can take care of myself. I'm not a child anymore, no matter how much she wishes I was."

"Are you two fighting again?" John asked. It felt like his wife and daughter had been arguing for years. They refused to agree on anything, preferring to battle it out over the most trivial matters. It made for an unsettled home life.

"Don't worry about it, Daddy. Mom's just being a pain in the ass as usual."

"Michelle! You can't talk about your mother like that, no matter how frustrating she can be," John said. Michelle pouted and apologized. She couldn't stand to have her father angry with her.

Outside, a car horn honked. Michelle glanced toward the front door in exasperation. She hated it when people used the horn to summon her. Her friend Jenny did it all the time, and it drove her batshit. It was rude and lazy. Was it so hard to switch the car off and come to the front door? Or better still, text her?

"I take it you're going out tonight," her father said. "Is that bozo going to come in and introduce himself to your old man?"

"Not tonight, Daddy. Maybe if I decide to go out with him again, I'll introduce you. I'd better hurry up and get out there before he goes crazy with the horn again. Can I grab twenty dollars?"

Her father stood up and went over to the hall table near the front door. He took a couple of bills from his wallet. "Here, Pumpkin." He winked at his daughter. "Make sure you are home by one-thirty, or your mom will flip."

Michelle took the money from her father and gave him a hug. "I love you, Daddy. I'll see you in the morning. We'll go get a coffee or something."

She grabbed her keys from the pottery bowl she'd made in the fifth grade, which was still proudly displayed on the hall table despite being undeniably hideous and misshapen. She walked out onto the front porch and shivered as a gust of wind blew at her hair. A thick cover of clouds had blown across the sky, blotting out the stars. The moon was nowhere in sight.

She pulled her jacket tight around her body and hurried down the path. Dan rolled down the driver's side window as she approached.

"Come on, babe! The boys have already started drinking."

Michelle stepped off the curb and deliberately took her time walking around the front of the car. The headlights illuminated her ass in the tightest pair of jeans she owned. She opened the car door, wincing at the awful creaking noise it made and sank into the seat beside Dan.

She scrutinized the car with distaste, kicking aside a collection of empty energy drink cans and fast-food wrappers to make room for her feet. "Maybe it's time to upgrade," she suggested dryly.

Dan scoffed. "Babe, this is a 1969 Dodge Charger. This car is an absolute classic. It was my dad's, and now it's mine. Hopefully, someday when I have kids, I'll get the chance to pass it down to my son."

"It looks like it's falling apart." It wasn't quite that bad, but to Michelle, "classic car" really meant some old junk overdue for the scrap heap. She had no interest in the history and status of owning an American muscle car, especially one in need of serious restoration. Her idea of a decent ride was the latest BMW SUV, not a rusty V8 full of empty cans and burger wrappers. She was starting to reconsider the whole idea of dating Daniel Cumberland, especially if he was more interested in drinking than being with her. There were plenty of guys who would kill to be on her radar.

"It might not look like much now, but I've got plans to restore her to her former glory. Dad didn't do much to her over the years, so she's looking kinda tired. I'm saving to have her resprayed and get all new tires. Just wait and see."

"OK, Dan," Michelle agreed, to shut him up. "Did you bring something to drink?"

"Yeah, there's some bourbon and colas on the back seat."

"I hope someone at the party brought some tequila," she said, sighing.

Dan worked the gearshift and pulled away from the curb, the engine growling rowdily as he floored it. It might not have looked like much on the outside, but the car had the goods under the hood.

A few minutes later they pulled up outside Tara Hoskin's house. Michelle examined the property with a critical eye. While the street was respectable enough—it was no Glenview Estate, but it wasn't a part of Crack Corridor either—the house was starting to show signs of neglect. The rain gutter sagged across the middle, and the window frames needed a fresh coat of paint, giving it a slightly rundown appearance. Tara was a year behind her at school. As far as Michelle was concerned, they had no business socializing with juniors, but she kept her opinion to herself.

If Dan became a regular thing, she'd have to educate him on the social hierarchy. He was too laid back, happy to go along with whatever his buddies were doing, and Michelle had it on good authority that one of those buddies was currently cock deep in Tara Hoskins and had been for the past few months—hence why they were parked out the front of her place on their first date.

Dan killed the engine and reached over to the back seat to grab the bourbon and colas. "Are you ready to go in?" he asked eagerly.

Michelle nodded and climbed out of the car. "Damn, it's cold. Do you think it will snow?" she asked as they walked around the cars parked on the front lawn.

"It feels that way," Dan said. Someone called out to him, and he jogged over to a group huddled beside a clump of bushes near the front door, passing a joint around. There was a burst of raucous laughter and elbow jabs and more than one salacious glance in her direction. She couldn't quite hear what they were saying, but she got the gist of it. Dan was obviously the hero of the night because he had bagged Michelle Tanner. Too bad the half-baked idiots didn't realize she had no intention of putting out tonight.

Tossing her hair over her shoulder, Michelle strutted past them and entered the house in search of some tequila and someone worth talking to. She found the alcohol in the kitchen, which was already crowded with empty bottles. The wooden counter was littered with abandoned snacks and the odd drink stuffed with cigarette butts. Keen to get a buzz on, she had three shots in a row, urged on by some kids in her math class.

The tequila was cheap and burned her throat, but its numbing warmth quickly spread through her limbs. Within minutes she was pleasantly smashed. Suddenly, it didn't matter so much that Dan seemed more interested in catching up with his pot-smoking friends out front. She allowed herself to be dragged off to the living room by a girl she had been friends with in middle school, where R&B was bumping. A group of girls were grinding against each other to the delight of half the football team, who were watching in awe.

Michelle wasn't that hammered. No one could lure her into any girl-on-girl action. But she found herself dancing suggestively in front of a guy she'd briefly dated as a sophomore. He had dumped her for some nerdy thing with a flat chest, greasy hair, and glasses, and the rejection still stung more than two years later. At the time, she was mortified. But a few months later, when Little Miss Mousy decided she could have more fun screwing all the guys in her science club, Michelle decided he had gotten what he deserved.

Now, as she lost herself in the moment, her inhibitions melted away by alcohol, she cared more about letting go and having fun than upholding her carefully constructed image. When one of the guys she'd had shots with found her and handed her another drink, she took it gratefully. She gulped it down, almost choking on the dreadful concoction. It tasted like a combination of muscle rub and cough syrup. Grimacing at the taste, she wiped her mouth with the back of her hand and leaned in close to the guy. Was his name Todd? She thought it was. They had talked a few times at school, where they shared a class, and he had helped her work through a difficult question.

"That was unbelievably bad," she shouted into his ear so he could hear her over the music.

He nodded, grinning like a cute, dopey monkey. "It tastes like shit, but it'll get you smashed hella fast." They laughed. It felt good to relax and have fun.

A hand wrapped around her forearm. Dan was at her side. "Are you all right? You seem pretty tanked."

She smiled cheekily, "I might have had one too many," she agreed. "Todd gave me something to drink that I swear killed every last one of my taste buds, but he assured me it would rock my world." She winked at Todd, who had retreated a respectful distance when Dan showed up.

Dan gave him the stink eye, and pulled Michelle close against him to let the jerk-off know his place. "Come on, baby. Let's go."

Michelle pouted. "Really? We only just got here."

Dan checked his cell. Michelle was right. They hadn't even been at the party for an hour. "Really. Let's go for a walk or something. You look like you could use some fresh air."

Michelle couldn't argue with that. That last drink Todd had given her was beginning to take effect. Her head was starting to spin, and she was grateful to lean against Dan for support. "OK. A walk is probably a good idea." She turned to Todd. "I had fun tonight. Maybe we can catch up later."

Todd smiled shyly and nodded. "Sure. I'll see you around." He gave Dan a sideways glance and turned away.

Dan led Michelle through the house and out the front door, doing his best to ignore the pleas from his buddies to stick around. He was helping Michelle into her jacket when her face soured.

"Looks like one of your stoner cronies is trying to get your attention."

Dan turned to the group he had hung out with earlier, and one of the guys waved him over. "I'll be back in a sec." Michelle rolled her eyes and walked across the lawn, concentrating on each step so as not to stumble and fall in a drunk girl heap.

Dan kept an eye on her while one of his friends passed him a blunt. He inhaled deeply and held the smoke before slowly exhaling. "Thanks, dude."

"Take it with you."

Dan took another hit before passing it back regretfully. "Nah, I don't think Michelle is a fan of weed. I'll see you Monday." He spent a minute saying goodbye to everyone before jogging after Michelle. He hopped over a kid who was spread out on the ground beside the mailbox, a puddle of vomit circling his head. Michelle sat waiting on the hood of his car.

She smiled as he crossed the yard, pulling him close when he reached her. "Warm me up," she purred as she rested her hands against his chest and leaned in to kiss him. When their lips touched, she let out a tiny moan, and Dan slid his arms around her, his hands cupping her ass, drawing her hard against him so she could feel his excitement. They kissed long and hard, the drugs and alcohol fueling the euphoria of making out with someone fresh and unfamiliar. Michelle's limbs turned to molten gold, the place between her legs throbbing with desire. Her breath came in ragged gasps, and she feared that if she didn't take a step back, they'd soon be fucking on the hood of his car.

That was a sobering thought. Michelle extricated herself from his embrace and shimmied out from against the hood of the car, relieved to have some space between them. She was unnerved by how quickly her body had reacted to Dan's touch.

"Maybe we could go for a drive or something," she suggested huskily—anything to give her time to sober up. She didn't put out on the first date. Never had, never would. But tonight, she felt dangerously close to spinning out of control and breaking her own rules. The combination of too much tequila and the thrill of finally making out with Dan after weeks of flirting had sent her libido into the stratosphere.

Dan cleared his throat and adjusted himself. His jeans were too tight to accommodate his raging boner. "Sure, babe, whatever you want," he said.

He walked around to the driver's side and climbed into the car. Michelle settled into the seat beside him and fumbled with the seatbelt.

"Where do you wanna go?" he asked after starting the Charger.

Michelle looked across at him and shrugged. "I don't know. Somewhere quiet, I guess, where people won't stare at us."

He knew just the spot. He put the car in reverse and gunned the engine. The tires spun on the slippery grass for a moment before gaining traction, and the car hurtled backward out into the street.

They drove across town, making a dizzying number of turns onto back streets to avoid any cops on patrol. They always prowled the town on the weekends, and Dan wasn't too keen on being busted for driving under the influence. They passed Crack Corridor, a three-block stretch on the wrong side of town notorious for its crackheads and tweakers. It was a relief when they turned onto Old South Road, a largely abandoned stretch of blacktop since the old granary had fallen into disrepair, followed not long after by complete abandonment in the nineties. Since then, it had become a popular spot for young couples seeking somewhere to partake in illicit activities.

Dan pressed down on the accelerator, and the engine reverberated as the Charger sprang forward with a thunderous growl. Michelle leaned over to check the speedometer. The needle crawled up past eighty-five. They glanced across at each other before bursting out laughing. The speed and sexual tension made them feel crazy and reckless.

A mile down the road, Dan rocketed past the entrance to the granary. "Shit! I missed the fucking driveway." Michelle threw her head back and started laughing all over again. She hadn't felt this carefree in months. Dan put his foot on the brake, and the tires squealed in protest. He did a U-turn and drove back toward the silo, which loomed like a massive pale phallus against the inky night sky.

Michelle shivered as they approached the abandoned silo. She had never much liked hanging out at the old granary. Every kid in Taylor's End had spent time out here at one time or another. Even during daylight, there was something unnerving about the location.

"This place gives me the creeps," she admitted. They pulled to a stop a short distance from the towering silo and the derelict outbuildings.

After Dan killed the engine, there was a period of awkward silence. Neither knew what to say.

"Do you want me to put the radio on?" Dan asked.

Michelle shrugged. "Sure."

Dan unbuckled his belt and fiddled with the dial until he found a station playing the current top fifty. He adjusted the seat, pushing it back as far as it would go, before sliding closer to Michelle. She followed his lead, releasing her belt and unzipping her jacket. Dan reached across and cupped one of her breasts through the soft cashmere fabric, kneading it gently. She wriggled closer and leaned in to kiss his neck, her lips barely grazing his skin. The contact, so subtle and teasing, drove him wild.

Michelle lightly flicked her tongue out between her lips, caressing the skin just behind his ear. As she slowly worked her way around to his lips, she found herself thinking about her ex. She knew it was wrong, but she couldn't help comparing the two. And sadly, there was no comparison. Randall won hands down. Dan was nothing more than a distraction.

When his tongue darted into her mouth hungrily, she forced herself to kiss him back, but he must have sensed her sudden reluctance. "What's wrong?" he asked.

"Nothing. Everything is fine," she assured him. But everything wasn't fine. Memories of Randall filled her head. She had spent months trying to forget him, to move on the same way he had when he went off to college and left her behind. But it wasn't that easy. Forcing aside thoughts of her ex, Michelle tried to match his enthusiasm, her hand running along the inside of his thigh to cup the bulge in his pants.

Breathing heavily, he reached up under her sweater to touch her breasts, the skin-on-skin contact sending a delightful shiver through him. Too worked up to wait, Dan hurriedly unbuttoned his jeans and freed his cock. It sprang up, and he groaned with relief and anticipation. "Suck it a bit before we fuck," he urged, pushing Michelle's head down toward his crotch.

Making out was one thing. Sucking him off was something else entirely. Michelle was still too hung up on her ex to do anything more than some harmless groping and no amount of alcohol could change that. She simply wasn't ready to put out for someone she wasn't totally into. She pulled away, suddenly repulsed by her proximity to his exposed erection.

"What the fuck?" he said in confusion.

Michelle shook her head and fumbled with the zipper on her jacket. "I'm sorry, but I'm not ready for that. I don't know if that's something I'll ever want to do."

Dan forced his boner back in his pants. "You fucking told me you wanted to go somewhere we wouldn't be disturbed."

"Yeah, because I was drunk and didn't want everyone watching us make out. It didn't mean that I wanted to fuck you."

"The guys were right about you," he said. "You truly are a fucking prick tease."

She scowled at him and opened the door. "You're a real jerk."

"Where are you going?" he asked incredulously. They were a couple of miles out of town, and the clouds were about to unleash a hellish storm.

"I'm going to find somewhere to pee. Then you are going to drive me home because whatever was happening between us is over." She slammed the door and stalked off in search of a private place to go to the bathroom. She was steaming mad. How had things turned so ugly between them so damn fast?

She hadn't meant to lead him on, but apparently that was exactly what she had done.

Away from the circle of light thrown by the headlights, it was difficult to see more than a few feet ahead. Her boot caught a tuft of grass growing up through the gravel. "Shit!" she yelled as she stumbled forward, her arms pinwheeling wildly. She barely kept from falling, which would have been the pinnacle of an already regrettable night. Her thoughts soured as she continued toward the outbuildings about hundred yards from the car.

Alone in the dark, the dilapidated outbuildings appeared suitably sinister. They squatted menacingly beside the concrete silo. The roof of the larger was collapsed in places. Weeds and overgrown shrubbery had reclaimed the land and grew high against the decaying buildings. Spindly branches poked through the broken windows like skeletal limbs.

If her bladder weren't so full, Michelle would have returned to the car and waited until she got home to relieve herself. "Pull yourself together," she whispered to herself. She made her way around the side of the larger building, ensuring she was out of sight. She pulled down her jeans and crouched behind a bunch of metal drums discarded beside the rotting wooden cladding. The air was cold on her bare backside as she balanced somewhat precariously on her toes to avoid pissing on herself. It would have been a challenge at the best of times, but squatting to urinate while drunk was downright impossible. Struggling to stay on her feet, she reached out and leaned against a barrel for support. She willed herself to finish, but the stream continued. All she wanted was to be at home, snuggled in bed under the covers. Instead, she was stuck out in the cold night air, the wind howling between the buildings eerily, while the tips of the weedy undergrowth tickled her backside like ghostly fingers.

When she finally finished, she gave herself a little shake and stood, pulling her jeans up and grimacing at the dampness in her panties. She zipped her fly and was wrestling with the button when she heard footsteps behind her. Abandoning the button on her jeans, she whipped her head around.

"Dan?" she called out uneasily. It was too dark, and she was still too tipsy to deal with this bullshit. "Dan? Stop messing around, OK?" Her eyes darted around nervously, searching for the source of the sound. The fine hairs on the back of her neck prickled, and she suppressed a frightened whimper.

A brittle twig snapped nearby. Michelle whirled around. "I told you to quit it!" she hissed angrily. "Huh? Who the hell are *you?*"

A slender girl with long dark hair hanging around her shoulders in limp tangles stood between the buildings. She was blocking the exit.

Michelle eyed the stranger nervously. "What are you doing out here?" she asked, wrapping her arms around her body protectively. Everything about this situation felt wrong.

The girl continued to stare at her with unblinking black eyes. She tilted her head like she was listening to a voice only she could hear. All she wore was a filmy slip, the fabric glued to her body by the blustery wind. It couldn't be more than forty degrees. She was liable to get hypothermia if she didn't get out of the cold soon.

Michelle risked a glance over her shoulder at the gap running between the two buildings, weighing up her options.

It was dark and thick with shadows. She would have to make her way around the back of the abandoned building, which was peppered with overhanging foliage, and other trip hazards, and come out the other side of the silo. Maybe she would have done it if she'd had her cell to use as a torch, but in her haste, she had left it in the car with Dan.

She took a faltering step toward the peculiar girl. "I don't know about you," she said, squeezing past the girl, "but I'm going to get out of this wind. It's brutal."

The dark-haired girl's arm shot out, and her fist slammed into Michelle's chest. Michelle went hurtling backward. The back of her head struck the raised metal edge of one of the barrels and she collapsed in a heap on the ground. Some old and rusted barrels toppled over with her, rolling along the ground with a hollow clatter.

Michelle groaned and dragged herself to her feet unsteadily. Her head was ringing, and her chest felt like an elephant had sat on her, snapping her ribs. Each breath caused excruciating pain; she could only manage the shallowest of breaths. "Somebody help me," she gasped pitifully, taking a step back. She tried to focus on her attacker, but the blow to the back of her head must have messed her up, because she wasn't seeing clearly. The girl's face was strangely distorted, her features appearing to shift and melt until they finally settled into a hideous rictus that turned Michelle's bowels to water. "Help me!" she cried out again, this time louder. She turned to run, the darkness beyond nothing compared to the black-eyed creature bearing down on her with gnashing teeth and hooked claws.

Before she took two steps, she was yanked back by her hair. She screamed, reaching over her head to bat away the fist dragging her. It was like hitting solid stone. "Dan! Help me. Please..." she sobbed, knowing he would never hear her over the howling wind. He was too far away. And the radio would be playing some lame song. She was helpless. It spun her around and shoved her to the ground, pinning her beneath its tremendous weight.

Its terrible eyes bore into her, promising the realization of every horror she'd ever imagined. "Please, don't hurt me. I just want to go home," she begged between sobs. Its mouth turned up into a parody of a smile, a hellish vision plucked straight from a dentist's nightmare: a cavernous maw crowded with rows of jagged teeth sharp as needles and ripe with the stench of decay. It waggled a talon in front of her face. The razor tip caught the side of her cheek, splitting the skin.

"When I'm through with you," it taunted, "you will go home in pieces. Many. Little. Pieces."

Michelle thrashed beneath its crushing weight and screamed for help once more.

The creature descended on her, tearing off her cheek from under the eye to the jawline. Its claws shredded her chest to ribbons. The deep lacerations welled with blood, staining the remains of her clothing.

Back at the car, Dan thought he heard a scream. He turned off the radio and listened. There was nothing but the constant whine of the wind blowing against the Charger. He checked his phone. It shouldn't take that long to take a piss. He knew she was mad at him, but it was frigging cold and miserable out there. Nobody would willingly linger around the old granary alone on a night like this. Plus, her phone was still in the car. She wouldn't have taken off without it. He was weighing his options when he heard a dreadful howling cut through the night.

"What the fuck was that?" he asked out loud, looking out of the windows nervously. They started to fog up, so he reached out and rubbed the driver's window and windscreen with the sleeve of his jacket to clear the condensation.

It was too dark to see much of anything. With growing unease, Dan started the Charger and flicked the headlights onto high beam. Michelle had stormed off toward the old buildings flanking the silo. He steered the Charger in a slow semicircle across the lot, crawling past the dilapidated structures in case she was crazy enough to have ventured inside.

Movement between the buildings caught his attention. A large pale smudge crouched low to the ground. For all he knew, it could have been an animal or even a sheet of plastic blowing in the wind. He threw the car into reverse and started rolling back when something landed on the trunk with a tremendous thud. Dan looked up into the rearview mirror, his mouth agape.

With outstretched arms, a demonic creature clung to the rear of the car, peering straight back at him. Its face was a violent red smear.

He slammed his foot on the accelerator, and the Charger rocketed backward. He switched his foot to the brake pedal. The car squealed to a stop, and the demon was sent hurtling.

Dan threw his arm back over the passenger seat and craned his neck around to look out the back window. *Where the fuck is it?* He wondered frantically. He wasn't left wondering for long. It rose from the ground behind the Charger, its hideous face contorted with hate. Dan knew it would kill him in a heartbeat. The only thing stopping him from putting the car in drive and getting the fuck out of there was the realization that Michelle was still out there somewhere. If he abandoned her now, she would be alone against that thing, and she wouldn't stand a chance.

The demon, seeming to sense his indecision, made its move. Darting forward, it leaped at the car, its long muscular arms outstretched, bloody talons poised to strike. Dan jammed his foot down on the accelerator once more, and the car lurched back, the powerful engine propelling the vehicle straight at the creature. The car struck it dead on, flinging the creature up into the air. It hit the ground with a bone-crunching thud.

Trembling, Dan watched in the rearview mirror. He held his foot above the accelerator, ready for round three should the damn thing try again. Its head slowly emerged a short distance behind the car. It craned its neck to glare at the vehicle. Dan revved the engine, hoping to deter the creature. The demon slowly turned away and lurched into the darkness.

Dan clutched the steering wheel and counted the seconds. Eventually, when the thing didn't return, he climbed out of the car and reached under the seat to retrieve the tire iron he kept there. With both hands firmly gripping the weapon, Dan eased the door closed and went off in search of Michelle. He ran over to the buildings, pulling his cell phone from his pocket. He switched on the flashlight and held it out in front, ready to swing the tire iron if anything so much as breathed in his direction.

Dan spotted Michelle's crumpled body lying midway between the two old sheds. "Oh fuck," he cried, running toward her. She was curled up on her side, one arm outstretched, her fingers clutching at a clump of weeds. "Michelle, are you all right?" he asked, dropping to his knees beside her. She moaned, her face concealed by her matted blond hair. "Come on, we have to get out of here," he urged. She reached out to him, and he placed his phone down on the ground so he could help her up. She whimpered as he pulled her into a sitting position, and he nearly dropped her when her hair fell away from her face, revealing her injuries. He stared in disbelief at what remained of her face. A ragged strip of skin dangled from her chin. The entire left side of her face was missing. Her underlying muscles, teeth, and ligaments, now exposed, reminded him of the plastic anatomy figure in the corner of the science lab at school —except this was the girl he'd been making out with only a short time ago. He had never seen such catastrophic wounds before.

Without warning, vomit erupted from his mouth, and he only just managed to turn his head away. When his stomach was empty, he shakily stood up and gently pulled Michelle to her feet. Once she was upright, he was able to see the full extent of her injuries. Deep gouges scored her chest, leaving her fluffy sweater in shredded tatters. He had no idea how much blood a person could lose before it was fatal, but surely she wasn't far from being critical.

Panicking, he scooped her up in his arms, apologizing every time she cried out in pain as he walked her back toward the Charger. Despite her slender size, she was a dead weight in his arms, and it was a struggle to reach the car without dropping her.

"It's going to be all right," he assured her. He gently propped her against him while he opened the passenger door. "I'll get you to the hospital, and they'll take care of you. I promise."

She mumbled something incomprehensible. He carefully bundled her into the car and closed the door, then ran around to the driver's side.

"Hold on, baby," he said, glancing across at her, but she was out cold. "Shit! Please don't die in my car," he muttered and thrust the car into gear. It fishtailed wildly before he regained control and sped away. He tapped the brake just enough to make the turn onto Old South Road, then floored it. The Charger obliged with raw enthusiasm, barreling along the road at astonishing speed.

The sky finally unleashed its burden of heavy raindrops, splashing the windshield and blurring Dan's view of the blacktop. He knew he should slow down, but fear kept his foot pressed down on the accelerator. What if the creature was following them? He kept seeing its dripping mouth and hellish eyes, eerily lit by the reverse lights when he'd tried to run it down.

The stop sign at the intersection of Old South Road and Francis Street loomed in front of him all too soon, and he slammed on the brakes to make the turn onto Francis Street. The back of the Charger slipped out behind him, and Dan fought to keep the vehicle on the road. He regained control in time to make a sharp right onto Hampton Street, and Michelle's head lolled to the side and whacked the door. He risked a glance in her direction, wondering if she was still alive.

The windshield wipers swished back and forth at high speed, but it was still a struggle to see through the rain. Dan turned onto Glebe Avenue, barely avoiding a scrape with a minivan parked away from the curb. At the end of Glebe Avenue, which ran diagonally between Hampton and Cressey Street, he turned left, followed shortly by a right onto Dermott Drive. The hospital grounds stretched the entire length of the following block, a mishmash of buildings and extensions added over the decades since the hospital's construction in the 1950s. He turned into the main driveway, which led to the emergency entrance and drove straight up to the sliding glass doors.

Dan shoved the car in park and honked the horn repeatedly. He leaped out without waiting to kill the engine and raced around to the passenger's side. In his haste to get her inside, he yanked the door open, and Michelle nearly tumbled out. He scooped her up in his arms and ran toward the reassuring light of the emergency room. His legs felt like jelly. He waited outside the glass doors until they opened wide enough to allow him to pass through. "Somebody help us!" he screamed frantically as he ran over to the nurses' station. The handful of miserable-looking people sitting in the waiting area watched with open curiosity as Dan burst into the hospital.

The nurse seated behind the station leaped to her feet and scurried around to where Dan stood with Michelle hanging limply in his arms. "You have to help her. She's lost so much blood," Dan pleaded.

The nurse took one look at Michelle and grabbed the phone. "I need a gurney immediately," she said, "and I need a doctor out here now. I have a female with extreme facial and chest trauma." She slammed the phone down and returned her attention to the unconscious girl slumped against Dan.

Moments later, a flurry of nurses rushed over with a gurney, followed shortly by the doctor on duty. Dan lowered Michelle onto the gurney and stepped out of the way. The doctor, a tired-looking man in his mid-fifties, checked her vitals and barked orders to the nurses surrounding Michelle. They nodded and started wheeling her away. He turned to Dan, his expression a combination of suspicion and concern. "Can you tell me what happened to her? Any information you can provide would be extremely helpful," he said, glancing over his shoulder as they wheeled her away from the prying eyes of the sick and injured seated on the plastic chairs in the waiting area. Dan started crying and shook his head, nervously rubbing at his hair, unaware that his hands were slick with Michelle's blood. He smeared it across his forehead and scalp.

Dan noticed the doctor quickly glance over at the nurse at the admissions desk. She gave an almost imperceptible nod of acknowledgment before picking up the phone and turning away from them as she spoke into the receiver. The doctor excused himself and hurried down the corridor after Michelle, leaving Dan to puzzle over the furtive exchange. A moment later, the nurse hung up the phone and plucked a handful of tissues from the box beside her computer. She cautiously made her way over to where Dan stood, sobbing, and led him over to a vacant chair as far away from everyone else as possible and gently urged him to sit.

He met her eyes and wiped at his running nose with the wad of tissues she had passed him. "I didn't hurt her, I swear. I would never do that to another person." He dropped his face into his hands and started sobbing uncontrollably. The nurse placed a comforting hand on his back. "Shhh. Dr. Preston will do everything he can to help your friend. Everything is going to be OK."

Dan's chest heaved as he tried to pull himself together. How had the night gotten so fucked up? Everything had turned to shit, and now he was sitting in a hospital waiting room with nearly a dozen pairs of eyes silently accusing him of unspeakable violence against a girl he cared about. And who would ever believe him if he told the truth about what happened? Everyone would think he was making up stories to avoid being held accountable for what he did.

Seven

Kate Lyttle folded the local newspaper and pushed it across the table in disgust. She couldn't help but feel that the paper's senior journalist, a man she had met at various social functions over the years, was sensationalizing the spate of violent attacks to sell copies. Had he even stopped to consider the damage his articles were inflicting on the township's collective psyche? He had splashed lurid descriptions of the crimes across the front page for close to two weeks now and whipped many people into a state of paranoid hysteria.

She pushed her stool back from the counter and padded over to the thermostat to bump up the heat a few degrees. The first snow of the season had fallen last week, and although it had melted almost as soon as it hit the ground, the chilly weather stuck around. Tightening her robe, Kate went over to the percolator and refilled her mug. The remains of her breakfast went into the bin, the plate stacked in the dishwasher.

Without a job to go to, Kate struggled to fill her days. Volunteer work helped, but she still had far too much time on her hands. Richard felt it would reflect poorly on him if his wife went out to work. He was a successful realtor and earned more than enough money to provide them with a comfortable existence. Whenever Kate mentioned her desire to enter the workforce, he would dismiss the idea outright. He was more concerned about living up to some outdated image he felt he had to uphold. It didn't matter if his wife was left feeling lonely and unfulfilled.

She was desperately envious of her working friends and the independence that paid employment provided. Without the distraction of a job, she found herself increasingly focusing on the woeful state of her marriage. And her marriage was not something she cared to dwell on. Ten years in, and it was glaringly obvious that she'd made a grievous error accepting Richard's proposal.

With her youth slipping away and the promise of a bright future turning out to be nothing more than an endless loop of empty days and lonely nights, Kate was at a crossroads. Something had to change.

The phone rang. Kate put her mug down on the counter and picked up the handset. "Hello."

"I left the folder containing the Walter Street documents on my desk in the office. I need you to drive them down to me," her husband explained.

"I'll take a quick shower and bring it down."

"I need the folder now. I have the vendors coming in to sign the paperwork this morning," he said.

Kate felt her jaw tighten. "I'm not about to drive down the street in my pajamas. I'll only be half an hour." She returned the handset to the cradle before Richard could argue.

After a blisteringly hot shower, Kate toweled herself dry and slipped into a pair of yoga pants and a long-sleeved T-shirt with a padded vest over the top. She took the time to rub moisturizer over her face and pulled her hair back into a neat ponytail. She snatched her coat off the hook in the hallway and headed outside with the file under her arm.

She hurried over to the blue hatchback that Richard had bought for her thirtieth birthday and climbed inside. The vehicle was frigid. She wished for the hundredth time that she could squeeze her car in the garage beside her husband's Mercedes. She started the engine, waiting for the car to warm up and for the windshield to thaw so she could make the trip downtown.

A short time later, Kate pulled into a vacant park beside Richard's German-made pride and joy outside the realty office. She fought the catty impulse to open the car door onto the Mercedes and dent its pristine surface. Richard would probably have a nervous breakdown if anyone so much as left a fingerprint on his car. If it were scratched or dented? He would completely flip his lid. It was almost worth it, just to get a reaction out of him. But her better nature won out, and she was careful not to open the hatchback's door too wide when she climbed out.

With the file clutched to her chest, she crossed the sidewalk and entered the realty office. It was warm and stuffy inside. Hot air blasted from the heater. Kate unbuttoned her coat before she started sweating. She stood at a respectful distance while the office assistant handed a handful of glossy brochures to a young couple. In the background, Richard's muted voice filtered through the closed door to his office.

"Can I help you?" the office assistant asked after the couple had left. Kate stepped over to the desk and studied the girl. What had happened to Gloria? Richard never mentioned hiring a new staff member. The very young, generously stacked office assistant looked at her expectantly. The overly stuffy office made so much more sense now. If you were going to wear a sleeveless, form-fitting mini dress during winter, then you'd sure as heck better make sure the heating was dialed all the way up.

"I don't think we've met. I'm Kate Lyttle. I have that file Richard asked for."

The girl smiled smugly. The expression did not quite reach her heavily made-up eyes. "Oh. So *you're* Dick's wife." Kate's eyebrows climbed her forehead. She didn't know what to say in response. It took a great deal of self-control to refrain from smoothing her ponytail, which had developed an abundance of flyaway hairs thanks to the wind. God, why hadn't she taken a few minutes extra to slap on some makeup and pull together an outfit that didn't involve lycra and sports shoes?

Finally, Kate found her voice. "I'll take this through to my husband. He's expecting me."

"He's pretty busy right now. It might be better if you leave it with me."

Kate smiled thinly. "You can sit back down. I've got it."

The girl opened her mouth to protest but thought better of it, sinking back into her chair with a sullen expression.

Kate strode over to Richard's office and rapped on the door before entering. Richard sat behind a massive glass desk, a laptop in front of him. There was a pile of manila folders stacked to his right and a sheaf of papers to his left. He dragged his eyes away from the computer screen long enough to reach across the desk and take the folder from his wife. "Thanks, but you could have left it out with Carly."

"Yeah, your new office assistant said that. I didn't realize Gloria was no longer working here."

"She left back in June. I thought I mentioned it."

"No, I would remember if you had. And I thought you hated being called Dick."

Richard placed the folder on the pile with the others and made a production of straightening them. "What are you talking about?" he asked in a tight voice.

"Your office girl called you Dick, but I was under the impression that you loathe it when people call you that."

Through the slatted blinds over the windows to his office, Richard glanced past his wife to where Carly sat at her station. He swallowed.

It was then that Kate knew he was banging the tart in the low-cut dress.

Unprepared to show her hand just yet, she maintained a neutral expression while he made some pathetic reply. It didn't matter. Nothing he said was of any consequence. Being bullied into staying at home and having no independence was one thing. She had learned to live in a loveless marriage, no matter how isolated it made her feel. But she wouldn't stick around while he was out sleeping with other women. That was too much. Her pride screamed at her to stand up for herself, for once, and walk away. So that's what she would do. He might not realize they were through just yet, but he would. Kate needed to be smart about this and sort out an exit strategy first.

"I can see you're busy, so I'll leave you to it," she said absently before turning to leave.

As she crossed the foyer, Carly chirruped, "Have a nice day, Mrs. Lyttle."

Kate's resolve cracked. "Go fuck yourself, Carly," she snapped icily and strode out of the office. She couldn't believe it. She never spoke to people like that. Although, under the circumstances, her outburst was probably justified. If Kate's hunch was correct, then it was far less than the girl deserved.

She reached her car and jerked open the door. It struck her husband's Mercedes with enough force to dent the door and remove a thick ribbon of paint. She glanced around to check that her petty act of vandalism had gone unnoticed, then quickly climbed into her car and reversed out. Driving down Main Street, she headed toward the police station hoping that Nick might be around.

Pulling into the small parking lot beside the police station, Kate killed the engine and did what she could to make herself more presentable. She pulled her hair up into a messy topknot. The wind had left her looking like a crazy bag lady. She dug around in her purse for some lipstick and gave her lips a quick coat before climbing out of the car.

It was only when she reached the sliding doors of the single-story red brick building that she thought of bringing Nick one of those sickeningly sweet vanilla lattes that he liked so much. It was too late now.

"Kate Lyttle to see Chief Bremner, if he's available." She flashed Joe her best beauty-pageant smile, a megawatt effort that belied the way she felt inside.

"He is swamped," Joe said, blushing, "but if you want to take a seat, I'll go check if he can spare a few minutes. Can I ask what it's regarding?"

"It's just a personal visit, so if he can't see me, I can always give him a call after work."

He motioned for her to take a seat and left the front counter to find the chief. Kate sat on one of the molded plastic chairs. She was glad she was only here visiting. How dreadful it must be waiting to see the police in connection with a criminal offense. Luckily, she wasn't left to ponder the prospect for long. Joe returned with Nick trailing behind, his phone at his ear. He held up his finger, and Kate stood up and draped her coat over her arm while he wrapped up the conversation.

Nick ended the call and pocketed his phone. He welcomed her warmly. "Hi, Kate, come on through."

She smiled weakly and followed him into the working heart of the station. He led her past a half dozen desks positioned around a large open room. Two officers, hunched over outdated computer screens, caught up on paperwork. They entered his office, and Nick motioned for her to take a seat. "Sorry I haven't been in touch, but it's been super hectic lately. I haven't had time to sleep, much less catch up with my friends," he admitted as he lowered himself into his worn leather office chair.

Kate placed her purse on the spare chair and clasped her hands together in her lap. "I've been following the stories in the paper. I can't believe some of the stuff being reported. Is it true, or is that idiot Fitzgerald exaggerating?"

Nick puckered his lips and blew air out between them while raking his fingers through his hair. "Fitzgerald is an obnoxious twerp, and I have zero time for the man, but on this subject, he is not exaggerating. But what you've read in the paper is just a fraction of the truth. The situation is honestly beyond my scope of experience. We have few leads and a disturbing degree of violence. I hope we catch a break before another body lands in the morgue." Nick shook his head slowly, his face showing signs of stress and fatigue. "Anyway, I know you didn't come all the way down here to listen to me vent. What's going on?"

"I don't mind listening to you vent. You should know that by now. But you're right. I needed someone to talk to, and you were the only person who would understand. You're obviously busy. We can catch up some other time." She stood to leave, feeling awkward and overwhelmed by the emotions competing inside her.

Realizing that his friend was wrestling with something upsetting, Nick jumped up, walked over to the door, and gently closed it to give them some privacy. Everyone in the station knew he and Kate had been friends for years, so he wasn't worried about setting tongues wagging. Besides, his staff knew better than to spread malicious gossip. He picked up her purse and placed it on the desk so that he could sit in the chair beside her. "It's all right. I can talk now," he assured her. Kate looked up at him, her hazel eyes moist with unshed tears. She wrung her hands, unsure of what to say or where to begin. "Kate, what's going on?" Nick asked with genuine concern. It pained him to see her suffering this way. He wanted to reach out and take her hands in his and assure her that everything would be all right. However, his sense of propriety kept his hands in place on his knees.

"Richard's having an affair," she blurted out. "I don't have any proof, but I know. It's that Carly girl he hired without even telling me." The tears started, and she sniffled. Nick took the box of tissues from his desk and offered them to her. She plucked a couple free and dabbed at her face. "You think I'm an idiot, don't you?"

Nick studied her for a moment before returning the box of tissues to the desk. "I don't think you're an idiot." The conversation had taken an unexpected turn. Eventually, he asked, "What makes you think he's cheating on you?"

Kate shifted in her chair and picked at her cuff. "We've been in a bad place for a long time. It's rare for us to even sit down to a meal together, and I couldn't tell you the last time we were intimate. I suppose I got so used to living that way that I thought it was normal."

"That doesn't sound like a happy couple to me," Nick admitted. He was always cautious about commenting on her relationship with Richard. He had warned her years ago that he thought criticizing someone's spouse was a guaranteed friendship killer, and he valued their friendship too much to risk saying anything that could offend her. Kate had always respected his desire to not get involved in the workings of her marriage, but right now she could really use some advice.

"You're right, of course," she said. She sighed and locked eyes with him, holding his gaze for a moment that felt like it stretched on forever. "Feeling lonely every single day is one thing. Knowingly tolerating infidelity is something else. I refuse to be with a man who cheats on me." She began sobbing in earnest, shame and hurt twisting her stomach into knots

Nick reached over, his hand hovering in the air between them before he finally lowered it over hers. Kate blinked, surprised by the rush of feelings the contact produced. Feelings that weren't platonic. She suppressed a nervous giggle, wondering briefly if she was losing her mind. First, there were tears; now laughter threatened to bubble out of her. Perhaps she was having some sort of mental breakdown.

Clearing his throat, he asked, "You still haven't told me why you think Richard's being unfaithful."

Kate placed her free hand on top of his, absently stroking the back of his hand with her thumb. "I spoke with his new office assistant before I came here, and she did a really poor job of concealing the true nature of their relationship. Oh, and Richard couldn't get me out of there quick enough." She looked at him, their faces only inches apart. Nick shifted his torso back to a more appropriate distance. "You know everything that goes on in Taylor's End. Have you ever heard any rumors about my husband?"

Nick sucked in a breath and freed his hands from hers. He had known that Richard was a cheating snake for almost all the time he had been friends with Kate. The sleazy bastard had a penchant for pretty, young women too naïve to see him for the pathetic loser that he was. "Kate, it's not fair to ask me that. It puts me in a tough position."

Her eyes widened, and she leaped to her feet, backing away from him in disgust. "You *knew* Richard was cheating on me, and you didn't bother to mention it?" she asked angrily.

Nick shook his head in dismay. "How was I supposed to tell you something like that? You would have hated me for suggesting that your husband was cheating, or you would have thought I was saying it to get in your pants. Either way, it would have ruined our friendship, and I'm too selfish to allow that."

"That's bullshit!" she shouted. The knowledge that her best friend had been withholding the truth from her was far more hurtful than discovering Richard's sordid affair.

"Is it?" Nick asked. "I've had my suspicions about Richard since shortly after we met at that charity golf tournament. Do you remember that?"

"I remember. You were wearing that hideous red-and-yellow striped polo shirt."

"That's right. You kept calling me Ronald." The ghost of a smile turned up the corners of his mouth as he remembered the way she had teased him about his choice of shirt.

"I was in an impossible situation. It tore me up inside, not being able to warn you about Richard, but I needed you in my life."

His admission diffused her anger, and Kate collapsed back into the chair. It was the first time Nick had ever spoken so openly about their friendship. It wasn't much, but it made her wonder if his feelings for her ran deeper than he'd let on. "I've been such a fool, Nick. I've wasted more than a decade of my life on a man who, as it turns out, doesn't care about me at all. What do I even do now? I have no job, no money of my own. I'm stuck right where the bastard wants me."

"We'll sort something out. Do you think you can stick it out a while longer? That way, you can talk to a lawyer and figure out the best way to proceed."

Kate rolled her eyes. "Spoken like a true cop," she said with a sigh. "I suppose I can stay put for now, but I don't like it."

"I have to get back to work, but I'll call you later and see how you're doing."

Kate stood up and collected her purse. "I'm sorry I unloaded all my crap on you."

Nick pulled her against him and wrapped his arms around her in a tight hug. Startled by his unusual display of affection, she returned the embrace, nestling against his chest. She couldn't recall the last time she had hugged someone. She was surprised by how comforting it felt.

"You can unload on me anytime you need to," he said into the top of her head. "Now, you'd better go before people start talking." They disengaged, and Kate followed Nick out to the waiting room.

Joe stood back, watching discreetly as the pair said their goodbyes. "Be careful, Kate," Nick said. "Taylor's End isn't safe right now. Lock your doors and avoid contact with anyone you don't know. I'll check in with you when I finish work."

Kate agreed to be vigilant and left the station. She had thought speaking to Nick would help clarify her situation, and it had to some degree. There was no longer any question about the state of her marriage. Richard was cheating scum, and it was time for her to leave him. He had kept her in the dark about his extramarital activities to preserve his image as the happily married successful businessman, lying to her and the community so he could keep the money rolling in and maintain the prestige associated with his name.

What she hadn't counted on was Nick's confession about his feelings for her. While they had always enjoyed a close bond, she assumed he saw her as one of the boys, someone to laugh and have a round of golf with on the weekends. Yes, they had always enjoyed each other's company and shared confidences, but never had he given her any reason to believe he saw her as more than a friend.

Their hug moments ago was the first real physical contact they had ever had, and it kindled something inside her that had long been missing from her life. Climbing into the hatchback, Kate saw a tiny glimmer of hope among the steaming pile of crap that was her life right now. Up until a few minutes ago, she could have seen her life going only one of two ways. Either she turned a blind eye to Richard's wandering cock and continued as usual, or she could leave and scrape by in some run-down studio apartment while working a dead-end job that barely covered the rent. But Nick had assured her that it didn't have to be such a dire outcome, and she believed him. He was a man of his word. If he said he'd help her through this, then that's exactly what he'd do.

Bremner sat at his desk, munching the end of a pencil while his mind kept circling the conversation he'd had with Kate earlier. He couldn't stop thinking about what might happen if she went ahead and left that douchebag husband of hers. There was no way of knowing if she would ever see him as anything but a friend, but at least she would be free if he ever plucked up the nerve to try for something more.

There was a knock on the door to his office. Joe poked his head inside. "Sorry to interrupt, Chief, but Fred Fitzgerald from the Taylor's End Gazette is asking to see you."

Nick groaned and tossed the chewed-up pencil down on his desk. "Are you kidding me? That's the last thing I need." Sighing theatrically, he motioned for Joe to send him in. "Show him through, but if he thinks I'm giving him anything after that travesty he printed in last Friday's paper, he's got rocks in his head." Joe ran off to collect the journalist while Bremner cleared his desk of anything relating to the Michelle Tanner attack or the rest stop murder. He scooped up the thick stack of crime scene photos and dropped them in one of the desk drawers along with the case files.

Fred Fitzgerald lumbered into the office after Joe, a tatty briefcase tucked under his arm. He was a few years younger than Bremner, but poor lifestyle choices and a knack for dressing in moth-eaten sweaters made him look much older. It didn't help that he was balding and tried to conceal it with a mussed-up hairstyle that only fourteen-year-old boys could pull off.

"Chief Bremner. I've got a few questions to ask about the rest stop killing if you don't mind." He took a seat and removed a pocket-sized voice recorder from the scuffed briefcase he insisted on carting everywhere as if it gave him intellectual authority. It didn't.

"I do mind, actually. You know damn well that I cannot comment on an ongoing investigation, so you can turn that damn thing off and go find someone else to annoy."

Fred did his best to look offended, but Bremner saw through his bullshit. Fred Fitzgerald was impervious to insults, whether by nature or gained over years of pissing people off with his insensitive snooping, Bremner would never know.

"Come on. You have to give me something. This is the biggest story in Taylor's End history."

"I find that very hard to believe," Bremner replied drily. Trust Fred to call a random act of violence the defining moment of a town that had been around for close to a hundred and fifty years.

"You sure about that?" Fred challenged. "A man traveling from Arizona on business shows up dead less than ten miles out of town, gutted like a deer, if my source is correct, and now one of our best and brightest is in the hospital with half her face ripped off. I think you're kidding yourself if you question the magnitude of this story."

Bremner resisted the urge to lunge across the table and jam the voice recorder down Fred Fitzgerald's throat. Now that would be a story, he thought.

"Fred, I don't deny the magnitude of the situation. I do, however, question your inflammatory articles and your complete disregard for the impact they are having. Half the town is too damn scared to leave their homes, and the other half have decided that carrying a firearm is the only way to stay safe—which, I'm sure you will agree, doesn't help anyone. It's especially unhelpful to me and the rest of the department since we have to run around calming hysterical, gun-toting folks ready to blow a hole in their neighbors because they mistook them for the killer."

"People should be scared," Fred said. "There could be a serial killer preying on the residents of Taylor's End, and what exactly are the police doing about it? By the look of it, a whole lot of nothing. Two weeks have passed, and neither the Michelle Tanner attack nor the rest stop murder is any closer to being solved. Or do you have something you would like to share with the Gazette's readership?"

Bremner took a moment to compose himself. "Be very careful about throwing around that term, Fred. Right now, we have no evidence to suggest the two crimes are related."

"Yeah, right. Next, you'll be telling me some hopped-up meth head is responsible," Fred replied sourly.

"It wouldn't be the first time some drug-addled idiot went homicidal. But I don't believe that that's the case here. I'll be sure to get one of my people to inform you the minute we have anything concrete to share," Bremner said dismissively.

"Of course you will." Fred rose from the chair with a huff, snatching up his briefcase. "I'll show myself out."

Bremner nodded and gave the other man a tight smile. "Bye, Fred." He waited until the reporter left before getting up and slipping into his jacket. He had to get out of the office and into some fresh air. Otherwise, his head might explode. And as much as he hated to admit it, Fred, the grubby weasel, had a valid point. People in Taylor's End should be scared. Bremner was scared. Although they were still searching for the connections, it couldn't be a coincidence that three violent acts were committed on the same day on different people.

One of the victims was dead. Another was in the hospital, facing countless reconstructive surgeries, and was too traumatized by the horrific assault to make any sense. The third was convalescing at home, waiting for his geriatric bones to heal. Bremner planted his hat on his head and headed out. It was time to have another crack at Tom McCormack. The old guy was holding something back, and Bremner needed to find out what that something was.

Eight

It was becoming uncomfortably warm in the basement, almost stifling with the furnace cranked up and the radiant heater in the corner pumping out the heat. Often, after the furnace had run for a couple of days, it became unbearably hot, and Connor would have to crack open the small window beside his bed to let in some cool air. When his father was being a miserly prick and turned off the furnace, the basement became an icebox. Luckily, because of tenant complaints, Jim refrained from cutting off the heating too often. The last thing he wanted to deal with was a bunch of irate winos hounding him about the cold.

Connor was in his bedroom in the basement playing video games with his buddy, Todd. Although Connor was a year older and had already left school, the pair remained friends and spent time together whenever they could. It was rare for Todd to visit Connor at the boarding house. Usually, they would hang out at Todd's place a few blocks away on Wentworth Street. He lived in a neat two-bedroom apartment with his mom, and although it was on the small side, both boys preferred it there than at Connor's, where they never knew if Jim was about to go mental and start beating on Sophie or the boys.

Tonight, it was either hang out in the basement or freeze out in the street. Todd's mom was entertaining Don, a douchebag she had been seeing for the past month or so. They worked together at the packing plant, and as far as Todd was concerned, the guy was a complete dick. He had a rudimentary understanding of his mom's loneliness, but surely it was better to remain single than demean herself by hanging out with a loser like Don. Regrettably, she had yet to reach this realization, so here they were, bunkered down in Connor's basement while his mom fawned over Don like he was some rich stud.

"Do you reckon your mom and Don are getting serious?" Connor asked. His eyes were glued to the television, which was propped up on a makeshift stand of cinderblocks and salvaged timber.

Todd jabbed his controller angrily. "I sure fuckin' hope not. I hate that prick. He's always eyeing her like she's a juicy steak he can't wait to sink his teeth into. It makes me wanna puke."

Connor gave his friend a quick sideways glance before returning his attention to the game. While he trusted Todd's judgment in most things, he wondered if he was being a bit unreasonable about his mom's choice of boyfriend. As long as Connor had known Todd, it had just been him and his mom. His old man had up and left when Todd was just a kid. He thought his friend might not be coping well with the prospect of sharing his mom. Todd had been moody and quick to anger ever since Rita Vincent had started dating Don. Connor asked, partly to stir the pot and distract his friend but also out of genuine curiosity, "What are you gonna do if she asks Don to move in?"

"Fuck off. There's no way she would ask that loser to move in."

"She might. She's been alone a long time. Waking up to Don's big schlong every day might be too much to resist," Connor teased.

"I think I'm going to kill you," Todd replied. Connor burst out laughing, barely maintaining his focus as Todd renewed his attack against Connor's onscreen character.

"Seriously," Connor said, "it could happen."

"If she asks Don to move in, I'm moving out. There is no way in hell that I'm sharing an apartment with that loser. He thinks he's so funny, but he's just a lame-ass motherfucker. And his teeth are gross. I mean, would it kill the guy to use a toothbrush occasionally?"

Distracted by his rant, Todd was a second too slow deflecting a fatal blow from Connor's character. Connor whooped in victory, throwing his controller down on the bed and jumping around like a hyped-up monkey at the circus. "Take that, motherfucker!" he taunted, grinning.

Todd sprang to his feet and cuffed Connor playfully, and then it was on. The pair wrestled and pummeled each other, grunting and laughing. Todd collapsed onto his back, panting and red in the face. "Time out," he cried. Connor dropped into the beanbag and wriggled around until he found a comfortable position.

"Hey, any chance you wanna go upstairs and get us a drink? All that messing around has made me thirsty as fuck."

Connor nodded. "Sure. I could use a soda. Wanna come up with me?"

"Nah, you go on up. I'll chill down here."

Connor struggled to extract himself from the squishy, underfilled beanbag, his body sinking back into the depression every time he moved. Eventually, he rolled himself out in an awkward tumble. He stood up and brushed off the front of his jeans. "I'll be back in a minute. Do you want anything else while I'm up there?"

Todd shook his head. "Just a soda is fine."

Connor started climbing the stairs, and when he was a few steps from the top, he heard his father shouting. He paused, listening for clues as to what had set him off this time. He glanced over his shoulder and saw Todd standing by the bottom of the stairs.

"You don't have to go up there," Todd said. "I'm not that thirsty."

Connor turned his back to Todd, ashamed that his friend was willing to make excuses for him. Overhead the conflict escalated. There was the familiar thud of furniture being overturned, followed shortly by his mother's muffled cries. "It's fine. I want a soda now. I'll be back soon." The last thing he wanted to do was enter his parents' apartment while his father was in a rage, but he didn't want Todd to think he was too scared to go and get them a couple of drinks. He eased open the basement door and slipped through the opening, bracing himself for the all too familiar nightmare he was about to enter.

Todd wandered back into the section of the basement that Connor had converted into a bedroom. He sat on the edge of the bed and looked around at the partially finished space. Connor had installed the drywall himself, and although it needed a coat of paint, he had done a decent job. It was especially impressive considering he had no prior building experience. Connor had watched a few DIY videos before getting stuck into it, and he had gotten some advice from the old guy down at the hardware store, but that was it. A doorway had been cut out and the frame installed, but the door itself was absent. Apparently, Connor was trying to save up for a door and a can of paint, but Todd doubted that it would happen anytime soon. Connor didn't even have a regular paying job.

There was a thump overhead, followed by more shouting. Todd peered up at the ceiling and deeply regretted sending Connor upstairs. He had sent his friend, unarmed, into a war zone. And all for a lousy soda. Something heavy clattered to the floor above him, and he flinched, trying to ignore the volley of curses directed at one of the Websters. He couldn't begin to imagine what it must be like living under the same roof as Jim Webster. He pitied Connor and his younger brother, Nathan. How Connor's mom stayed married to a violent drunk like that was a mystery. He supposed she must be too scared to try and leave. The mad bastard would probably kill her if she tried.

While he waited for Connor to return, he recalled a story that Chad had told him a year or two ago. Chad and Connor used to hang out until Chad was busted for a string of break-ins on Glenview Estate and sent to prison for four years. A month or so before Chad was caught, Todd had found himself hanging out with him and a couple of other kids he hardly knew. It had been a dry autumn afternoon, and Todd was walking home from school after cutting gym class. He had no plans other than to avoid running laps with all the other obedient sheep, so once he had safely skipped class, he took his sweet time covering the two blocks to his apartment. He turned the corner and spotted Chad headed in his direction, kicking an empty can along the road.

"Hey, Chad!" Todd called out.

Chad gave the can one final kick, sending it skittering across the ground with a clatter. He jogged down the street to greet Todd. Chad had half a packet of cigarettes, so they made their way over to the vacant lot on Ribald Street. It was only a short walk from Todd's place, and he often went there to smoke and watch porn on his cell phone.

The boys reached the lot and followed a narrow path, cut through the knee-high weeds by all the kids who frequented the garage for various illicit activities. For some reason, the garage still stood, even after the old house was gutted by a fire one winter and later demolished. And although the peeling paint and the debris accumulating around it made the garage look ready to collapse, the structure itself was sound.

The boys slipped inside the shadowy interior and sank onto an old rear car seat, ripped from a wreck. The place didn't look like much, but it was somewhere to smoke or drink or fuck if you could find a girl willing to lower her standards and put out in such a hovel. Chad took the pack of cigarettes from his shirt pocket and plucked one out. He offered the packet to Todd. With their cigarettes lit, the boys sat in the gloom, making small talk while they smoked. The conversation got around to Connor and, more specifically, his father, Jim. Chad grew excited at the mention of Jim Webster, and he quickly ground out his cigarette butt and absently lit another. He offered the pack to Todd, but he shook his head.

"Man, have I got a story for you!" Chad exclaimed eagerly. "I'd forgotten all about it until you mentioned Connor's dad."

"All right then, tell me about it," Todd urged, mildly intrigued by Chad's enthusiasm. Whatever gossip the older boy had on Jim, it was obviously something juicy.

"I was at a buddy's place two, maybe three weeks ago. There was a group of us, and we were smoking some weed, playing *Call of Duty,* and shooting the shit. One of the guys, some dude from Minneapolis that I'd never met before, started telling a story about his uncle who drives trucks for a living. Not a riveting start to a story, by any means, but I was fuckin' baked, so I listened on anyway. And it's a good thing that I did because no sooner had I packed my next bowl that the story got a whole lot more interesting. Apparently, this trucking uncle of his had to stop over in Taylor's End for the night on his way to someplace I don't fuckin' remember. It was during that lame folk music festival that the town hosts every year, and all the motels were booked out, so he tried the only place with a vacancy. Christ, not even those stinky-ass hippies will stay at Webster's Boarding House. That should tell you something." He took a long drag from his cigarette, which had burned down to the last quarter-inch of tobacco. "Anyway, I'm getting sidetracked. This trucker walks up to the boarding house, and it's late—after ten at least. When he knocks on the door, big ol' Jim is drunk and half asleep, so he sends the guy straight up to the room, telling him he can settle the bill in the morning.

"So morning rolls around, and the truck driver decides to push off without paying for the room. It's early, and the neighborhood is a bit rough, so he thinks it's unlikely anyone paid too much attention to the plates on the semi parked across the street. He manages to sneak off, and thinking his escape has gone unnoticed, he drives the truck through town, admiring the clear, bright morning. It's not until he's turned onto the highway that he checks the rearview mirror and sees a car hurtling toward him at what he guesses to be a good eighty-five miles an hour. It doesn't take long for the car to catch up with him. The semi hadn't warmed up yet, so he's being gentle with her. The car veers around the truck erratically and rockets past him, cutting back into the lane only a few feet in front of him. The trucker brakes to avoid smashing into the rear end of the car, and now he's starting to wonder what the hell is going on."

"Tell me it wasn't Connor's old man," Todd asked, unable to contain himself.

Chad nodded and continued the story. "He doesn't have to wonder long because the car shoots off ahead before screaming to a stop three hundred yards down the road. And who do you think leaps out waving a handgun in the air like a fuckin' maniac?"

"No way!" Todd leaped up and danced around the shed, too excited to contain himself.

Grinning at Todd's reaction, Chad pressed on with the story. "Sure enough, Jim Webster was standing out in the middle of the highway in a stained wifebeater and pajama bottoms, impervious to the 70,000 pounds of truck barreling toward him. He plants his feet and aims the gun directly at the truck."

Todd scoffed incredulously.

"Wait, it gets better. Now, my buddy's friend, who is the trucker's nephew, promises me this next part is 100 percent true. Jim fires the gun at the truck, and the bullet slams through the windscreen, lodging itself in the passenger's-side headrest. Naturally, the trucker shits his pants and slams on the brakes. Obviously, Jim Webster means business, and the guy has no desire to die over twenty dollars. Not only is this poor guy worried he's taking his last breaths, but there is also a serious possibility that he has soiled his pants. Frozen by fear, he remains in the truck's cab, his hands clutching the steering wheel, watching with apprehension as Jim strides toward the truck with the gun pointed straight at him."

"Couldn't he have just run Jim over? I mean, the guy *was* driving a semi," Todd mused.

Chad shrugged. "Maybe. I guess having a gun fired at him freaked him out too much. Do you want me to finish the story or not?" Todd nodded and motioned for another cigarette. "So Jim walks up to the truck, the gun still pointed at the trucker's head, and he tells him to roll down the window. The trucker is trembling so bad that it takes a couple of attempts to press the window button. He risks a nervous glance out the window and doesn't know what's worse: peering down the barrel of the gun or witnessing the maniacal grin plastered on Jim's face.

'Hey, asshole,' Jim says, 'I believe you owe me twenty dollars for the room. But since you made me chase you down, I think we can agree that forty is fair compensation for all the trouble you've caused.' Naturally, the fear of being shot dead by a gun-toting booze-addled nutjob was enough to silence any protests regarding the satisfactory payment of his outstanding bill.

"By now, he is blubbering like a baby, his face slick with snot and tears. He cracks open his wallet, pulls out two twenties, and hands them down to Jim. Jim pockets the cash, slips the gun into the waistband of his pajama pants, and calmly walks back to his car. Apparently, he even waved at the trucker as he drove by on his way back to town."

Todd thought it was a load of shit and said so. Chad assured him every word of it was true. Except for the part about him blubbering. That had been thrown in for dramatic effect. Todd still didn't believe it, but he let it go. Even if it wasn't true, it was still a good story that helped pass the time.

As he sat in the basement, listening to the shouting upstairs, Todd wondered if there had been any truth to the story after all. When Connor got back, he would ask if he knew whether his dad owned a gun. It was taking Connor a long time to grab a couple of sodas, and the fighting upstairs was getting worse. The floor between them muffled the sound, but he thought he heard Jim bellow, "Get over here and say that to my face, ya little prick!" A moment later, there was a loud crash. Todd assumed it was one of the Websters being tossed around like a ragdoll.

That was enough. It was time to get the fuck out of there before something bad happened. Todd's mom would kill him if he got caught up in the Webster family drama, and he was too scared of Jim Webster to stick around. He felt around under the bed for the old wooden stepladder that Connor kept for these very occasions. Brushing aside some balled-up tissues, which he refused to think too much about, he grabbed the stepladder and pulled it out from under the bed, placing it on the floor beneath the window.

He felt guilty sneaking off without saying goodbye, but he figured Connor would understand since he frequently used the small basement window as an escape hatch when things got too ugly. His friend knew how Todd felt about Jim. Nobody wanted to be in the same zip code as the guy when he was going off, much less the same building.

A blast of frigid air whipped at his face when Todd cracked open the basement window. Remembering his jacket, he jumped down to retrieve it. He tossed it outside and hoisted himself up through the opening. It was a tight fit. The opening was small, and he must have gone through a growth spurt since the last time he left through the basement window. His feet pedaled the air as he dragged himself up, his shoulders scraping the window frame. For a second, panic constricted his chest as he got stuck, but then he was through, crawling out onto the snow-covered walkway alongside the house.

Brushing snow from his hands and feet, he pulled his jacket on and zipped it up, flipping the hood up over his head to block out the cold. He shivered, burying his hands deep in his jacket pockets, and trod quietly along the path beside the house. Rebel was chained up out the back and he didn't want to set the dog off. He was so intent on sneaking away that he didn't notice the girl standing at the living room window until he was almost upon her.

Todd froze, watching the girl that Connor's buddies had harassed downtown a few weeks ago. He remembered Connor mentioning something about her staying at the boarding house. It didn't explain why she was out in the cold, peeping through a two-inch gap between the curtains.

Todd couldn't fathom why she would be so mesmerized by the violence unfolding inside the house, nor did he wish to draw her attention. Her lips were turned up into an ugly smirk as she spied Jim pummeling his youngest son Nathan. There was something very wrong with her. It was more than just the late-night voyeurism; the night felt darker and more dangerous around her. For the second time that night, Todd regretted his decision to hang out with Connor at the boarding house.

Hoping to retreat unseen, he took a step backward, followed by another. Ella stood at the window, her full attention on the beating taking place inside. Todd thought he would escape unnoticed until his heel caught in a crack in the concrete path, and he fell to the ground with a loud thud.

Ella's head whipped around at the sound, her coal-black eyes boring into him. The sickly yellow light spilling out from between the curtains cast strange shadows across her face. Their eyes locked. Her brows knitted together in a frown, and her fists slowly clenched at her sides. Todd dared not move, afraid that she would dash forward and attack him while he was vulnerable on the ground.

Inside the house, Sophie screamed. It was the distraction Todd needed. Hating himself for taking advantage of Mrs. Webster's suffering, he scooted backward while the girl's attention momentarily returned to the brutality taking place inside. He scrambled to his feet and ran along the side of the house, his arms pumping as he fled. He vaulted the chain-link gate and bolted across the front lawn. The Websters' pit bull started barking frantically from its enclosure on the opposite side of the house, setting off the other dogs in the neighborhood. Todd ran on, ignoring the cacophony of barking that his escape had caused. He raced west along Bourke Street until his lungs burned and his legs felt like lead. Unable to continue, he slowed to a walk and took some deep breaths, wincing at the sharp pain in his side.

Now that he was a safe distance from the boarding house, he wondered if he had overreacted. Sure, catching some weirdo peeping at a family fighting was somewhat unsettling, but did it warrant the cowardly dash from Connor's place? A sense of shame settled over him, and Todd hoped Mrs. Webster and the boys weren't too badly hurt. He knew it was wishful thinking.

No doubt, the boys would be mottled with purplish-black bruises the next time he saw them. At least the cold weather meant they could hide much of the damage beneath long sleeves and bulky winter coats with the hoods pulled low over their faces. Bruises were easier to conceal than broken bones. Last year, before he had dropped out of school, Connor showed up to school with his arm in a cast. He hadn't bothered making up any bullshit story about falling down the stairs or whatever. Everyone knew what his father did to him. Even the teachers had learned to stop asking about the split lips and black eyes.

Todd's mom had once said Jim Webster deserved a bullet for the dreadful things he did to his family. Now, after running off into the night to avoid getting caught up in the violence, Todd wholeheartedly agreed. Someone ought to put a bullet in Jim's head. The world would be a better place without scum like that, especially for his wife and two sons.

Turning right onto Wentworth Street, Todd almost bumped into a dark figure walking toward him. He hurriedly stepped back, relieved that he'd managed to suppress the startled scream threatening to escape his lips. It was just a couple of kids he saw around town from time to time.

"Hey, man, sorry if we frightened you. I thought you saw us coming."

"No problem. I guess I wasn't paying attention," Todd replied. He grappled to remember the boy's name. Wade? Wayne. That was it. He was a year older than Todd and worked part-time at the dry cleaners on Robinson Street. His girlfriend was a chubby thing with poorly applied makeup and an even worse dye job. Wayne asked if he could bum a smoke, and Todd nodded. "Yeah, sure." He handed them each a cigarette and fumbled in his pocket for a lighter. The tiny blue flame danced behind his cupped hand as they leaned close.

"Thanks, man," Wayne said. "I'll pay you back next time I see you." His girlfriend smiled shyly at Todd, and the pair walked off hand in hand, puffing on the smokes he had given them.

Todd tapped a cigarette free from the pack for himself and lit it, inhaling deeply. Smoking might cause cancer, but it sure as shit helped calm his nerves. By the time he finished it and flicked the smoldering butt into the gutter, his paranoia had all but vanished.

When he reached the row of apartments where he lived, he was disappointed to see Don's pickup still parked in one of the visitor parking spaces. It was five minutes after ten. Obviously, their cozy evening was going well—too well, as far as Todd was concerned. If the shady bastard thought he was sleeping over, he could fucking think again. Feeling jealous and put out by his mom's new squeeze, he sidled over to Don's pickup and checked that no one was watching before he grabbed hold of the side mirror on the driver's side and yanked it off.

Pleased with his spiteful act of vandalism, Todd hurled the broken mirror into the garden bordering the small parking lot. Good luck finding your mirror now, asshole, he thought triumphantly. It had landed with a thud among the overgrown bushes.

Reluctant to enter the apartment while Don was inside, Todd walked over to his mom's car and crouched beside the front tire on the driver's side. He felt under the wheel well until his fingers closed around the small magnetized box containing the spare key. He removed the key from the box and slipped it into the lock. He'd give them another hour max. After that, he was going inside to break up the party. In the meantime, he would have to wait in the car. It wouldn't be much fun, but it sure as hell beat sitting out in the snow, getting hypothermia.

Climbing into the back seat, he eased the car door shut and pulled a crocheted blanket down from the rear deck. His elderly neighbor had given it to his mom as a housewarming present when they first moved into the complex. Arranging the blanket over himself, he lay on his side across the length of the seat. He folded his knees up near his chest. It was cramped and not particularly comfortable, but it was only for an hour or so. Sighing, he shifted his weight, searching for a better position, and closed his eyes.

His thoughts drifted to Michelle Tanner. Last he had heard, she had been transferred to a private hospital in the city to undergo a series of reconstructive surgeries. He hadn't gone and visited her when she was at Taylor's End Community Hospital. Her condition had been too precarious to allow visitors. Besides, he doubted she would want to see some random guy she hardly knew.

It was difficult to reconcile all the grisly details of her attack with the gorgeous, fun-loving girl he had danced with at Tara's party earlier that same night. Despite knowing that there was nothing he could have done to prevent it, Todd felt a pang of guilt about what had happened. If only he had stopped her from leaving with that muscled-up jerk, Dan, maybe she wouldn't have gone out to the old granary where the psycho had been lurking.

Todd wrapped the blanket tightly around himself and wished he hadn't started thinking about what had happened to Michelle out at the silo. He was beginning to feel jumpy and on edge all over again. What a load of bullshit! Why should he be stuck out in his mom's car when it was snowing, for fuck's sake? It wasn't fair that Don the jerk got to cozy up to his mom inside *his* home while Todd had to freeze his balls off outside.

A noise outside the car caught his attention. He pushed himself up on his elbows to peer out the window, which was already beginning to fog over from his breath. Expecting to see Don and his mom parting company for the night, Todd was puzzled when he saw nothing but the dim outline of lamplight creeping out from between the curtains of old Mrs. Walsh's living room window.

He settled back, draping the old blanket around himself once more, when he heard it again. Nope, that wasn't his imagination working overtime. The sound of gravel crunching underfoot was unmistakable from the otherwise silent car. Flinging the blanket off, he cracked open the car door and listened intently. His mom's easy-listening music filtered across the small parking lot, but that was all.

The creepy feeling he'd experienced back at the boarding house was back. His skin prickled as he scanned the darkness, his eyes unable to penetrate the thick black shadows bordering the apartment complex. The squat lamps along the garden edge did nothing to illuminate the overgrown shrubbery. It didn't help that nearly a third of the bulbs were blown and needed replacing. For the first time since living there, Todd wondered what the maintenance guy did to earn his money. Sweet fuck all, judging by the unkempt garden bordering the property and blown lightbulbs leaving much of the complex in complete darkness.

Pressing the car door shut with his backside, Todd stepped away from the security of his mom's car. Every shadow took on a sinister outline. Every sound made his stomach do a little flip. He pulled out his cell and switched on the flashlight function, swinging it in a slow arc around the parking lot. He walked around Mrs. Walsh's faded green Escort to get a better look at the far side of the parking space, where the bins stood behind a privacy screen.

A woman's flirty laughter caught his attention, and he turned to see his mom standing in the doorway to their apartment. Don stood on the threshold, leaning in close to his mom, whispering something in her ear. She laughed again. It was high and girlish, unlike her usual laugh. Mystified by this new side to his mom, Todd crouched behind the Escort to avoid being caught gawking. He poked his head around the small front end of the Escort just as Don moved in for a goodnight kiss.

Todd couldn't decide whether he wanted to puke or leap out from behind the old lady's car and pummel Don's face into hamburger meat. Knowing his mom would be seriously pissed if he tried anything, he remained behind the vehicle until the couple eventually separated. His legs were numb from crouching for so long. He hunkered down even lower when Don crossed the driveway, barely containing a snigger when the douche discovered he was missing a side mirror.

Don kept his cool until Todd's mom waved goodbye and closed the front door. The second that door clicked shut, he kicked the tire in frustration and cursed profusely while his fingers felt the empty socket where the mirror belonged. After a half-hearted search in the dark, Don climbed into the truck and threw it into reverse, spitting up gravel as he beat a hasty retreat. *Take that, motherfucker*, Todd thought as he watched the truck's taillights disappear down the street.

Now that the sleazy bastard had gone, he could go inside and get out of the cold. The snow continued its steady descent, finely coating his shoulders. Not wanting his mom to think he had been skulking around outside while she was entertaining Don, Todd thought it was best to wait a few minutes before venturing inside. Besides, he needed to get his story straight before he faced his mom. He couldn't exactly tell her the truth. She already disapproved of him spending time with Connor. If he admitted that Jim had flipped his lid while Todd was visiting, she would go out of her way to make it difficult for the boys to spend time together in the future.

He would tell her he had forgotten about a biology assignment that was due tomorrow. That was plausible enough. All he had to do now was wait a couple of minutes, and he would be inside, thawing out in front of the heater in the living room. Hell, since his mom was obviously in a good mood, she might even be amenable to making him a sandwich or two.

He was trying to remember if there was any turkey in the refrigerator when he heard gravel crunching underfoot behind him. Before he could turn to see who was there, an arm hooked around his throat, and he was jerked backward across the hood of the Escort. The metal buckled under his weight, his heels making a hollow thumping noise as he kicked. He clawed at the arm locking him in a deadly chokehold, and his fingers scratched and tore at the pale flesh tightening around his windpipe. Its grip only tightened, and Todd fought back panic as he felt the world beginning to fade. He slid off the edge of the hood, and with a violent thrust, he kicked back against the side of the car.

The sudden motion caught his attacker off guard and sent them tumbling backward. As they hit the ground, the grip around Todd's throat momentarily relaxed, and he rolled free, scrambling across the snow-covered gravel back toward the parked cars. Sucking in lungfuls of air as he crawled toward the cars, he risked a hurried glance over his shoulder. The girl from the boarding house was slowly getting to her feet, her hair falling in thick tangles over her face.

Todd climbed to his feet, using the Escort for balance, and ran between the cars toward the row of apartments. Should he make a dash for his place, which was the second apartment in the row, or head over to Mrs. Walsh's apartment, which was closer, and hope to heck the old bag heard him? In the split second he had to decide, he opted for the closest option.

He assumed she'd followed his path around the front of the car and was taken by surprise when she intercepted him in the middle of the driveway. Spotting the pale creature hurtling at him, Todd barely had enough time to brace himself. Ella tackled him hard and sent them both tumbling across the driveway in an awkward dance to stay on their feet.

He felt his ribs crack as she clutched him. Her breath, steaming and rank with the smell of decay, burned his cheek. He fought as she dragged him back toward the dark outline of the garden, but she was so much stronger than him. What the fuck? He had to outweigh her by forty pounds or more, yet he felt powerless against her. He battered against her with his fists and feet, kicking out at her shins with little effect.

"Let me go," he croaked, "Help me! Somebody help!" The searing pain in his ribs prevented him from inhaling deeply enough to make noise that could be heard by anyone but his attacker.

"Nobody can hear you," Ella said, chuckling darkly. "You're a dead boy. And dead boys don't talk." She squeezed him, pulling him up over the weathered sleepers that lined the garden bed.

"No, no, no," Todd wheezed.

He reached up and grabbed a handful of her hair as hard as he could. It wasn't much, but it seemed to catch her by surprise. She loosened her grip on him enough so he could squirm free, leaving her holding his jacket. Lunging forward, clutching his ribs, he managed one frantic cry before she caught him by the ankle. He fell forward onto his hands and knees.

She leaped onto his back, riding him like he was a pony at the fairground, her hands wrapped around his throat. He bucked and twisted as she throttled him, trying in vain to unseat her before he passed out.

Tiring of the game, Ella reached around with one hand while maintaining her grip on Todd's throat with the other. Her clawed fingers forced their way into Todd's open mouth and wrapped around his tongue in an iron grip. He retched, grabbing at her wrist as nails as sharp as slivers of glass sank into the soft meat of his tongue. Tears squirted from his eyes, and his bowels let go.

With a savage twist, the creature ripped his tongue out at the root and greedily stuffed the dripping meat into its mouth. It slackened its grip on Todd, and he managed to crawl out from beneath it. He climbed to his feet unsteadily, and his trembling hands rose to his chin in shock. Blood poured over his lips, streaming between his fingers and down his wrists. It spilled over his chin and stained his sweater like a macabre bib.

Pushing through the haze of shock and pain, Todd took an unsteady step toward the soft glow of light spilling from his apartment. It wasn't so far away. Not really. If he could convince his legs to move with a bit more coordination, he could reach the front door in seconds. Once inside, he would be safe from the insanity of flesh-eating monsters in the guise of young girls.

He remembered his cell phone and patted his pockets. Nothing. It was gone. He must have dropped it during the scuffle. Blood pooled in his mouth, seeping out from between his lips and trickling down his throat. A coughing fit shook his body and he dropped to his knees, overcome by a wave of dizziness.

Panic constricted his chest. Focusing on the light illuminating the front door of his apartment, Todd crawled forward. Gravel gouged his palms and knees. He saw his mom's car through the blur of tears. Should he lock himself in the car instead? It was much closer than the apartment. Shock and blood loss had robbed him of his remaining strength. It would be so much easier to climb up into the car than try to cross the driveway, but being locked up in the dark was too much. The dark harbored unspeakable things that filled him with terror.

No, he couldn't take refuge in the car. He had to push through the light-headed feeling eroding his thoughts and reach the apartment. His mom was inside, and she would make everything better. She always did. No matter what was wrong with him, she always seemed to know what to say and do to fix everything. He almost smiled when he thought of his mom. Almost. He didn't have far to go now. A little farther and his mom would be there to help him inside and keep the sharp-toothed shadows at bay.

With all his energy focused on finding refuge before he passed out, Todd failed to hear its approach. Ella stalked him silently. It waited in the shadows while he made the fateful decision to carry on. Nostrils quivering, it inhaled the intoxicating scent of fear and freshly spilled blood. It trailed behind Todd as he stumbled toward the apartment.

The creature lunged forward with a throaty snarl. Todd whirled around at the sound, his feet tangling together, and he fell forward, his bloody mouth a surprised O as he went crashing to the ground. Before he could recover, it grabbed his ankles and pulled him back toward the far end of the apartment complex, where the shadows would swallow them. His cries for help came out wet and muffled, a fine spray of blood splattering the snow as it dragged him away.

The creature flung him over onto his back with a violent jerk of its powerful wrists and stooped down over him menacingly. "Shhh," it hissed, raising a finger to its misshapen mouth. "No waking the neighbors." Then, with a crooked grin, it backhanded him with such force that it knocked two teeth out of his mouth and sent them skittering across the ground like playing dice.

The blow knocked Todd senseless. Consciousness receded into the background as a blanket of darkness enveloped him. While he lay limp and unable to put up a fight, the creature grabbed him by the ankles once more and hauled him back to the garden at the rear of the property.

Todd's eyes fluttered open when the back of his head bounced over the timber edging that acted as a border between the garden bed and driveway. He moaned as the jolt sent a wave of pain through his battered face. He almost fainted again. Instead, he folded his torso forward so he could bat at the creature as it tugged his legs. It pulled him over the rough wood chips covering the ground and left drag marks in the snow, but they would soon disappear beneath the steady flurry of snow falling.

The creature hunkered down to squeeze between a pair of shrubs, ignoring Todd's pitiful attempts to swat it away. Brittle, snow-covered branches scratched and tore at their skin as they made their way to the furthest corner of the property, where they were completely hidden from view. Half dead and delirious, Todd sobbed, realizing the end was near. Nothing he did would change it. Despite this, he still tried to crawl beneath the nearest bush to escape. The creature chuckled at his feeble attempt and pinned him in place with one hand. It traced a clawed finger along his trembling jaw, its ink-black eyes captivated by his dread. He tried to plead for his life, but his stump of a tongue wouldn't form the words.

Straddling him, it pinned his arms beneath its knees and covered his mouth with the palm of its hand, its fingers latching onto his jaw. It forced his head to the side, exposing his throat. Todd was still conscious when its needle teeth sank into the tender flesh of his neck below his earlobe. He was aware when it started chewing on him like he was a steakhouse special.

Then he faded away. From blood loss or shock, it didn't matter. He was gone. His eyes stared up sightlessly at the spindly branches entwined above him, his head lolling slightly each time the creature gnawed at his body, giving the impression that he was still alive. But he wasn't. Todd was very much dead. His fate had been sealed the moment he climbed out of Connor's basement window and caught Ella spying on the Websters.

Across the parking lot, Mrs. Walsh poured herself a mug of milk—full fat, not the watered-down rubbish people mostly drank nowadays, thinking they were being healthy—and popped it in the microwave to warm. Since her daughter had given her the microwave as a seventy-fifth birthday present two years ago, Mrs. Walsh had grown accustomed to a mug of warm milk paired with a sleeping tablet to help her get a decent night's rest. The older a person got, the more elusive sleep became, but a sedative and warm milk seemed to do the trick. She waited by the microwave, marveling at the technology as the turntable rotated, heating her beverage.

Was that someone screaming? She quickly pressed the stop button on the microwave and listened. Princess, her beloved silky terrier, must have heard it too. The dog raced through the eat-in kitchen to the living room. It jumped up onto its hind legs at the large window and yapped its head off, running back and forth from one side of the window to the other until Mrs. Walsh came shuffling over. The cold caused her joints to seize.

"Shhh now, Princess. You'll disturb the neighbors with all that yapping," she admonished the little dog. Deep down, she was alarmed by the dog's reaction. If Princess was carrying on like this, then maybe she *had* heard someone scream, or perhaps an animal crying out in pain. She pulled back the heavy floral drapes and peered outside. There wasn't much to see. The security light at the front door had blown sometime last week, and she was still waiting for the maintenance guy to climb up and replace it for her. It didn't help that her glasses were sitting beside her bed.

It was much too dark to see anything outside. Wait. Was that just a harmless shadow over by the cars, or was it something more sinister? Her heart constricted in her narrow chest, and she hurriedly drew the curtain back across the window.

Uncomfortably aware of her vulnerability, she checked the deadbolt on the front door and placed the chain across as an extra precaution. She had read too many stories about elderly people being bashed and robbed in their own homes—or worse, though she tried not to think about the other possibility. That sort of degeneracy hadn't yet spread to

Taylor's End, but the way the world was these days, who could tell? Kids were taking all kinds of mind-altering drugs that made them do crazy things. She briefly considered calling the police, but the thought of her children finding out that something had spooked her badly enough to contact the authorities was enough to keep her hand away from the telephone. She simply couldn't give her family any reason to pack her off to a nursing home.

The following morning the incessant beeping of the alarm clock woke up Todd's mom. It was five-fifteen. She groaned and reached across the bed to press the button. It was a challenge dragging herself out of her cozy bed so early when it was cold and dark outside, but she did it for a good reason. Taking the early shift at the plant meant that she got home shortly after Todd finished school in the afternoon. Not that he wanted to hang out with his mom much, now that he was getting older. Sadly, the days when he came running home from school, full of enthusiasm and eager to tell her about his day over a cookie and glass of milk, had long since passed. Still, Rita tried to be at home in the afternoons if she could. The early shift also meant she could have dinner on the table at a decent hour.

Thinking about dinner as she filled the drip filter for a much-needed coffee, she then went over to the refrigerator and pulled a couple of steaks out of the freezer to defrost. She scribbled a note on the magnetized whiteboard on the fridge for Todd when he woke up. *Sorry, I missed you last night. I must have already been asleep when you got home. You can tell me about your day over dinner. Steak and potato salad—your favorite. Love Mom.* Although he'd never admit it, especially not in front of his friends, she knew he enjoyed the sappy messages she wrote for him. And there was always a happy face at the end. When the coffee was ready, she poured herself a mug and took it into the bathroom with her while she showered.

Twenty minutes later, she slipped outside and locked the door. She pulled on her thick hand-knitted beanie. It didn't look like much, but it sure as heck kept her head warm during the colder months. In the gloom of the early morning, she carefully made her way across the snow and hopped inside her car. She shoved the key into the ignition and started the car. It reluctantly turned over, and she gave the accelerator a pump to get the engine going before switching on the headlights.

The tip of Todd's sneaker poking out from beneath a bush at the rear of the garden was still visible when Rita put the car in reverse and swung out of the parking space, unaware of her son's body lying nearby.

Nine

Christian hefted himself off the worn couch. He parted the dusty Venetian blind over the small living room window to check the weather outside. It didn't look very encouraging: dull and overcast, the sun hidden behind a mass of heavy clouds that promised more snow. He sighed, making a mental note to dig his boots out of the bottom of the crowded wardrobe in his bedroom.

His roommate Dale had mentioned something about the possibility of the town being hit by a blizzard sometime over the next few days, but Christian was skeptical. Just because they had received about an inch of snow during the past twenty-four hours didn't mean they were in for an apocalyptic winter storm. As far as he was concerned, they'd be lucky to get any more snow before the weekend.

He let the blinds flick back into place and slowly turned to survey the small apartment. The two-bedroom apartment was on the first floor of a blond-brick complex built in the seventies. It was in original condition except for a handful of slapdash paint jobs over the years. It was nothing flashy, but it was cheap and served its purpose.

Still, it wasn't exactly the sort of place he would want to bring a girl. And while he had hooked up a few times over recent months when he was away at motocross meets, there hadn't been anyone in Taylor's End that he had considered bringing back to the apartment. But since meeting the girl with the long dark hair at the diner the other week, he had been unable to get her out of his head. There was something about her. Despite her tough, independent pretense, there was also a vulnerability that intrigued him. After thinking about her for several days, he plucked up the courage to track her down at the boarding house. It had been a bit of a long shot. He hadn't known for sure if that was where she ended up, but it was worth a try. It turned out he was on the money. She had taken a room at the seedy dump over on Faithful Street.

Surprisingly, when he called up that gangster wannabe Connor, from whom he'd bought weed on occasion, she took his call. It hadn't been easy at first. The conversation was jilted and awkward, but they slowly developed a comfortable rhythm. It wasn't until it was getting close to the start of his shift at the hospital that he blurted out the invitation. It was a now-or-never kind of situation.

There was a long pause. He was sure she would turn him down, but then she did the unthinkable: Ella agreed to meet him for a drink on Saturday night. Christian couldn't believe it. She was cagey and didn't seem likely to want to meet up, and then she said yes. Finding himself placed on the spot, he blurted out the first place that came to mind: Blue Two Tavern, probably the shittiest dive in Taylor's End. And that was the place he invited Ella for a few drinks. What the fuck was wrong with him?

Now he was faced with the possibility, as remote as it was, of bringing her back to his apartment afterward. Maybe, by some miracle, she would feel inclined to get naked and swap bodily fluids.

Panicking, Christian ran around the apartment, tidying as best he could. He couldn't much about the curbside collection of furniture, interspersed with the occasional piece from Ikea. Failing a win on his weekly lotto tickets, the shitty couch and scuffed up coffee table had to stay. The fast-food wrappers littering the coffee table and dirty plates piled in the kitchen sink were another matter. It probably wouldn't hurt to change the sheets on his bed either. He couldn't recall the last time he put them through the wash.

Was he being presumptuous? Fuck yeah. Better to be prepared than caught short. Today was his day off, and he wasn't due back at the hospital until the following afternoon, so he had plenty of time to get the apartment cleaned up.

His stomach grumbled loudly. It was lunchtime, and he hadn't eaten since the day before. He went into the poky kitchen, with its lime-green cabinetry and chipped countertop, and took some leftover hotdogs from the fridge. He threw them between two slices of stale bread with a generous squirt of ketchup.

Taking a seat at the table jammed against the wall behind the couch, he took a bite of the sandwich. Sauce oozed out from between the bread and trickled down his fingers. It was probably the least sophisticated food he could eat, but he couldn't deny the pleasure of a simple hotdog. Sure, it would have been better if the bread was fresh and he had some mustard and onions to go with it, but beggars can't be choosers.

He spotted a note lying beside Dale's empty breakfast bowl. He plucked it free and read the scribbled message with a sinking heart. The rent was due. Somehow, Christian had completely forgotten about it. He jumped up and grabbed his wallet off the coffee table. There was a whopping fifty dollars and seventy-five cents. Fuck.

"How could I forget something like that?" he admonished himself as he crumpled the note and tossed it on the overflowing bin in the corner of the kitchen. His roommate would go ballistic if he found out he couldn't cover his share of the rent. He crammed the last of the sandwich into his mouth and wiped his fingers on the dishtowel beside the sink before going into Dale's room to retrieve his roommate's share of the rent from the old coffee jar he kept stashed in the top drawer of the battered dresser. Christian removed the wad of bills from the jar and counted out four hundred and ten dollars.

For a moment, he was tempted to take what he needed to cover his share of the rent and replace it the following week when he got paid. Dale probably wouldn't notice. Christian lingered beside the drawers, his hand hovering over the jar.

It would be so damn easy.

He pushed the drawer shut and stalked out of the room, slamming the door shut behind him.

He wasn't that person anymore. All that shit was in the past, and he wasn't about to risk everything unraveling over one tiny mistake. Still, he was going to have to do something to fix his situation. Dale was fanatical about paying the bills on time, and he would kick Christian's ass if they were late with the rent. If he wanted to get out of this in one piece, he would have to find some way to cover his share of the rent. Stealing was out. Christian had been down that path before, and it was a hard-fought battle to regain the trust of the people in his life. He couldn't risk disappointing them again. People could forgive someone's mistakes only so many times before they washed their hands and cut ties. Borrowing wasn't an option either. No one he knew would be willing to front him the money for fear of a repeat of his previous behavior. Fair enough. He'd fucked over enough people during his addiction. His mom had passed away from cancer nearly three years ago, and his dad was who-the-fuck-knew-where. His friends were in the same boat as him, living paycheck to paycheck, and he'd die before asking Anna for a handout. That left begging. Not exactly the most dignified option available, but what choice did he have? The rent had to be paid. He had fucked up and didn't have the money, and he had to make it right. To hell with dignity. He grabbed his coat and headed downstairs to the carport, where he kept his bike.

A short time later, he was idling at the traffic light over the intersection of Main Street and Poplar. Scanning the street for an available parking space, he failed to notice when the light changed. An impatient driver behind him, driving a late-model Volvo, beeped his horn. Startled, Christian gave him the finger and took off. The bike rushed forward with a deafening roar. A couple of old ladies in their winter woollies and blue-rinsed hair stopped outside Barry's Footwear to scowl at him in disapproval. The decrepit pair shook their heads and clucked in distaste at his loutish behavior.

Whatever. Christian had more important things to worry about than the opinions of a pair of dried-up old women. He spotted a parking space on the opposite side of the street and zipped into the space before some other asshole could take it. Ordinarily, he reserved that sort of riding for the track, but the asshole in the Volvo had embarrassed him and made him drive like a jerk. He climbed off his bike and waited for a break in the traffic before jogging across the road. Feeling the chill air on his ears, he removed the beanie from his pocket and pulled it down over his head.

He pushed open the glass door and stepped inside out of the cold. It was too warm and smelled mildly like reheated food. He hastily removed his beanie and smoothed his hair down before unzipping his jacket. Looking like a crackhead wouldn't help his cause. He took a deep breath and strode over to the reception desk. The blonde seated behind the desk didn't look much older than he was, despite the heavy makeup she troweled onto her face. She looked up and gave him a megawatt smile that she surely practiced in front of the bathroom mirror at home.

"Hi. How can I help you?" the receptionist asked in a chirpy voice. "I'm here to pay the rent," Christian replied, his armpits moistening with sweat.

"Sure. What address?" He told her, and she quickly typed it into the computer. She waited briefly while the computer loaded the details. "That will be eight hundred and twenty dollars for the month," she said. Christian hesitated before taking out his wallet and removing Dale's share of the rent plus his own meager contribution. He handed it to the secretary and watched as she counted the bills. Frowning, she looked up at him questioningly. "Is this a joke? You're short three hundred and sixty dollars."

"I know," he laughed nervously. "Funny thing, that. I'm a bit strapped for cash this week, but I swear I can have the rest of the money to you next Thursday when I get paid." He felt heat rush to his cheeks as Carly glared up at him like he was something distasteful on the bottom of her shoe.

"I'm sorry, but that isn't my problem. We have a strict policy about money owed. You agreed to it when you signed the rental contract. If you fail to pay the rent by the due date, which is by close of business today, I'll have no choice but to forward the matter to management. Your tenancy will be terminated."

"There is no way I can get the money to you today. Please, I swear I will have the money for you first thing next Thursday," he pleaded.

The secretary shook her head. "I'm sorry, but we can't go making exceptions. You will need to provide the outstanding amount by 5:00 p.m. today. Otherwise . . ." She shrugged and placed the money into a small lockbox kept in the drawer at her desk.

"Come on. You can't kick us out." Christian abhorred begging, but he was desperate. Dale would never forgive him if they got kicked out because he had fucked up and failed to put his share of the rent money aside.

"As I already said, I can't help you," the secretary snapped.

He was wasting his time trying to elicit any sympathy; the girl was pure ice. Shaking his head, he collected his helmet and turned to leave.

Kate Lyttle emerged from her husband's office. She had been working on a new property listing while Richard was out with clients. She still hadn't confronted Richard about his infidelity, so it was business as usual for now. Nevertheless, it killed her to be civil to her cheating pig of a husband or the vapid tart he was banging. But it couldn't go on for much longer. Now that she knew, Kate had to confront him. However, she chose to heed Nick's advice and seek legal representation before doing anything rash, which meant being stuck in the office with Carly. How delightful.

She walked over to the reception desk and asked what the problem was, even though she had stood on the other side of the door to the spare office and heard the entire exchange.

"This *gentleman* can pay only part of the rent, and I was informing him of our zero-tolerance policy." Carly scowled across at Christian, who was standing by the door clutching the handle, ready to get the hell out of there like he committed a capital offense.

"Zero-tolerance policy?" Kate said, arching a brow in bemusement. "I'm sorry, I thought this was a realty, not a law enforcement agency." Christian fought to contain the smirk.

"We are," Carly replied curtly, "but Mr. Lyttle has told me numerous times that tenants are to pay the rent on time or face eviction."

Kate gave Christian the once-over. "Have you ever had trouble paying the rent before? Sorry, what was your name again?"

He cleared his throat and fidgeted with the visor on his helmet under the intensity of her appraisal. "I'm Christian."

"It's nice to meet you, Christian. I'm Kate." She smiled at him, and he was floored by how radiantly beautiful she was. Whoever put that gold band on her finger was one lucky bastard. "Well?" she prompted.

"Oh yeah, sorry. We've never paid the rent late. This is the first time we've been short, and it's entirely my fault," he admitted. "My bike needed repairs, and I forgot to put money aside for the rent."

Kate turned to Carly and whispered something. Carly frowned and shook her head in defiance. Kate glared at the younger woman before returning her attention to Christian. "I asked Carly if perhaps she could make an exception just this once. But it appears she is committed to implementing my husband's ridiculously rigid rules." It was hard to miss the venomous look the two women exchanged. He had no clue what was going on here, but he suspected it had nothing to do with his inability to make the rent.

When he could stand the tension no longer, he blurted, "I'm sorry if I've caused any trouble. I'll go and see if I can find the rest of the money. If not, then I guess you'll have to do whatever you have to do."

Kate wasn't about to let it go. "Nonsense. I just had a thought," she smiled triumphantly. Carly's overdone eyes narrowed suspiciously. "I'll lend you the money, and you can reimburse me next week when you get paid."

Christian was speechless. They were complete strangers. Why would she offer to help him out?

"Well? Does that work for you?" she asked.

"I couldn't let you do that," he muttered.

"Sure you can. All you have to do is smile and say yes."

She dazzled him with another smile of encouragement, and he nodded. "OK. That would be great. But only if it won't leave you short or anything."

Kate chuckled. "That shouldn't be a problem."

Carly sat behind her computer stiffly, her face as dark and apoplectic as the storm clouds outside. Ignoring the glowering secretary, Kate beckoned for Christian to follow her into the spare office she used when Richard needed a hand. She took a pen and scribbled a name on a notepad, then tore it free and handed it to him. "When you have the money, you can drop it off here."

"You're a jeweler?" he asked in confusion.

Kate laughed and shook her head, hunting around in her purse. "Nope. I've recently started working there part-time as a sales assistant. I work Thursday and Friday. It's not much, but it gets me out of the house." She gave him the money, "Here, take this out to Carly before she sends the Gestapo after you."

Christian grinned. "Thanks so much. You're way too generous." He pocketed the piece of paper and handed the money to Carly. "All sorted. You can call off the dogs now."

She snatched the money from him and watched sullenly as he strode out of the office with a new air of confidence. She grabbed her cell phone and messaged Dick, informing him about what his interfering wife had been getting up to in his absence.

Ten

The officer at the front desk called across the station to Joe. "Hey. Go get the chief, would you? And it's important, so hurry up." Joe leaped up and ran between the desks, pausing briefly to knock on the chief's door before entering the office.

Bremner gave the young officer a dark look. "Can you hold for a moment?" he spoke into the phone. "What is it, Joe? I'm on a call," he held out the receiver for emphasis, "and I'm crazy busy."

That was an understatement. His day had begun before dawn with a five-mile jog. It was a slog running through the snow, but he ignored the urge to quit and curl back up in bed for an extra hour of sleep. With his daily run behind him, Bremner had made his way into the station to get an early start on the mountain of work piling up. And no doubt he would still be chained to the desk long after his shift finished later that evening.

"Sorry to interrupt, but an urgent call has come through at the front desk. Phil said it couldn't wait."

"Can't you transfer it through to my office?"

Joe's face turned an unflattering shade of red, and he shook his head regretfully. "I already tried transferring the call. All I managed to do was put him on hold."

Bremner sighed wearily and stood up. He could feel the beginnings of what promised to be a terrific headache forming behind his left eye. "Joe, do me a favor and go grab me a coffee."

"Yes, boss," Joe agreed.

"Make it a strong one. I think I'm gonna need it." Bremner said as he made his way to the front desk.

He picked up the phone and said, "Hello. What's going on? Joe said it was urgent."

"Hi, Boss. A body has been discovered at an apartment complex a few blocks from the high school."

Bremner groaned. "How bad is it?"

"It's not good."

"Alright. Give me the address, and I'll be there shortly."

After Phil told him the location, he returned the receiver to the cradle and strode away from the front desk with a mug of coffee, and returned to his office. He raised the steaming drink to his lips and sipped. He had asked for strong, and strong was what he got. There was enough caffeine here to keep him buzzing for a week. Hell, it was practically a mug of caffeine syrup. Judging by the conversation he just had, a near-lethal dose of caffeine was the only way he would make it through the rest of the day.

Once back inside his office, he abandoned the mug and pulled on his jacket and hat. "Where's Chandler?" he asked Joe as he shut the door behind him on his way out.

Joe shrugged. "I think he went with DeAngelo to a call out about a break-in at Glenview Estate."

"OK. See if you can get hold of Chandler and tell him to meet me at the apartments at 62 Wentworth Street."

It wasn't long before he was pulling up to the curb outside the apartment complex. He planted his hand on the horn to move the gaggle of onlookers eager to get an eyeful of whatever atrocity had occurred behind the yellow tape strung across the property. He killed the engine and climbed out of the cruiser, tamping down the anger he felt at people's morbid fascination with death and tragedy. They got so caught up in the drama that they failed to comprehend the crimes or accidents that take others' lives. A loved one's passing and how it would forever impact a family were forgotten in the ghoulish thrill of the unexpected.

Aggrieved by the human vultures milling about, Bremner stalked over to the crowd with a dirty scowl. Richards, an officer with twenty-odd years of service behind him, was doing his best to keep the group under control, but he was slowly losing the battle. They smelled blood, and with the series of recent attacks, macabre curiosity won out over the weary directives of a lone police officer.

Raising both his hands, Bremner yelled, "This is an active crime scene, folks. Anyone still loitering thirty seconds from now will be arrested and taken down to the station. Now get the hell out of here!"

The crowd looked at him sheepishly before shuffling off one by one. Bremner stood in the center of the driveway until everyone had either given up and left or retreated a respectful distance. When he was satisfied they wouldn't regroup, he turned his attention to Richards, who no longer looked like he was about to have a major coronary episode.

"Thanks, Chief," Richards said. "Some people have no sense of decency. I kept telling them to step back, but they wouldn't listen. All they cared about was catching a glimpse of the body so they could be the first to post it on social media and get likes or whatever." Bremner hadn't realized that Richards was even aware of social media.

Bremner ducked under the crime tape and squinted as he surveyed the scene. A row of five apartments ran the length of the property. A pitted gravel driveway extended to a compact parking lot at the rear of the complex. The door to the third apartment stood open despite the cold, and a woman sat crumpled on the stoop. She wailed uncontrollably, and an elderly lady tried to console her.

Richard's partner stood nearby. His hands were clasped in front of him. He was clearly unnerved by the emotional outpouring.

"Where is the body?" Bremner asked.

Richards waved toward the end of the complex. "It's up behind the garbage bins at the back of the garden."

"And that woman crying over there," Bremner nodded in Rita's direction, "I'm guessing she knows the deceased."

"Yep. That would be the boy's mother. Regrettably, she saw the body, which, I will tell you right now, is not in a good way. No parent should have to see something like that."

"Shit," Bremner said. "This day keeps on getting better. Call for the paramedics if you haven't already. I'd say she'll require sedation. Keep a close eye out for the onlookers. If they start gathering again, make some arrests. This woman has been through enough. She doesn't need a bunch of strangers gawking at her tragedy."

Bremer walked down the driveway toward the rear of the property. God, he truly hated this aspect of the job. Viewing a corpse at a funeral was vastly different than witnessing devastation inflicted on the human body, by accident or otherwise. The coffee he drank earlier sloshed around in his stomach and made him queasy.

He reached the end of the drive and stepped into the garden. The ground was uneven beneath a thick blanket of snow. Carefully picking his way between the lumpy outlines of stubby plants, Bremner was stopped by an abandoned sneaker brushed clear of snow by curious paws. Sadness settled over him. He stood transfixed by the shoe, the mother of its owner wailing in the background.

From the sneaker, it was easy to follow the trail of paw prints leading to the larger bushes at the back of the garden, where a foot peeked out from beneath the snow. A toe stuck out from the worn tip of the Looney Tunes sock. Bremner took a steadying breath, bracing himself for what was to come.

The bushes had protected much of the body from snow. His jumper and the T-shirt beneath had ridden up, exposing waxy skin. Bremner crouched down so he could crawl into the bushes to get a better look. Mindful of contaminating the scene, he eased forward, careful to avoid touching the outstretched hand. The nails were chipped and broken, the palm grazed and bloodied. Whatever had happened, judging by the damage to his hands, he had put up a fight. Why wasn't he wearing a jacket? A few weeks ago, it wouldn't have been necessary, but now? Nobody was heading outdoors without throwing a coat on.

Despite the cold, ants trailed across the corpse's shredded torso, along his mangled throat, and over his bloodstained chin, where they disappeared between his swollen purple lips. Bremner leaned under the thorny branches.

He was just a boy.

Anger and grief competed inside him, and he had to blink away the tears threatening to spill down his cheeks. He was relieved that there was no one to witness his weakness. Once he regained his composure, he returned his attention to the body. The boy's head rested against his shoulder at an unnatural angle. Were these atrocities inflicted on him before or after his neck was snapped? According to the defensive wounds on the boy's hands, it was probably the former.

Thoroughly unnerved by the discovery, Bremner eased himself out from the undergrowth and turned away from the dead boy. What the hell was going on in Taylor's End? He didn't need the coroner to tell him the kid was a victim of foul play. It was possible some hungry critters had nibbled away at the body postmortem, but his instincts suggested otherwise. As much as he wanted the recent wave of violence to be unrelated, it was becoming more and more difficult to swallow the truth. Michelle Tanner had barely survived the assault at the old granary. If Dan Cumberland hadn't intervened, he had little doubt that she would have ended up in the morgue. Two bodies and a violent assault added up to a shitstorm of trouble. Something was seriously amiss in the town. If Bremner didn't catch the killer soon, the locals would be asking for his badge.

He stepped out of the garden and crossed the driveway, taking a moment to collect his thoughts before he rapped lightly on the door to the fourth apartment and waited. The door opened, and Phil stepped aside to let him in. Since the old lady had the heater going, Bremner quickly closed the door to keep the cold out.

"Did you see it?" Phil asked in a hushed voice.

Bremner nodded. "I saw it. Richards said the old lady discovered the body. Is that correct?"

"Technically, it was the yappy little mutt that found him, but it's not like we can interview a dog, so its owner is the next best thing, right?"

Bremner's mouth set in a hard line. He silently counted to ten. The day kept going from bad to worse. "Does she have a name?"

"I think she's called Princess," Phil replied.

"Not the dog, Phil, the woman. What is the woman's name?"

"Oh. The dog's owner is Mrs. Walsh. She lives alone in the apartment. Her husband died a few years ago. I think she said it was a stroke."

"And where is she now? I thought you brought her inside so we could have a chat away from the boy's mother."

Phil pointed along a short hall toward the back of the apartment. "She needed a moment to freshen up. She'll be back in a minute."

They waited in silence until the bathroom door opened, and Mrs. Walsh came shuffling down the hall. "Sorry to keep you waiting, gentlemen. Would you like to sit at the dining table in the kitchen? I can make a pot of tea or coffee if you prefer."

"That's kind of you to offer, but we are fine, thanks." Bremner followed her into the kitchen and sat at the dark wooden table polished to a high shine.

"I'm going to brew a pot of tea for myself if you don't mind. Tea helps calm my nerves."

"Go ahead," Phil encouraged.

"I wish we were meeting under different circumstances, Chief Bremner. I had the pleasure of seeing your picture in the paper a couple of times: once when you were elected chief of police, and the other time was for some charity event, I think. The pictures didn't do you justice. You are far more handsome in person. It's hard to believe you are still single. Surely, the local ladies are throwing themselves at you." Phil stifled a chuckle, and Bremner gave his shin a sharp kick under the table. Mrs. Walsh turned her faded blue eyes to Phil. "It's all right for you. Tonight, when this dreadful day comes to an end, you get to go home and take comfort in the arms of your wife. But this one?" She nodded in Bremner's direction. "I'm guessing with no motivation to clock off, he'll keep working until some ungodly hour to avoid going home to an empty house. Am I right?"

Bremner shifted in his seat, hoping his discomfort wasn't visible. The old woman was closer to the truth than he cared to admit.

"I apologize," she said. "I tend to prattle on when I'm upset."

"That is perfectly understandable, Mrs. Walsh. I imagine that you are quite rattled by what you discovered this morning. Do you think you can tell us about what happened?" Bremner shifted in his seat and waited patiently for the elderly woman to reply.

Mrs. Walsh clutched the edges of her heavy knitted cardigan, pulling them tight across her chest at the memory. "It wasn't me that found that poor, poor boy," she admitted.

Bremner glanced up sharply, pen poised above his notebook. "I'm sorry. Phil told me you discovered the body. Is that incorrect?"

She reached for the teacup and took a trembling sip. There was a long stretch of silence. Bremner was about to prompt the old woman when she finally shared her story.

"I was deep in the fourth chapter of *Beauchamp Hall* by Danielle Steele. She is my absolute favorite author. I just *love* her stories. I put the book down to put the kettle on to make my morning coffee. I have to make them half-strength these days. Otherwise, I would never get to sleep at night."

"Too much caffeine can have that effect," Phil agreed.

She clutched her hands together in her lap and continued. "Princess jumped off her special cushion beside my recliner and ran over to the door and started yapping. She doesn't usually make much noise. I try to discourage her from barking because of the neighbors, but she hasn't stopped since we heard that noise the other night. I don't often let her out the front to go potty. I'm afraid she will run off down the street and get hit by a car. But she was so insistent that I gave in and opened the front door, and the second that door opened, she ran outside. I thought she was going to run away, but she started sniffing around the driveway, then disappeared into the garden behind where the garbage cans are kept. She started yapping again, but she sounded different than usual. More upset. Now, you probably think I'm some crazy old lady, but I know my dog, and she sounded distressed."

"I believe you, Mrs. Walsh. People develop close relationships with their pets and learn to read their different moods."

"I knew something was wrong, so I went into the garden after her, and that's when . . ."

Bremner reached across the table and gently patted her hand. "Are you all right? I know this must be very difficult for you."

She nodded, taking a moment to compose herself. "Yes, I'm all right. It's nothing compared to what poor Rita must be feeling. I cannot begin to imagine her grief right now."

"Can you tell me what you saw when you went searching the garden?" Bremner asked, steering her back to the story.

"Princess dug a shoe out from beneath the snow, and I knew who it belonged to immediately. Rita's son wore the same type of shoe. It was red and black and flashy, like the ones those basketball players wear. Anyway, Princess was still barking, so I pushed between the bushes to get to her. They are overgrown. The gardener needs to give them a hard prune. The branches scratched at me and caught on my clothes, but I pressed on. And then I saw Todd lying on the ground. He was bloody and mutilated, and he looked so scared. I suppose wild animals must have got to him because he looked all chewed up." Her chest hitched. She removed a handkerchief from the pocket of her cardigan and dabbed at her eyes.

"I sure do appreciate your telling me what happened, Mrs. Walsh. I know it wasn't easy for you, and I'm truly sorry that you had to witness such a dreadful thing. I'll need you to come down to the station and provide a formal statement, but you don't need to do so right away—maybe in a day or two when you feel up to it. Until we get this situation sorted out, could you stay with any family nearby for a few days? I don't think it is a good idea to be alone at a time like this. Is there someone Phil can call for you?" Bremner asked.

"Maybe he could ring my daughter. I haven't seen my grandchildren for a while. But I wouldn't want to impose. I know they lead such busy lives."

Phil stood up, careful to avoid pushing his chair into the kitchen wall. It was a tight squeeze. "I think they would be more than happy to have you once I explain the situation. Why don't you get me your daughter's number so I can call her for you?"

She stood up and walked halfway to the buffet in the living room, and paused. She turned to him and said, "I heard something the night before last. I think it might have been when poor Todd was killed."

Bremner pushed his chair back and followed her into the living room. "What did you say?" he asked.

She took a small address book from one of the drawers in the buffet and flipped through the pages until she found her daughter's phone number. She passed it to Phil before turning to Bremner. "I said I think I may have also heard it happen. Although I can't be certain. It could have been the television next door, but I doubt it."

"What exactly do you mean?"

"Sometime between ten-thirty and a quarter to eleven, I heard a scream. Princess became rather agitated and was at the window scratching and barking. I heard it only once, so I didn't call the police. I thought it must have been my imagination, but now I'm not so sure." Her face crumpled. "If I had gone outside to investigate or called for help, Todd would probably still be alive. Rita will never forgive me."

Bremner quickly scribbled down everything. "Can you repeat that for me? When did you hear the scream?"

"The night before last. Rita knocked on the door the following afternoon and asked if I had seen Todd. I honestly didn't think anything of it."

Bremner tucked his notebook in his pocket and mustered up a smile. "Mrs. Walsh, I don't want you to go blaming yourself for any of this. We don't know what happened to Todd just yet, and it won't do you any good thinking it's somehow your fault. Now, if you don't mind, I'll leave you with Phil while he calls your daughter."

Bremner let himself out of the apartment and took a moment to survey the scene. What the old woman had said might have been nothing, the imaginings of an overactive mind. Or it could be an important factor in the timeline of the boy's death. He was mulling it over when he spotted Chandler and DeAngelo walking up the driveway toward him. Sighing, he made his way over to them, bracing himself for the inevitable encounter with the dead boy's mother. What a frigging nightmare, he thought as he strode down the driveway.

Eleven

Nick Bremner pulled into his driveway well after nine that night, just as Mrs. Walsh had sagely predicted. He put the car in park, pulled on the handbrake, and killed the engine. He remained in the car, listening to the ticking of the engine as it cooled. What a truly awful day it had been. Watching the savaged body of Todd Vincent loaded into a van and taken to the morgue was one of the most heartbreaking things he had ever witnessed.

The boy's mother was taken to the hospital. It was a precautionary measure because of her state and so she didn't have to watch the body being taken away. Not that it made much difference. The woman had seen her son lying dead and defenseless among the shrubs, his mangled body discarded by a callous killer.

He rubbed his eyes with the palms of his hands, wishing he had eased off the caffeine earlier in the day. Between the artificial stimulation from the coffee and his inability to switch off his brain when he clocked out for the day, Bremner knew that it would likely be a long, sleepless night despite the deep exhaustion he felt.

Looking up at the lightless bulk of his house, acutely aware of the emptiness within, he knew the only comfort he would find inside would come from the half-empty bottle of scotch sitting on the kitchen counter.

Realizing he couldn't spend the rest of the night in his car, he climbed out and made his way up the walk to the front door. Usually, he was unfazed by coming home to an empty house. Tonight, though, it felt like the sparsely furnished bachelor pad that it was. Despite being large enough to contain a boisterous young family, it was wasted on a man too busy trying to maintain law and order to fill it with the love and laughter it had been built to accommodate. Plus, finding the right woman wasn't exactly easy. Taylor's End was a small town, and most eligible women already had a ring on their finger. And those he did manage to date simply held no genuine connection with him.

As he closed the front door, he switched on the lights and laughed at himself. The Vincent boy's death had left him feeling maudlin. If he didn't do something to distract himself, he would end up crying in front of the TV, watching some pathetic rom-com on cable. Screw that. If he couldn't go to sleep, he would keep working until he was too tired to keep his eyes open.

He dumped his pile of case files onto the coffee table and continued through to the kitchen. His last meal had been breakfast: a soggy cheese and tomato sandwich he had found in the staffroom at the station. He went to the refrigerator and checked for anything remotely appetizing. Unsurprisingly, nothing jumped out at him. There were a couple of containers of leftovers, but they had probably evolved into a biohazard by now. Eating them would be digestive suicide. He shut the door. He unscrewed the lid from the bottle of scotch and poured himself a finger of the amber liquid. Reconsidering, he added in a little more before taking a sip. It burned going down, spreading its warmth through his empty stomach, and by the time he returned to the living room and planted himself on the couch in front of the case files, the alcohol had dissolved some of the tension winding him up.

Before long, the seed of an idea crept into his head. The alcohol, exhaustion, and loneliness led him to what could only end in disaster. It disturbed him. Nonetheless, he found himself scrolling through the contacts on his cell phone and hitting the call button before he could talk himself out of it. The phone rang once, twice, three times. By the fourth ring, he was relieved nobody was going to pick up, but then:

"Hello?"

"Kate."

"Nick. Is everything all right?"

"Yeah, it's been a rough day, and I guess I just needed to hear a friendly voice. But it's late. I shouldn't have called."

"I don't mind," she assured him gently. "Truthfully, I'm glad you called. We haven't spoken since I burst into your office the other day like a madwoman. I'm so embarrassed for acting like that."

"Don't be embarrassed. We've been friends for a long time, and friends look out for each other, right?"

"Right."

There was a pause on the other end of the line.

"Nick, do you want me to come over?"

His breath caught as he mulled over her words. He knew he should say no. She was married, and he was a public figure, but her husband was a cheating jerk, and he was so damn lonely.

"Well?" she asked when he didn't respond. "You sound like you could use some company."

"Yeah, I want you to come over, but it's probably not a good idea."

"Probably not," she agreed, "but at this point, I couldn't give a shit whether it's a good idea. I'll be there in ten." Kate hung up.

Nick was left holding the phone to his ear, wondering what he had just set in motion. His head swam with all sorts of crazy thoughts. Was Kate coming over as a friend to provide support when he was overwhelmed? Or was she coming over for something else? He had always felt the chemistry between them, and if she weren't married, he would have done anything to be with her, but did she feel the same way?

He placed his cell phone down on the coffee table and returned to the kitchen for a second drink. He had to fortify himself against whatever was about to transpire. Kate would arrive in minutes. An anxious glance around the house confirmed his suspicions—the place was a complete mess. Ordinarily, he kept the house tidy, but with the recent increase in his workload, he had struggled to find time for some shut-eye, let alone the housework.

Without much hope of making a dent in the mess, he collected all the empty takeout containers piled on every available surface and dumped them in the trash. He dashed upstairs two at a time to change out of his uniform and freshen up a bit. He slipped on a pair of jeans and a comfy long-sleeved tee, wishing he had time for a shower. A fresh spray of antiperspirant would have to do the job. He splashed some water on his face and dabbed it dry with a clean towel.

He caught his reflection in the mirror above the vanity. Although Mrs. Walsh had been on the mark regarding his empty home, she was freaking nuts if she thought he was handsome. Not that it mattered. Enforcing the law didn't require dashing good looks. But damn, he wasn't looking good. His eyes were red and tired-looking, and the fine lines on his forehead and around his eyes were more pronounced than usual. His skin was dull. To top it all off, he needed a haircut. At least he wouldn't have to worry about Kate trying to jump his bones.

Disheartened, he switched off the light and headed back downstairs. Not wanting Kate to see the gruesome contents of the case files, he shuffled the papers and photographs in the manila folders and placed them beneath the newspapers long overdue for the recycle bin. He scooped up a pair of stray socks in front of the TV and straightened a pile of books he had been meaning to read.

A tremendous crashing sound outside startled him. "What the hell was that?" he wondered aloud, dropping the socks on his way toward the rear of the house.

He flicked on the exterior light and flung open the back door, sending the screen smacking against the wall. The recycle bin lay on its side. Empty bottles and cans rolled across the concrete walkway that ran the length of the rear of the house. Many of the bottles smashed in the impact, creating a lethal carpet of glass that glittered in the light cast by the bulb above the back door. Bremner tried to see into the darkness beyond the weak circle of light illuminating the back steps. The shadows were too dense beyond the perimeter of his yard, but he wasn't too concerned. The cold drove the local wildlife to act more boldly than they would during the warmer months when food was more abundant. It was most likely a hungry raccoon.

The doorbell rang. He hurried back through the house and let Kate inside before the neighbors noticed. As she squeezed past him, her hair brushed Bremner's cheek, tickling his skin. He inhaled the light floral scent that trailed after her and quickly closed the door.

Kate smiled up at him sheepishly. "I feel like a naughty teenager sneaking out after curfew. I hope none of your neighbors saw me. I would hate to send the nosy gossips into overdrive."

Bremner helped her out of her coat and hung it on a hook by the door. "The porch light is out, so I think we might have sneaked you in unseen," he winked conspiratorially. He could already feel his mood lifting.

She smiled up at him warmly and looked around the room. A lengthy silence stretched between them, neither person sure about how to proceed.

Finally, Kate broke the awkward silence. "This is stupid. We've never had trouble talking before."

Bremner laughed nervously. "I know. It feels different somehow. I'm not sure why."

Kate circled the room, too keyed up to stay still. She walked over to the bay window and pulled the curtains closed.

Bremner swallowed. The tension in the room was unbearable. He would explode if something didn't happen soon.

She crossed the floor and stood only inches from him. A rosy glow stained her cheeks, and he could see by the rise and fall of her chest that she was just as excited as he was.

Her hand trembling, she reached out and clasped his hand in hers. "I'm tired of feeling alone, Nick. I want more from life. I need love and warmth and laughter. And I want all that with you. If you'll have me."

Bremner stared down at her for the longest time, then pulled her close, wrapping his arms around her. The physical contact, missing from both their lives for too long, was a pleasure neither wanted to end.

At some point, her hand found its way down the waistband of his jeans. Her fingers slid beneath his underwear to cup the muscular curve of his buttock, pressing him close against her so she could feel his growing hardness against her stomach.

"Kate?" he asked huskily. He wanted to give her one last chance to change her mind before they did something that would forever change the dynamics of their relationship.

"Shhh," she replied. She reached up on her tiptoes and kissed him. Their lips melted together hungrily. He pushed her skirt down over her hips and let it fall to her feet. He continued stripping her while his tongue slipped into her mouth, and she wrapped her arms around his neck, returning his enthusiasm.

Fumbling with the clasp on her bra, he eventually got it off. He was rusty. She stood before him in nothing but pale pink underwear, and Nick took a moment to appreciate the view before he stripped off his T-shirt and unbuttoned his jeans. He pulled her against him once more. The heat of their touching flesh was almost dizzying. The cool air made Kate's nipples jut out. He cupped her breasts, reveling in their weight, and gently caressed them. She moaned, and her head tilted back, exposing her neck. He kissed her throat and slowly made his way down to her collarbone, teasing her with each featherlight kiss.

"Nick, please. I can't wait," she whispered.

He felt the same sense of urgency, but he wasn't willing to rush things. He had waited too damn long for this moment. Kate guided his hand down between her legs, and he could feel the dampness through her underwear. He reached into his jeans and freed his cock. She stroked him eagerly. He wanted to fuck her then and there, but he held back, slipping his fingers inside her instead. She pressed down against them, pushing them deeper into her body and kissing him with wild abandon. Then, when neither of them could take it anymore, they sank to the floor. Kate straddled him, rubbing herself along his length, watching him with heavy-lidded eyes. Her hair fell around her shoulders in loose waves, and Bremner had never seen her look so beautiful and carefree. If she kept on teasing, he would blow his load before they even made love.

"Get on," he growled, grabbing her hips and pressing her body down on his. A cry of delight escaped her lips as she sank onto his cock, and Bremner watched, open-mouthed, as he disappeared into her moist center. She rode him without inhibition. Her breasts bounced to the frantic rhythm of her hips as she slid up and down the length of his cock. A faint sheen of sweat gathered on her forehead, and she panted like an animal.

"Nick," she gasped as she rocked back and forth, "this feels so good."

Although he enjoyed her riding him, Bremner knew he wouldn't last much longer, and he wanted his turn at pleasing her. He gripped her buttocks and rolled her onto her back. He took her legs and placed them on his shoulders, then plunged deep inside her. He thrust again and again, delighting in the sensation of her pelvic muscles contracting as she climaxed. Her nails dug into his back as she cried out in pleasure. Unable to control himself any longer, Bremner exploded inside her before slowly pulling out and lying beside her.

They lay with their limbs entwined, his erection slowly softening between them. The sweat cooled on their bodies. He smoothed the hair back from Kate's face and gently planted a kiss on her forehead.

"I love you, Kate. I've always loved you."

She smiled momentarily, but the expression dropped from her face, and she scrambled to her feet, one hand covering her breasts, the other between her legs. "There was a face at the back door. Somebody was looking in through the glass at us!" she cried hysterically.

Bremner leaped up, confused by her sudden outburst. He was still in a daze. "Kate, it's OK." He reached out and put a hand on her arm to try to calm her. "Do you honestly think there would be someone lurking around my backyard, waiting to catch us in the act?"

Kate peered up at him, "Nick, I'm not imagining things. I saw someone watching us at the back door. It looked like they were wearing a Halloween mask or something." She shivered and snatched the blanket from the back of the couch, wrapping it around herself. He didn't want to dismiss her concerns, but seriously? The likelihood of a peeping Tom choosing the house of a man that rarely got any action seemed highly implausible.

Kate scooped up her clothes and quickly got dressed. She was visibly shaken by the incident, which made Bremner wonder if he wasn't taking it seriously enough. Something had knocked over the recycling bin just before she arrived. "Do you think it was a raccoon or maybe a stray dog?" he dared to ask.

Kate's eyes narrowed. "Only if it was the world's tallest raccoon," she responded drily.

There was a muffled thud overhead. They both looked up.

"Is there someone else here?" Kate whispered.

Bremner shook his head. He held a finger to his lips. "Stay put while I go upstairs and check it out. I won't be gone long, I promise." She nodded and moved behind the wall dividing the living area from the kitchen so that nobody could spot her from the rear of the house.

Bremner crept upstairs quietly, his bare feet hardly making a sound on the carpeted floor. He switched off the hall light and waited a few seconds for his eyes to adjust to the darkness. His gun was in a secure box under his bed, less than twenty steps away. He heard another noise. It came from the guest bedroom off to his right. It was a stealthy sound like someone was trying to pry open the window. He didn't like their chances.

He decided against taking the extra time to retrieve his gun. Instead, Bremner stepped up beside the door to the guest bedroom and eased it open an inch so he could steal a look before he burst inside. There was nobody there. He had accidentally painted the window shut a few years back, and cracking the seal was on his ever-growing to-do list. He kept the door to the spare room closed since guests rarely used it, and he had a habit of tossing all his junk in there. Out of sight, out of mind.

Bremner swung the door open and switched on the light. He caught a glimpse of a pale, long-fingered hand groping along the edges of the window frame from the outside. Then it vanished. He raced over to the window in time to hear the heavy thud of something or someone hitting the ground below the window. He spun around and flew down the stairs two at a time, using the wall for support as he descended. Regretting his decision to not take the time to retrieve his gun, Bremner grabbed the baseball bat he kept in the plant pot with the umbrellas near the base of the stairs. He raced past Kate, who shrank against the wall, and ran toward the French doors at the back of the house. "There's someone out there, all right. Lock the door behind me."

"Should I call the police?" she asked, following him into the dining room.

He unlocked the door and shook his head. "I am the police. Now make sure you lock it behind me." He crept down the concrete steps. She quickly pulled the door shut and turned the lock before ducking behind the kitchen counter.

Bremner readied the bat. The concrete was miserably cold beneath his bare feet, and the icy air wrapped around his naked torso like a frigid blanket. He stepped across the snowy ground and toward the second-story window where he had spotted the intruder. The light from above the back door ended three feet from the steps, leaving him to edge along the side of the house in near pitch darkness. When he finally reached the area below the guest room window, Bremner crouched. Using the bat for support, he ran his hand across the ground until he found the two craters in the thin layer of snow. Indents created by someone landing on the ground from a considerable height.

Standing up again, he scanned the yard. Every shadow was a potential threat. The thick row of pines at the rear of the property could easily conceal someone, but it would be risky to hide there. A person could easily poke out an eye on a protruding branch or trip over a tree root in the dark. He turned toward his neighbors on the left. Their properties were separated by a six-foot fence and a vociferous Staffordshire Terrier who would like nothing more than to shred the pants off an intruder. That left his neighbors on the right—and the gate between the two properties.

He ran along the back of the house. His foot caught on the garden hose loosely coiled on the ground. He lost his balance, and the baseball bat flew out of his hands as he fell forward. He reached out and steadied himself against the cladding, narrowly missing a nasty tumble onto the unforgiving concrete.

Before he regained his footing, a dark shape materialized from out of the shadows and charged straight for him. He ducked instinctively, bracing himself for the impact, but his reflexes weren't quite quick enough. The creature struck out at the shirtless, shoeless chief of police with an openhanded swipe that knocked him across the side of the jaw and sent him sprawling to the ground. With his head ringing from the impact, he crawled across the frigid ground to snatch up the baseball bat.

His fingers wrapped around the smooth wooden handle with seconds to spare. The creature lashed out at the spot where Bremner had been kneeling only moments earlier. But this time, he was prepared. He sprang to his feet and swung the baseball bat at the hulking shape in front of him. It hit the creature dead center in the chest, sending it staggering back a step. While the blow slowed the attacker down, it didn't stop it altogether. Bremner raised the bat for round two. But before he could swing the bat a second time, the creature barged into him and fled toward the narrow path to the gate, flinging him back against the house. His elbow smashed through the glass in the French doors.

By the time Bremner extricated himself from the broken pane, the creature had escaped through the side gate and out into the night. He felt the back of his arm and plucked a shard of glass from the meat above his elbow. Blood flowed freely from the wound, running down his forearm to drip from the tips of his fingers. He was about to make his way back inside when he heard the screech of tires, accompanied by a car horn.

Mustering the last of his energy, Bremner rounded the corner of the house and slipped through the open gate into the street. He jogged toward the car that had stopped in the middle of the road. Forgetting how intimidating he must look, half-naked and bleeding, he knocked on the driver's side window. He immediately recognized the startled face behind the steering wheel. Mrs. Walden was a secretary at the Bowen Medical Center, and she lived six houses up from Bremner.

He knocked on the window again. "Mrs. Walden, could you roll down the window, please? It's Nick Bremner." She looked at him dumbly, clearly not recognizing him. He repeated himself. "Mrs. Walden, it's Nick Bremner, Taylor's End chief of police. I need you to roll down your window. It's an emergency."

The woman cracked open the window slightly. "Nick, the policeman?" she asked cautiously.

Nick nodded vigorously, although it hurt his injured face to do so. "That's correct. I know I must look like a mess, but I've had a bit of a scuffle with an intruder. Unfortunately, they got away. Did you see anything?"

Her hands shook as they clutched the steering wheel. He was just a beaten and bloody cop with a baseball bat. She rolled down the window a little further, letting in the cold air. "Some fool girl ran straight out in front of the car. I slammed on the brakes. It was so close. I must have missed her by inches. She didn't even check the road for traffic."

"Are you sure it was a girl?" Bremner asked.

"Yes, I'm sure it was a girl. The headlights lit her right up. She turned her face away from the car, but she had long dark hair, unkempt like it needed a good wash and brush. That's about all I can tell you. Was she the one that attacked you?"

"It doesn't seem likely. Will you be all right to drive the rest of the way home?"

"I'll be fine. Frankly, I'm more concerned about you. You need medical attention and some warm clothes. Let me drive you to the hospital."

"Thanks for the offer, Mrs. Walden, but I'll manage. Be sure to lock your doors when you get home," he said before patting the roof of her car and turning away. He limped across the road and slowly made his way up the path to his house. The soles of his feet were lacerated from the broken glass scattered across the ground where the recycle bin had been tipped over. Some of the cuts still contained jagged shards of glass that buried deeper into his flesh with each step, and he winced at the sharp stinging pain.

Kate was waiting by the front door when he knocked to be let in. She held a kitchen knife.

"Jesus, put that thing down before you hurt someone," Bremner joked as he hobbled inside. Now, as the initial rush of adrenaline wore off, he felt every single injury he had incurred. Wanting to impress Kate, he did his best to push through the pain as he slowly made his way through to the kitchen. He grabbed a dish towel and wrapped it around his bleeding arm.

Kate placed the knife down on the kitchen counter and examined Bremner's injuries. He flinched when she knelt in front of him and plucked a small sliver of glass from his heel. She managed to remove two more pieces before she stood back up. "What the hell happened out there?" she asked as she tenderly traced her fingers across the scratches on his cheek. He shied away from the touch.

"I got my ass whipped. That's what happened. I walloped them with the baseball bat, but it did sweet fuck all. And I've got a good swing on me. I don't know what I'm dealing with here."

"Maybe they were crazy high on drugs? You told me that happens sometimes," Kate reminded him.

"Yeah, sometimes. Look, I'm going to have to go to the hospital and get some of these cuts stitched up."

"I can drive you."

"No, I don't want anyone knowing that you were here. As far as everyone knows, you and Richard are still a happy couple. Best to let people keep thinking that until you officially separate."

"Nick, I don't care what people think."

"Well, I do. I'm a public figure, and it wouldn't reflect well. But more importantly, I don't want people saying bad things about you. Go home, make sure all the doors and windows are locked, and if you hear anything suspicious, call the police immediately."

"Will you at least let me know how it goes at the hospital?"

"Sure. I'm not nearly as badly hurt as I look. A couple of painkillers and a few stitches, and I'll be as good as new." He smiled weakly. She reached up and kissed his uninjured cheek before collecting her purse and heading out to her car. Bremner stood in the doorway and watched as she reversed out into the street and drove off. His mind was reeling. So much had happened since he had dragged himself out of bed that morning. He needed time to mull over what had just transpired and put his jumbled thoughts in order. But first, he needed to get dressed and drive himself over to the hospital to get patched up.

Twelve

The lateness of the hour had done little to diminish the crowd at the Blue Two Tavern. Once the domain of the bikers passing through town, the tavern had become a regular haunt for anyone looking to get blitzed and have a good time in Taylor's End. Most of the action happened on the weekend when people were keen to forget the mundane workday grind, but tonight, the place was positively bustling.

Ordinarily, a Wednesday night consisted of half a dozen dedicated alcoholics doing their best to drink away their miserable existence. Tonight, however, was no ordinary night. The news of Todd Vincent's violent demise had spread through the community with the speed only a small town could manage. Details of the gruesome discovery—some accurate, others way off base, cooked up by overactive imaginations—had set everyone on edge. It was inconceivable that such heinous attacks could occur in the sleepy town.

Owen, owner and manager of the Blue Two Tavern for more than eight long years, stood behind the bar polishing the glassware with a clean dish towel. A couple of guys that weren't part of the regular Wednesday night crowd sat at the bar nursing their beers. They looked twitchy and on edge. "I ain't ever heard anything like it," the guy with the thick salt and pepper mustache said. He peered into his glass before raising it slowly to his lips and draining the remaining beer. "I know," his friend agreed. "I don't feel comfortable taking the trash out once the sun goes down. Suddenly, I'm scared I'm going to be the next person to have their face ripped off or their guts strewn across the ground."

"Yeah, you're too damn good-looking for that," the guy with the mustache joked, pushing his empty glass across the bar. Owen took the empty glass away and replaced it with a fresh beer.

There must have been close to two dozen people in the bar tonight, and it was late. Most of the tables were occupied. A bunch of drinkers had already had their fill and left for the night, aware that it was only mid-week and they would have to go to work tomorrow. If he'd known it would be so packed, he would have rostered on extra staff. Tragedy had a way of making people examine the frailty of their existence. And often, that was accompanied by the fortifying effects of a stiff drink or two.

Most people in Taylor's End were born and raised there. They played in the streets as children, and when they grew up and had families of their own, they didn't think twice about letting their kids do the same. A woman could walk home from the cinema after a late showing and not fear for her safety. The can of mace she carried, just in case, was forgotten in the bottom of her handbag.

Not so anymore. People were scared, and it was starting to show. Todd's death heralded the demise of the simplistic but much-cherished view of the town. While some immediately recognized the implications of the violent attacks and mourned the loss of the town's almost childlike innocence, others struggled in a fog of confusion and loss, not yet aware of what it all meant. Others still had gathered at the Blue Two Tavern to drink away their anxiety before returning to empty homes where the most innocuous shadows took on sinister shapes. Fear ran through people like a powerful undercurrent. It was understood by all but the most ignorant or inebriated of residents that absolutely anybody could be next to end up in a body bag.

The somber mood inside the tavern was indicative of just how shaken people felt by the news. Rita Vincent was a Taylor's End lifer, and the brutal death of her only son had dealt a devastating blow. The jukebox had remained ominously silent early in the evening. Nobody dared slip a coin into the slot. The hushed tones of grim conversation felt more appropriate than the grating riffs of some well-worn rock song. But as the liquor lubricated the patrons, one of the tavern's regulars stumbled over, fed a coin into the slot, and picked his favorite song, breaking the unnatural hush gripping the bar.

Owen had witnessed almost every human emotional response imaginable. Running an establishment that catered to the indecorous had opened his eyes to the darker aspects of human nature, which had gradually hardened him to the countless stories of suffering and woe that flowed freely from tongues loosened by alcohol.

Although the crowd had eventually relaxed, there was still a heavy sense of suspicion and distrust in the air. As closing time approached, Owen was relieved that they'd made it through the night without the usual bar fights and bloodshed that had earned the tavern its notoriety. He called for last drinks, his voice carrying across the bar with practiced ease. Kenny Stewart was losing a game of pool to a smug-looking out-of-towner, and he didn't seem happy about it. He raised his empty bottle and hollered across the bar for another. Owen gave the man a slight nod of acknowledgment and was glad they were closing. With a few more drinks in him, Kenny was liable to turn mean.

Many slurped the last of their drinks and pushed their empty glasses and bottles aside before leaving. Among those that stayed for a final drink was Jeb McCormack. His bourbon and cola had grown warm in his hands. He only half-listened to the crude anecdote being retold by his friend Cameron. The other guys around the table burst into laughter at the appropriate moment, and Jeb plastered a smile on his face as though he too were amused. And he had been—the first time he had heard the story. Besides, he wasn't in much of a laughing mood. Nobody in the tavern was, except for the clowns he was drinking with.

When the laughter died down, Jeb was elected to get the final round. Another drink was the last thing he wanted. He gulped down the warm, watered-down dregs of his drink and gathered a handful of crumpled notes from the center of the table. As he made his way over to the bar, he wondered how his grandfather was doing. Earlier in the evening, when Jeb had finished work, he had returned to the farmhouse to find his grandfather lying in bed. He was still in yesterday's clothes, and the room reeked of booze and old-man stink. After weeks of encouraging Tom to return to his routines, Jeb had all but given up on his grandfather ever returning to normal. Losing their dog Rosie in such a senseless and cruel manner shook them both, and they were still grieving her passing. A lot of people would dismiss the loss as trivial. She was only a dog, after all, but to Jeb and his grandfather, Rosie had been the only other family they had.

But it was more than just the death of their dog. Though Tom's wrist was healing nicely and the bruises on his face had almost faded away, the old guy was a complete wreck psychologically. The day after the attack, Jeb replaced all the locks on the doors and checked the latches on the windows while his grandfather was still in the hospital. The farmhouse was as safe as he could make it. But Tom still felt vulnerable, although he wouldn't come right out and say so. It was the furtive glances out the window or his insistence on checking the deadbolts three or four times before he would sit down to his TV dinner. This behavior convinced Jeb he was living in constant fear of his assailant returning to finish the job. Jeb couldn't even persuade Tom to continue his duties on the farm. When Nick Bremner had dropped by to check how he was recovering, Tom had made some lame excuse about still being unable to perform the chores that would usually fill his day.

With Tom out of commission, it was up to Jeb to keep the farm running during the few hours each day that he wasn't elbow-deep in clogged drains or leaking pipes. So, even though drinking at the tavern hadn't been the most appealing of invitations, it sure beat plumbing or sitting at home, trying to coax Tom out of his malaise.

"Hey, Andrea, can I get four beers?"

The petite barmaid regarded him curiously and glanced across the dimly lit tavern to the table where he and his buddies had spent the evening chowing down on buffalo wings and drinking. "You don't want another bourbon and Coke?"

Jeb shook his head. "No thanks, I've got an early start tomorrow. How have things been with you? I haven't seen you around much lately."

Andrea took a clean glass from the tray beside the dishwasher and began filling it. "I've been working mostly, getting as many shifts here as I can. Plus, I picked up some work cleaning at one of the motels. I'm saving like crazy so I can get out of Taylor's End once and for all. The plan is to stay with my sister in St. Louis for a few weeks until I find a place of my own."

"Sounds cool. Can I come?"

Andrea smiled. He had been a few years ahead of her at school. When the other kids bullied her, calling her an ugly muff-muncher and throwing trash at her whenever she walked down the hall to class, he would tell them to fuck off and leave her alone. It hadn't been much, but on more than one occasion, it had been the only thing getting her through the day.

"Sure. My sister always wanted to open a refuge for Taylor's End rejects," she teased.

"Who you callin' a reject?"

Andrea chuckled as she poured the final beer. "Seriously, I thought you were happy here with the farm and your friends, although I'm not entirely sure what you see in them." She glanced at the raucous bunch before placing the tray of beers on the counter.

Jeb shrugged. "Yeah, I am most of the time. But lately, I've been feeling restless, like it would be good to jump on my bike and get the fuck out of here."

"I hear you. Tell you what, when I get settled, you should come visit. Clear out the cobwebs and have some fun. What do you say?"

"I say you have yourself a deal," he said, smiling.

She rang up the beers, and he handed over the money. Jeb collected the tray from the counter, slopping some beer over the rim of the glasses on his way back to the table. He was glad to have a chance to catch up with Andrea. She was a nice girl and super easy to talk to. He would take her up on the offer to visit once she found a place to live. A break from Taylor's End and the monotony of life on the farm sounded fantastic. But first, he would have to help his grandfather get back on track.

Once back at the table, he handed the boys their beers and said his goodbyes. They protested, but it was late, and he was tired. He waved to Andrea on his way out as he zipped up his leather motorcycle jacket.

As he crossed the parking lot, for a second, he thought he saw the girl that Christian had been talking about nonstop, over by a parked car. But it must have been his imagination because there was no one there when he did a double-take. He was alone in the parking lot.

Not too long after Jeb left the tavern, Owen hustled the remaining patrons out into the night and locked the door behind them. In the early days, he had made the mistake of leaving closing to a less experienced staff member, and a cunning stewbum had sneaked back inside. He hid until the staff left, then indulged in the abundance of booze. He was discovered the following morning, unconscious in a puddle of piss and vomit. Owen learned to lock the doors the moment the last of his customers stepped outside. Some of the hardcore alcoholics still tried begging for one more drink for the road, and when that failed, they would turn nasty and cuss him out with language that would make a sailor blush.

It was all part of the job.

As it was midweek, he and Andrea would take care of closing. Between them, it would take only thirty or forty minutes to clean the place for the next day.

He had a wife with a warm, pliable body waiting for him at home, and he was keen to finish up at the bar so he could climb into bed and snuggle her. As he sprayed the bar and wiped the sticky surface clean, he kept an eye on the girl as she went from table to table collecting bottles and glasses.

Losing her as an employee would hurt, but it was difficult to begrudge her wanting more from life. From the snatches of information she shared throughout her time at the tavern, Owen got the impression her mother was deeply disapproving, picking at every decision the girl made. And while she hadn't come right out and admitted as much, he assumed her sexuality was an issue too. He sincerely hoped Andrea would find a better life when she left the restrictive mindset of Taylor's End. She was still so young and deserved to experience the giddy highs, and heartbreaking lows of love, something he doubted would happen if she stuck around.

"Hey, Andrea, can you empty the ashtrays and take out the trash while I tackle the bathrooms?" he called across the empty room. Unlike many of his former bosses, he rotated the cleaning of the bathrooms to avoid resentment among the staff. Working at the tavern could be a hard slog, especially when the crowd got rowdy. Sharing the unpleasant tasks was a small incentive to stick it out.

"Sure thing. I'll finish loading the dirties into the dishwasher, then I'll get right on it."

"You know where I'll be if you need anything. I saw Mickey Devlin head into the bathroom earlier. I swear, if he's shit up the walls again, I'm giving him a lifetime ban."

Andrea laughed. "In that case, you'd better get out the high-pressure hose. That man is worse than an animal."

Owen wished she was exaggerating, but truthfully, she was on the money. Every time Mickey Devlin emptied his bowels, it looked and smelled like an excrement bomb had exploded in the stall. He collected a mop and bucket from the cleaning closet and headed for the bathrooms.

Eager to get home and wind down with some Netflix before bed, Andrea set to work cleaning the ashtrays. After stacking the dirty ashtrays into a bucket, she returned to the bar and emptied the stale-smelling contents of each one into the trash before piling them in the sink to be washed when the dishwasher had finished its current cycle.

She collected the trash bags from the bins along the bar and tied them off before making her way out to the double dumpsters at the back of the tavern.

Loaded up with heavy trash bags, it took a couple of attempts to turn the deadbolt, but she managed to push the heavy door open with her hip. As she stepped out into the halo of light above the entrance, she immediately regretted her decision to forgo her coat. With little body fat to insulate her and dressed only in jeans and a thin cotton blouse, Andrea's teeth were chattering before she had taken three steps.

As she made her way over to the dumpsters, she heard the door click shut behind her. The automatic closing hinges ensured that the door was never inadvertently left open. Blinking away the flakes of snow that settled on her eyelashes, she was glad she didn't bother with makeup. Otherwise, she'd be rocking the raccoon look once she returned to the stale, smoky interior of the bar.

One of her trash bags caught on a stack of wooden pallets leaning against the wall beside the dumpsters. A sharp splinter tore a hole in the bag, spilling trash all over the ground. Andrea cursed angrily and plonked the heavy bags down. She kneeled in the grubby snow, trodden to a brownish slush, and picked up the partially eaten buffalo wings, peanut shells, and cigarette butts sucked on by mouths that had done God only knew what in the bathrooms or out in the parking lot behind the privacy of a car. There was chewing gum and used napkins, and for just a moment, she considered leaving it there for some other asshole to clean up tomorrow. But that wasn't her way. It was better to do it now and be done with it. Picking up the litter with a grimace, she paused over chicken bones wadded up in a napkin.

Snow crunched underfoot, and a young woman emerged from around the corner of the building. She wore dark jeans and an oversize black jumper, her arms crossing her body protectively, her hands clutching at her elbows. She sniffled, raising a hand to wipe her nose. She was pretty, in a waifish, little-girl-lost sort of way. Tears welled in the girl's dark eyes, and there was a flush to her cheeks. She took a reluctant step toward Andrea, who stood up. Something didn't feel right. Working in a dive like the Blue Two Tavern had honed her senses, and they rarely let her down. The hairs on the back of her neck rose. She looked over her shoulder at the door. It wasn't far. Surely, she could reach it if need be.

"I'm sorry about this," the girl said, her chest hitching as she took in a lungful of air. "I swear I don't want to. It's not me. Do you understand what I'm telling you?" She took another faltering step toward Andrea. Was she mentally unstable? The girl's brow furrowed. She shook her head and clutched it, wailing mournfully. "Run! Run now!" she cried out. Confused by the girl's erratic behavior, Andrea did the exact opposite. Dropping the napkin and the buffalo wing bones it contained, she stepped toward the girl. How could she leave when she was clearly in distress?

"Are you all right? What are you doing out here all alone?"

The girl lowered her hands from her face, and her dead black eyes locked onto Andrea's startled grey ones. The waifish girl was barely recognizable; her delicate features transformed into a twisted mask of hate. Andrea swallowed, realizing too late that she had made a terrible error.

"What are you doing out here all alone?" it mocked. Its mouth turned up into a cruel grin as it slowly closed the distance between them.

Fumbling with the keychain clipped to the apron wrapped around her waist, she turned to run, her fingers groping the keys, but she was too slow. Fingers wrapped around her throat and yanked her back, stifling her cries for help. Owen would rescue her, she thought, even as she was dragged toward the dumpsters, farther away from the reassuring circle of light above the entrance.

Owen checked the time on his phone and wondered what the heck was taking Andrea so long. He had already dealt with the bathrooms, a relatively easy job after all, as Mickey hadn't destroyed the stall as he had feared. Now he was almost done balancing the registers, and there was still no sign of her.

Growing increasingly irritated, Owen stalked over to the kitchen to check if she was inside. The kitchen was empty. The stainless-steel surfaces were wiped clean, and everything was washed and in its place. He switched off the bright fluorescent overhead lights, plunging the kitchen into darkness, and crossed the hall to the staffroom.

"Hey, Andrea, you in here?" he called out. The compact room was stuffed with a row of lockers along one wall and a two-seater sofa that had seen better days. There was a single toilet for the staff in the far corner, but the door stood open. Andrea's coat was still hanging on one of the coat hooks, so she had couldn't have gone too far.

Had she slipped and fallen on her way to the dumpster? He hadn't had time to salt the walkway today. The last thing he needed was a lawsuit. If Andrea fell and broke her arm or snapped her ankle, she would be well within her rights to sue for negligence. She was a good kid and a real asset to the tavern, but if something happened and she decided to take him to court? The tavern wouldn't survive something like that.

He opened the door and stepped outside, looking around for trouble. The drunks didn't always disperse right away after closing, but tonight it looked like everyone had made their way home.

"Andrea? Quit fucking around, would you? It's late, and I'd like to get home before midnight for a change. Andrea?" He noticed the bags of trash abandoned on the ground. Something was wrong.

He flashed back to the incident four years ago when one of his barmaids had been attacked at the end of her shift. Some horny drunk bastard had thought it was a good idea to force himself on her, pressing her hard up against her car when she had gone to unlock the door. Fortunately, one of the regulars had stopped to piss in the fresh night air and interrupted the would-be rapist with a punch to the side of the head, followed by a kicking that would prevent future attempts at procreation. After that, Owen had installed security cameras, covering the parking lot and the front and side entrances to the tavern. He hadn't thought it was necessary to place a camera at the employee entrance. The equipment cost a bundle as it was, and he needed to save money where he could.

"Andrea?" He hurried over to the garbage scattered over the ground. Beyond them, poking out from behind the furthest dumpster, was a Converse sneaker. "Jesus Christ, Andrea! Are you all right?" he cried in a panic as he half-ran, half-skidded across the treacherous ground. Placing a hand on the frigid metal dumpster for support, he peeked around it and froze.

Andrea sat propped on an empty beer keg. Her body slumped sideways against the dumpster, her chin resting on her chest. Her shirt was ripped open, and its small black buttons were scattered on the ground around her. And the blood. There was so much blood. It was everywhere. Her body was soaked, and the dumpster and the wall behind her were splashed with crimson.

Owen turned away from the sight and took a steadying breath. He had witnessed plenty of bloody noses, and the occasional tooth knocked from someone's mouth during a drunken altercation, but he had never seen a dead person before. He reluctantly turned back to the dumpster, and Andrea's body slouched against it. She really was dead. As desperately as Owen wanted to believe it was all just some sick prank, he knew that was nothing more than wishful thinking.

Retrieving his cell phone from the back pocket of his jeans, he dialed 911 and lurched back to the door on legs that felt like Jell-O. His eyes darted back and forth, nervously searching for the sicko that had killed Andrea. Holding the phone to his ear with one hand, he jabbed the key into the lock and pushed the door open, not daring to breathe until he was safely inside. When the dispatch operator finally answered, he wept with relief.

***

While waiting to be treated, Bremner dozed in a plastic chair in the waiting area of the hospital emergency room. His injuries were far from life-threatening, so patients with more serious medical issues received treatment before him. He didn't mind; it gave him a chance to get some shut-eye, which had been in short supply lately.

When the nurse came over and gently tapped his shoulder, Bremner jolted awake, momentarily disorientated. He'd been dreaming of monsters with razor-sharp claws and snapping jaws, and he swiped at the nurse's hand in confusion. The nurse smiled reassuringly. "I'm sorry if I startled you. The doctor can see you now, Chief Bremner."

Bremner glanced around the waiting area. Some of the sick and injured people that had been waiting were now gone. He pinched the bridge of his nose and rubbed his eyes, hoping to clear his head, but the fog of sleep persisted. "How long was I asleep?" he asked drowsily.

The nurse checked the watch dangling from a pin on her uniform. "Forty minutes or so. Come on through to the examination room." She led him down the corridor, her shoes squeaking on the highly polished linoleum. She stopped outside the examination room and motioned for him to head inside.

The doctor on duty greeted him while polishing his spectacles with a bunched-up tissue. "I'm Dr. Marmont. And you must be Chief Bremner." He gave his spectacles a final inspection and placed them over his beak of a nose. "For a moment, I didn't recognize you without the uniform."

"Yes, that's me. You can call me Nick. We didn't meet under the best of circumstances."

Dr. Marmont nodded gravely. "Yes, I remember. Dr. Preston was on duty that night, but I was called in to assist. Poor Michelle. It was such a nasty business. I hear she began a series of reconstructive surgeries, but it will be a long and unpleasant journey, I'm afraid. Is the perpetrator still on the loose? Do you think it's the same person who killed that young man?"

"The investigation is ongoing," Bremner replied. He settled himself on the reexamination table, wishing the doctor would just shut the hell up and stitch him up so he could go home. He wasn't about to be drawn into a conversation on the case. It was too late, and he was too sore to invest the energy required for such an exchange. Michelle Tanner hadn't been able to identify her attacker. And if the psychiatrist treating her during her recovery was correct, it was unlikely she would ever remember the event. The trauma was too deep.

The doctor unraveled the blood-soaked bandage around Bremner's arm and examined the wound. He prodded the injury, making a clucking noise at the back of his throat. "It's a good thing you came in. The cut will need suturing. And those scratches require cleaning. I think a course of antibiotics would be prudent also. Whoever scratched your cheek must have a serious set of nails. Acrylic would be my guess."

Bremner shrugged, unwilling to discuss the situation. Dr. Marmont prepared a suture tray, placed it on the overbed rolling table beside him, and dragged a stool over. "You'll be my first victim for the night," the doctor joked. He injected a local anesthetic around the wound.

"Huh?"

"I've been treating colds and stomachaches all night. You're my first stitch-up so far," the doctor said. He began irrigating the wound. "Did this happen while you were on the job?"

"I'm afraid not. Someone was lurking outside my house, and there was a scuffle when I went out to confront them. A window got smashed, and I came out second best, hence why I'm here getting stitched up instead of curled up in bed."

When Dr. Marmont had finished closing the gash on Bremner's arm, he set about cleaning the scratches on his face. "Nick, would you mind if I gave you a proper physical? It's somewhat unorthodox when you are visiting the ER, but I'm concerned about you. I've seen it too many times before: guys push themselves too hard for too long, and they drop dead of a heart attack after slurping on a double-shot grande."

"I thought I was the only one that noticed I look like crap, but I guess I was wrong," Bremner managed a half-assed grin. "If you want to examine me, knock yourself out."

"You know," said the doctor, "I look like a well-worn road map because I've got well over a decade on you. I'm also a sucker for punishment, and I volunteer for the graveyard shift as often as not. But when I'm not here taking care of patients, I'm taking care of myself by getting a solid seven hours of sleep each night or spending time with my family. Both serve to balance out my hectic profession."

Dr. Marmont read the blood pressure cuff and shook his head. "Your blood pressure is higher than I'd like. That could be attributable to the incident that occurred tonight, or it could indicate a broader problem. Hop on the scales for me, and we'll check your weight."

Bremner groaned. The checkup was not going well. He stood on the scales and waited for the doctor to share his opinion.

"Good. You're in the healthy weight range, and it's obvious you go to the gym, so that's a plus. When was the last time you had a good night's sleep?"

Bremner shrugged as he stepped off the scales. "I honestly couldn't tell you. Probably not since before we found the body out at the rest stop. Between trying to track down a psycho killer and keeping on top of the usual crackheads and granny bashers, sleep has been low on my list of priorities."

"I understand that," Dr. Marmont replied as he scribbled out a prescription, "but you must prioritize your health. You are displaying all the signs of exhaustion. I'd hate for it to escalate into something more serious. Ease up on the caffeine and get some sleep." He tore the prescription from the pad and handed it to Bremner.

On his way out to the car, Bremner checked his cell phone for messages. There were four: one was from Kate, asking him to call when he finished at the hospital. Three were about work, each more urgent than the last. So much for getting a decent night's sleep, he thought ruefully as he hopped into his car. He quickly called the station and listened intently as the voice on the other end of the line informed him of a situation at a local bar. Bremner tossed his cell phone down on the passenger seat and started the engine. He reversed out of the parking space and sped toward the Blue Two Tavern, all thoughts of his time with Kate momentarily forgotten.

Thirteen

ate in the afternoon, the police showed up at the boarding house and requested that both Connor and his father accompany them to the station to "help with inquiries relating to the death of Todd Vincent." That's how the stupid cunts worded it. *Help with inquiries relating to the death of Todd Vincent.* Connor wanted to punch a hole in the fucking wall and scream until his lungs burst. How could those numb fucks ever think he would be involved in killing his best friend? Todd was the one consistently good thing in his life: a small beacon of light in a dreary existence filled with poverty and violence. The prospect of living in this shithole of a town, trapped in the constant state of fear his cum-stain of a father elicited, was more than Connor could bear. Even in his drug-addled state, the loss of his best friend caused a pain inside him so profound that he couldn't see past it.

The fuckin' cops hounded him for hours. They asked him where he was on the night that Todd disappeared. If everything was cool, why would Todd leave without saying goodbye? Connor cocked an eyebrow. His hands clenched on his knees to stop his legs from jittering from nerves and lack of nicotine. Then he asked them if they understood who his dad was. They knew Jim Webster. How could they not? They had been called out to enough domestics over the years to be quite familiar with the man. His history of violence was likely the very reason they grilled Connor so hard about the old man's whereabouts once they were satisfied that he hadn't murdered his friend. No matter how much he hated his father and would gladly see him rot in jail, he couldn't bring himself to lie. Jim Webster had been at home when Todd left the boarding house.

True, he was the reason why Todd escaped into the night without saying goodbye, but that was the arrangement the boys had. When Jim was having one of his episodes, Todd left.

Nothing he said seemed to deter the cops from the idea that Jim Webster had finally flipped out and killed someone. Hating himself for defending the man he despised more than anything, Connor continued to protest his father's innocence. Still, it did sweet fuck all to persuade the cops he hadn't gone after Todd in one of his alcohol-fueled rages.

They started to ease up when Nathan and his mom came down to the station. Bruised and unbearably pathetic as they clung to each other for reassurance, they confirmed that Jim never left the boarding house that night. Mrs. Webster admitted the family got into a heated argument but politely refused to elaborate.

Connor had no choice but to corroborate their statement, although he wondered what the consequences might be for such a traitorous admission. Thinking his mom had finally found the courage to speak out, Connor told them everything. Yes, his father had started smacking his mom around when she'd made the grievous error of trying to protect Nathan from her husband's vicious outburst; the kid had bumped the old man's chair as he was squeezing past to get to the couch. In dishing out some discipline, Jim had also managed to smash a lamp, break a picture frame, and crack the leg of the coffee table. Afterward, his energy spent, Jim stumbled off to bed, where he slept soundly until morning. By the time Connor cleaned Nathan's split lip, gave him a bag of frozen peas for the swelling, and helped his mom tidy the living room, Todd was long gone.

Connor admitted he expected to catch up with Todd the following day, but his texts went unanswered. It was only when Rita Vincent called the boarding house looking for him and accusing Connor of corrupting her son that he started to wonder what the fuck was going on. Todd wasn't the sort of kid to run off without telling anyone, and nothing he said that night indicated anything out of the ordinary was bothering him.

After the cops finally decided he didn't know anything about Todd's death and released him, Connor made a lengthy pit stop at his dealer's. A while later, he found his way home and collapsed onto the couch, which was where he had remained for the last few hours, trying but failing to avoid thinking about Todd.

They had been through so much shit together since they had first become friends in grade school. Even in Connor's darkest moments, Todd always managed to help him feel better, lifting him out of the hopelessness that sometimes clouded his thinking. Now he was on his own. While reflecting on this, he heard the front door open and who should show up but that freak show staying in the room at the top of the stairs.

After their first encounter, Connor had gone to great lengths to avoid her. He did not want to be seen now. He already had grave misgivings about Ella, or whatever the fuck it was, parading around as some helpless girl with no history. All the bad shit that had been happening around town coincided with Ella's arrival. As implausible as it seemed that a five-foot-nothing wisp of a girl could tear people to shreds, Connor saw what lurked beneath the surface, and whatever it was, it was more than capable of causing such carnage.

Ella failed to notice Connor when she entered the boarding house. But he saw her, and he watched with interest as she crept along the front entry toward the staircase. He had been smoking weed and munching a combination of pills potent enough to take down a racehorse since finding out about Todd. It was late. How late exactly, Connor had no idea. He had been sitting on the couch in the dark for so long that he was beginning to wonder if his ass had melted into the cushions. Initially, he had planned on watching some TV, but he hadn't gotten around to picking up the remote off the coffee table and pressing the power button.

Shortly after he swallowed the pills he scored from his dealer, time ceased to have any meaning. Once they hit, combined with the weed, he was flying high enough to avoid collapsing in a sniveling heap over Todd. All he knew for sure was that when that thing posing as Ella came creeping into the boarding house, everyone else had already gone to bed. Even that crusty wino Reggie Billets had stumbled in after the last of the bars had closed and trudged upstairs to his stinky bedroom.

Since then, he had sat in the dark, thinking about Todd and listening to the sounds the house made at night. The quiet thrum of the furnace was a comforting contrast to the groaning wooden frame, buffeted by strong gusts of wind. He should get up and go downstairs to his room, but his brain wouldn't communicate the command to his body. If he weren't so shit scared, he would have pointed the cops in her direction, but he had learned long ago that you never rat anyone out. Ever.

So, when she slipped inside the house, gently closing the heavy hardwood door behind her, her boots hardly making a sound as she crossed the entry, Connor remained motionless. With only a single bulb lighting the staircase, his presence in the living room would go unnoticed. Sure, it was creepy sitting around in the dark, watching her as she stealthily entered the house, but he was in no state to interact with another person, especially not someone that threatened to tear the limbs from his family if he so much as looked in her direction.

Where was Rebel? He hadn't barked once yet. The dog never bothered raising the alarm when any family members came or went, but he went berserk whenever anyone else entered the property. Not this time. Tonight, he was silent.

Creeping across the entry toward the staircase, she skillfully avoided the floorboards that squeaked underfoot like a dying mouse caught in a trap. What was up with that? Even in his compromised state, it seemed odd that she felt the need to be so damn stealthy. Yes, it was late, and she probably didn't want to wake everyone in the house, but what the fuck was up with sneaking around like a fifteen-year-old girl getting home hours after curfew?

When she reached the foot of the stairs, she paused and glanced over her shoulder. Her eyes narrowed, and she stared straight at him. He held his breath. Did his breathing alert her to his location? With a slight shake of her head, she continued up the stairs.

Connor waited until she was upstairs before he relaxed. Were the drugs making him see things that weren't really there? If that wasn't the case, then he had to wonder what the fuck Ella had been up to. When she had turned back in his direction, he could have sworn that her face was flecked with inky dark splatters. Splatters that looked a lot like dried blood. The poor light made it difficult to know for certain. But he sure as shit wasn't about to chase her up the stairs to find out.

He was high as fuck, and he was just having a bad reaction brought on by the trauma of finding out what had happened to his best friend. He just had to stay put and ride it out, and in the morning, this crazy hallucination would be nothing more than a regrettable self-inflicted trip best forgotten.

And yet, curiosity gnawed at him. He peered up at the dimly lit staircase, contemplating following Ella upstairs to get a better look at her. It was pure insanity. What he should do is march his stoned ass downstairs to the basement and stream some music until he fell asleep.

Instead, living up to his father's constant reminders that he was a good-for-nothing half-wit, Connor let himself into the family's apartment and took the master key off the hook on the wall inside the door.

After gently closing the door to the apartment, he crept over to the staircase. He paused for a moment, trying to convince himself to head down to the basement instead. Nope, it wasn't going to happen. Now the idea was firmly planted in his head. He had to follow through no matter what.

Using the banister for support, he slowly climbed the stairs. Although he had lived in the boarding house for over half of his life, he wasn't nearly as successful at avoiding the creaky floorboards as Ella was. Halfway up he paused to stifle a cough. Too many cigarettes had left him wheezing for breath. The narrow stairs to the attic were draped in darkness so complete he couldn't see beyond the first three steps. Fuck it. There was no point breaking his neck before he even reached her room. Connor flipped the switch, casting the attic staircase in a dim light that vanished two-thirds of the way up.

Wincing at every little noise he made on his way up, he stopped at the top of the stairs and pressed his ear to Ella's door. He stood very still, listening for any sounds of activity inside the room that might indicate she was still awake. After listening for nearly a minute, he heard nothing.

He gripped the keyring tightly in his fist to prevent the other keys from jangling and carefully slotted the master key into the lock. With one firm twist of his wrist, the door clicked open. Connor waited on the threshold until he felt confident that his entry had gone unnoticed. He carefully removed the key from the lock and stashed the keyring in the front pocket of his jeans before he stepped into the room. He stood for a long time, waiting for his eyes to adjust to the darkness. It was impossible to shrug off the feeling that his curiosity was causing him to act like a creepy stalker. No normal guy broke into a girl's room in the middle of the night.

But Ella was not an ordinary girl.

He crossed the room, approaching the bed as quietly as possible. In the dim light, he could make out the lump of her backpack propped on the chair in the corner and a pile of clothes discarded on the floor beside the drawers. As he edged closer to the bed, he could see she was lying on her side, facing away from him. The covers were tucked up to her chin.

Damn it. He would have to creep all the way around to the other side of the bed if he wanted to get a decent look at her face. As Connor stepped around the end of the bed, his foot caught on one of her boots, and he tripped. His hand shot out, and he caught hold of the set of drawers, steadying himself before he went crashing to the floor. Still, his near-miss hadn't been completely silent. He studied the bed, expecting her to leap up and scream the house down. Instead, she moaned and shifted the covers tighter around her. Her breathing resumed a steady rhythm.

It briefly occurred to him that something was deeply wrong. There was no way anyone could sleep through the racket he had made. Dismissing the thought, he sneaked over to the bed and leaned down to try to get a better look at Ella's face. Stooped over, he angled himself beside the sliver of moonlight filtering through the window, straining to see the substance splattered on the sleeping girl's face. It was useless. In the dark, it could have been blood, chocolate, ketchup—anything, really. There was only one way to know for sure. He slipped a hand into the back pocket of his jeans and retrieved his cigarette lighter. It was risky, but he had to know. So far, all he had were suspicions. If Ella had killed Todd, he needed proof.

He held out the lighter and rolled his thumb across the flint wheel. A small yellow flame appeared. For a second, her face was lit by the flickering flame. There was dried blood all around her mouth and chin. It was splattered across her cheeks and crusted in her eyebrows.

Then all hell broke loose.

Her eyes flew open, black and empty like before. Her hand whipped out, knocking the lighter across the room, where it skittered across the floor to land under the window. Unable to step back quickly enough, he felt her fingers hook around his throat and drag him down toward her face. Dropping to his knees, he braced himself against the bed for leverage, but it made little difference.

She pulled him closer to those dead black eyes, her fingers tightening around his throat until his breath was nothing more than a thin whining whistle. Sneering, she breathed out a puff of putrid air that smelled of blood and decay.

"You shouldn't be in here," Ella hissed. Connor continued to push back against the bed frame. His sneakers skidded across the floor as she dragged him closer, all the while squeezing tighter and tighter on his throat. "You've been a bad boy," she taunted, "snooping around, just like that friend of yours. Maybe I should fix you like I fixed him." "I'm sorry. It was a mistake. Please let me go," he stammered. It slowly raised itself up into a kneeling position on the mattress. Connor fought back against it, punching ineffectually at its chest, the blows hardly registering.

"What do you think?" the demon asked. "Kill the worthless half-wit stoner, or go after the pathetic punching bags downstairs?"

Oxygen-deprived and desperate to escape, Connor pulled back as far as it would allow before driving his head forward with all his strength. Their heads collided with a jarring force, and the demon released him as it fell back on the bed. Connor went sprawling backward, crashing into the chair and knocking it to the floor with a loud thud. Wasting no time, he scrambled to his feet and lurched toward the door, still woozy.

The demon sprang off the bed and landed between Connor and the door. Shaking its head, it blocked Connor's exit.

"I can't let you leave," it growled.

Plucking up courage he never knew he'd possessed, Connor stood his ground. "If you let me leave now, I won't breathe a word of this to anyone. I don't know what you are, and I don't want to know. I just wanna get the fuck out of here and forget any of this happened." He tried to sound braver than he felt. You had to stand your ground and avoid showing fear when confronted by a bully—at least, that's what he had read somewhere. The author had probably never run into a blood-thirsty killer, or Connor's father, for that matter.

With narrowed eyes, the creature held tight to the door with one clawed hand. Realizing that the vile little stoner could be problematic if it went ahead and killed him in the same house it was using as a refuge, the demon refrained from tearing him into countless pieces of human meat. "If you ever even think of mentioning what you saw here tonight, I'll paint this decrepit shithole red with the blood of your loved ones. Do you understand me?"

Connor scrutinized the creature, searching for any sign of the girl within, but there was no evidence that she was there. Whether she ever had been, he had no idea. All he knew for sure was that it had killed his friend, and, judging by its gore-crusted face, it wasn't about to stop.

"I won't breathe a word to anyone," he croaked.

Stepping aside with a smile that would haunt his sleeping hours for many nights to come, the demon pulled the door wide to allow him to pass. Connor couldn't believe his luck, nor was he about to look a gift horse in the mouth. He shot past the creature and half-slid, half-ran down the stairs, not caring if he woke the rest of the house as he descended. Near the bottom of the staircase, he looked back to check if he was being followed and cried out when a hand wrapped around his wrist. He shook himself free and shrank against the wall.

Jim stood at the base of the stairs in his stained long-johns, bleary-eyed and only half awake. "What the hell is up with you?" he mumbled. "You're gonna wake up everyone in the house with that racket. I know you're fucked up over your friend and all, but you need to settle the fuck down." A run-in with the old man was the very last thing Connor wanted to deal with right now.

"Fuck off and leave me alone," he shouted before bolting across the entry and ripping the front door open. He slammed it shut behind him as he ran out onto the porch.

Fuck! It was fucking freezing outside. He zipped up his sweatshirt and pulled the hood up over his head, wincing as his hand brushed against his ear. What the fuck? He rubbed his fingers together, and sure enough, they were sticky with blood. That fucking thing must have slashed his ear with its gross-ass claws or something. Now that he was aware of it, his ear throbbed miserably. Cupping a hand over it, he jogged down the path and hopped over the gate, continuing across the road.

Jim opened the front door in time to see his eldest son leap over the gate and jog off down the street in nothing more than a hooded sweatshirt. It was nearly one in the morning, for Christ's sake. Jim knew the boy had been smoking the wacky tabaccy ever since the cops had released them late in the afternoon. The fucking house reeked of the shit. If he thought smoking it in the basement while burning some god-awful incense somehow disguised the smell, he was even stupider than Jim thought.

If the kid wanted to flip out in the middle of the night when it was cold enough to freeze a red-blooded man's balls off, then he could go right ahead and do it. Jim sure as fuck wasn't about to head out in the snow and chase him down. Not that it would make any difference anyway. The kid hated him, and nothing he could say would make any difference. Jim closed the door, farted loudly, and headed back to bed. Sophie could deal with the little turd tomorrow, assuming the kid didn't freeze to death first.

Connor jogged along Bourke Street, squinting against the icy wind whipping at his face. Between his throbbing ear and the pain in his throat every time he took a labored breath, he was beginning to wonder if the bitch in the attic had caused serious damage. He was crossing Kadwell Street when it dawned on him: he was on his way to Todd's place.

The realization was like a punch to the stomach. He doubled over, hands on his knees, wheezing painfully. Todd was dead.

He was murdered and partially eaten, and it was all his fault. He had known about that thing in the attic and stood by while it went around town attacking people. Even though he knew his dad was a fucked-up bastard that could go off the deep end at any time, he had still invited Todd over to hang out.

It was all on him, every last bit of it. He was a worthless piece of shit, just like his old man had told him all his life. It had taken his best friend's murder for the cruel reality of his miserable existence to hit home. There was no hope. He was never getting out of Taylor's End. Living in the basement like a rodent while his fucked-up family fought upstairs was the best he could expect from life.

He fought back tears and stood up, jamming his hands deep into his pockets. There was nowhere for him to go. As a last resort, he could hunker down in the shed on Ribald Street. It was an excellent chance to die of hypothermia, but he didn't much care at this point. With no other options, Connor headed for Ribald Street and its tattered, cum-stained mattress.

Behind him, lights flashed red and blue. *Fuckin' cops!* He took his hands out of his pockets and took off at a sprint, knowing full well there was no way he could maintain his speed. Still, if he could get around the corner before they reached him, there were plenty of places to hunker down and hide until they passed, provided they weren't too invested in tracking him down. A flashlight would easily illuminate his footprints in the snow.

Running along the gutter, his arms pumping and his head thrown back, Connor wanted to believe he could make it onto Ribald Street before the cruiser reached him. But he was riding out one hell of a bender, and to top it all off, he had a seriously damaged windpipe. He had no chance. The cops prowled along behind him before they surged ahead and cut him off. The cop in the passenger seat leaped out and gave chase.

It didn't last long. They had him beat, and he honestly couldn't give a fuck. Any other time he could have outrun the pigs no problem, but after his altercation with the creature back at the boarding house, he was too hurt and exhausted. He knew the joint in his pocket was probably enough to get him locked up for the night. At least then, he would have somewhere warm to sleep.

When the officer pursuing him caught up and grabbed a handful of his clothes, Connor lashed out, twirling around, trying to shrug out of the sweatshirt and escape. But the officer had a good hold of him and wasn't about to give up without a fight. Their feet got tangled up in the tussle, and they tumbled to the ground. The officer pinned him to the icy sidewalk and bent Connor's arms behind him, then whacked him in a pair of handcuffs for good measure. He read Connor his rights.

Struggling to their feet, the officer pointed Connor toward the patrol car. "You've just earned yourself a ride down to the station, son."

"Can't fuckin' wait," Connor replied. "Do I get a free donut with that, officer?" The officer, his cheeks ruddy from the exertion, shoved him against the cruiser, opened the back door, and guided him inside before slamming the door.

"Larry, does that kid look familiar to you?" the driver asked, flicking on the overhead light to get a better look at Connor. The arresting officer, who was still standing in the gutter beside the car, removed the flashlight from his belt and pointed it at the back seat.

Connor squinted and turned his face away from the light. "Get that fuckin' thing outta my face, would you? Jesus, man, what the fuck?"

"Hey, watch your mouth," said the officer sitting in front. Turning to Larry, who had lowered his flashlight, he said, "Isn't that the kid that was brought in for questioning this afternoon over the Vincent murder?"

Larry slowly nodded. "I reckon it might be. Got any ID, kid?" Connor shook his head. His wallet was still sitting on the coffee table back at the boarding house. "Want to explain why you look like you've gone a few rounds with Connor McGregor and got your ass whopped?"

The officer sitting in the driver's seat turned to get a better look at the boy. "Damn. I've seen roadkill that looks better than you. Wanna tell us what happened?"

"Wanna stop sweet-talking me like you wanna fuck me up the ass and take me to the station already?"

"Suit yourself. You can tell us now, or we'll get it out of you back at the station. Either way, you will tell us what we wanna know." Larry slammed the back door and walked around the rear of the car to climb in beside his partner.

It had been one hell of a crazy night. And while the kid might have been cut loose for the Todd Vincent killing, with his injuries, which were inflicted in the past half an hour or so— hell, the kid's mangled ear was still leaking—he may well know something about the dead waitress at the Blue Two Tavern. It wasn't likely, but neither officer was about to risk his career over some potty-mouthed punk.

After a short ride across town, Connor was escorted back into the warm interior of the Taylor's End Police Station, where he received a thorough frisking. With a smirk, Officer Larry confiscated the fat joint stashed with his cigarettes. Connor was surprised by how busy the station was, especially so late at night. There were cops everywhere. Some wandered around with steaming mugs of coffee, while others had phones glued to their ears and tapped madly at keyboards in front of computer screens. Something major was going down, and he doubted it had anything to do with finding his friend's killer.

The two officers led him through to a room painted a drab green that reminded him of baby shit. Officer Larry removed the cuffs and directed him to take a seat. "Someone will be in to talk to you shortly."

"Can I get a drink or something? My mouth is as dry as fuck." The officer stared at him with disdain, noting the bloodshot eyes and the distinctive reek of marijuana. Left alone in the same room used to question him earlier that day, Connor began to feel the aches and pains inflicted by the demon. He sat thinking about the day's events as he slowly sobered up, wishing the assholes hadn't confiscated his weed. The pills were starting to wear off too, and the prospect of coming down in a cramped room in the police station was enough to give him the jitters.

After what felt like half the night but was probably only half an hour, Chief Bremner opened the door, looking less than impressed to see him. He closed the door behind him and handed Connor a can of soda. Bremner sat on the metal seat screwed to the floor on the opposite side of the table and let out a long sigh.

"I can't say I was expecting to see you in here again quite so soon. My officers tell me you resisted arrest when they found you running along..." he said, taking a moment to consult his notebook, "Smith Street. That isn't too far from where someone killed your friend. Would you like to explain to me why you were running like the devil was after you at twelve twenty-three in the morning when it's cold as heck outside, and you are obviously wasted? It seems a bit odd, wouldn't you agree? Not to mention that part of your ear is hanging off, and the ugly bruises around your neck suggest someone tried to choke the shit out of you. Maybe you can appreciate why my men and I are concerned."

"I was feeling restless. With everything that's happened, I couldn't sleep, so I thought a jog might wear me out."

"Forget that bullshit story for a minute, because let's face it: the only time you're going to run anywhere is if you have the cops on your tail."

Connor crossed his arms and glared across the table at Bremner. The bastard had a valid point that was useless trying to dispute.

"The inability to sleep after the day you've had," Bremner said, "I can believe. Even the need to get out of the house and take a walk around the block makes sense. True, you aren't exactly dressed for the weather, but I suppose when you're fucked up on whatever it is you've been taking, appropriate clothing might not be a priority, wouldn't you agree?"

Connor nodded with as much enthusiasm as he could muster, hoping for a way out.

Bremner stared hard at him across the table, his fingers drumming a slow tattoo on the scratched and dented surface. "The problem, though, is that mere hours after you were brought in for questioning over your friend's horrific murder, it looks very much like someone tried to do the same to you. Possibly right after they murdered a young waitress over at the Blue Two Tavern, which is less than two miles from where you live. Do you see any connections there?"

"You don't look so good yourself, Chief Bremner," Connor replied sourly. "Maybe you need to worry more about what's happening to you and get the fuck outta my business."

Bremner rubbed a hand through his stubble and sat back in his chair, allowing the tension to deflate before he continued. "I know you and Todd were close. It must be tough losing him like that. You must feel awfully lonely without him."

Connor sniffed. He looked down at his hands clasped on the table in front of him. No way would he let Chief Pig get under his skin. "I'll get over it," he mumbled.

"Did Jim do that to you? Is that why you're not talking? I know what your father is like when he loses his temper."

"Oh yeah?" Connor's voice took on a dangerous edge. "You know how he has been beating the living shit out of me and Nathan since before we were old enough to go to school? The broken bones, black eyes, sprained wrists—did you know about all that too? What about Mom? All the trips to the emergency room for those clumsy accidents? Or better yet, the countless times he raped her so hard she couldn't sit down for days. Are you admitting that you know what he does, but you still sit around with your thumb up your ass and do sweet fuck all? Cause that's what it sounds like to me."

Bremner's face reddened. The boy was right. Although Bremner had been aware of Jim's nasty streak, he hadn't known it was anywhere near as bad as Connor described.

"I am truly sorry, Connor, for the terrible abuse you and your family have endured at the hands of your father. What he has done is unforgivable, but someone extremely dangerous is terrorizing Taylor's End right now, and it looks like they're escalating. You could have valuable information that can help us catch them."

Connor kept his eyes trained on the wall behind Bremner. "It wasn't the old man."

"No?"

"No. Jim's a fuckin' prick bastard, but he knows better than to draw attention to himself when the cops are sniffing around. Now, can't you just let it go? It doesn't matter."

Bremner folded his hands on the table, shocked by the boy's sudden indifference. "Connor, you are missing a chunk of your ear, and the bruising around your neck suggests that someone made a determined attempt at throttling the life out of you. Who knows? Maybe they will try again, make sure they do a proper job of it."

Connor's lip trembled. He glared at the scratched and chipped tabletop, willing his emotions under control. He wasn't going to start weeping like some piss-weak baby just because some asshole cop tried to freak him out. When he felt the wave of emotion pass, he sneered at Bremner. "You've seen that shithole I call home? You know what I am, who my parents are. If they wanna come back and finish the job, then..." he said, shrugging nonchalantly.

"Connor, please." Bremner continued undeterred, recognizing the boy's performance for what it was. "Tell me who attacked you. I can keep you safe. They won't be able to hurt you anymore."

Connor scoffed. "Like you kept us safe from Jim all these years? I don't think so." Silence was his only option. If he weakened and blabbed, his Mom and Nathan were dead. He had no doubt the demon would fulfill its promise if he caved and talked to the cops. No matter how desperately he wanted to unburden himself, he had no choice but to keep his mouth shut, for their sake as well as his own.

"If you don't care about yourself, what about Todd or the poor girl finishing up her shift at the tavern tonight? Hell, the same person might have assaulted me. Any information you can share will help us stop them before they get someone else."

The world started swimming in nauseating circles. Connor pushed his chair back and stood up unsteadily. His breathing was shallow. All the pieces began to fit together. It was no longer the half-baked conspiracy theory of a kid spending too much time alone in the basement. It all made sense now. The blood splattered over Ella's face—it wasn't her blood at all. It must have belonged to the murdered waitress; that's why Ella had entered the boarding house so sneakily. He had caught her returning from killing someone.

Before he could stop himself, Connor doubled over and puked on the floor between his feet. There wasn't much to it. He couldn't recall the last time he ate. It was mostly bile and watery liquid that filled the small room with an unpleasant odor. He wiped his mouth on his sleeve.

"Sorry," he said.

Bremner sat in his chair, unfazed by the incident.

"Don't worry about it," he said. "Believe me, I've seen a lot worse than a puddle of vomit. Did I say something to upset you?"

Connor shook his head. "No, a sick feeling came over me suddenly. Do you have something I can clean it up with?"

"Like I said, don't worry about it. I'll get someone to clean it up after we finish talking. Do you feel better now?"

"I'm fine."

Not likely, Bremner thought as he surveyed the boy. With a bloody ear, ugly purple bruising around his neck, and vomit on his sweatshirt, Connor Webster was a long way from being fine. "OK then, if there isn't anything else you want to tell me, I'll arrange for Officer Jenkins to take you over to the hospital to get that ear treated."

"I don't need to go to the hospital," Connor protested.

"Yeah, actually, you do. If you don't get some treatment for that ear, it's liable to turn septic. Then it will probably drop off. You are going to the hospital, you will accept any treatment required, and you can spend the rest of the night there to sleep off whatever drugs you've taken. Alternatively, Larry can drive you back to the boarding house." The last bit was cruel but necessary. Bremner wanted the boy to get checked out. If he went to the hospital, at least there would be an official record of the injuries.

Connor considered the offer. It was a no-brainer. He couldn't return to the boarding house, at least not tonight. It was too soon. He needed time to collect his thoughts and figure out the best course of action. "All right, I'll go to the hospital, but does Officer Jenkins have to take me? The guy is a total dickbag."

Bremner blinked and rubbed a hand over his mouth to cover a smile. "It's *Officer* Dickbag, or you'll spend the rest of the night stuck in here with your vomit."

Connor rolled his eyes. "Officer Dickbag it is."

Fourteen

After a restless night's sleep, Kate Lyttle awoke before seven on Saturday morning to the alarm clock going off on Richard's nightstand. She scowled at her husband as he continued to sleep, oblivious to the incessant beeping. It was the weekend. He should have remembered to switch the alarm off before going to bed the previous night.

Kate threw back the covers on her side of the king-size bed and pressed the button on the alarm. She stood in her pajamas, looking down at her sleeping husband, wondering how she could have remained with him all these years devoid of love and intimacy.

He stirred in his sleep and farted, his brow furrowing as he let go. God, how she despised him. All these years wasted on a man who didn't even see her. Since finally consummating her relationship with Nick, she truly understood what she had cheated herself out of by sticking by Richard. Sighing at her poor judgment and complacency, Kate returned to her side of the bed. She slipped her feet into her fleecy slippers next to the nightstand and wrapped herself in the robe flung over the reading chair in the corner.

With the curtains pulled closed against the cold, the house remained draped in darkness. She pulled the bedroom door shut behind her, hoping to leave Richard sleeping for as long as possible. The longer he stayed in bed, the more pleasant and peaceful the start of her morning. She opened the curtains in the living room and let in the early morning light. The front garden was an icy wonderland draped in a thick cover of glittering snow. It hurt her eyes to stare at it. A small bird fluttered from a branch to the ground in search of its breakfast, then back to the tree it went. Kate admired the simplicity of its existence.

Turning away from the window, Kate walked into the kitchen and filled the percolator. She promised herself that when she moved out, the first thing she would purchase would be one of those fancy coffee machines that automatically make a cappuccino or latte at the press of the button.

Of course, she would have to leave Richard first. Separate from her spouse, *then* buy the fancy coffee machine.

It wouldn't be long now. It was simply a matter of finding the right moment, though her friend Kim assured her that there was no such thing as the perfect time to end a marriage. She was probably right. Being asscrtive had never been one of Kate's strengths.

This new development with Nick, however, had changed her perception of her capabilities. Somehow, he gave her the confidence to be herself in a way Richard never had. She felt happy and light inside, and the sex was truly mind-blowing. It was all she could think about, and finding a time when he wasn't working a case was the only reason they weren't screwing every minute of the day. She blushed as she opened the front door to retrieve the weekend paper from the step, wrapping her robe around herself more tightly to keep out the cold.

Sex with Nick wasn't just a sordid fling to satisfy some sexual need. They had been best friends for years, and the addition of the physical aspect of the relationship sent their connection into the stratosphere. If they went public with the relationship, she hoped that it wouldn't hurt Nick's career. Taylor's End was a small town, and people could be extremely judgmental.

It was painful to reconcile wasting so much time with a man who never truly noticed her. Still, she couldn't go back and undo over a decade of marriage. The focus now was confronting Richard and getting out of the relationship with minimal drama. Hopefully, his monumental ego would prevent him from creating a scene that the boozed-up country club would spread around town. They had nothing better to do than discuss, in salacious detail, the destruction of someone else's marriage while being secretly relieved that it wasn't their dirty laundry bandied about.

Kate returned inside with the rolled-up newspaper in hand, where Richard removed a couple of mugs from the overhead cupboard.

She took a step back. "You startled me," she said when he looked over at her curiously. "It's Saturday. I thought you were sleeping in."

"I set the alarm because I have two showings this morning." He poured two mugs of coffee and handed one to his wife. They had avoided spending any time alone together in recent days. Fear of the dreaded *d*-word hung heavy between them.

Finally, Kate could take it no more.

"Richard, we have to talk," she blurted. It wasn't quite the smooth transition into the conversation she had rehearsed in her head for days, but it was a start.

"Now isn't the best time. As I already mentioned, I've got to go to work this morning."

"Surely you can spare a few minutes to have a conversation." Kate placed her mug on the countertop, not trusting herself with the scalding liquid. Her hands were trembling.

"Fine," he replied tightly. "What is it that is so important that it can't wait until later this afternoon?"

"I know about you and Carly. We can't go on like this anymore. Neither of us is happy."

Richard looked across the kitchen island at his wife. The last thing he needed was some over the top, hysterical reaction. It was too goddamn early in the morning for that crap. "People have affairs all the time. It's only natural after you've been together for as long as we have. The key is discretion."

Kate gaped at him, unsure if she wanted to hurl her mug of coffee at his head or fall onto the floor in a weeping heap. She took a calming breath and did neither. It shouldn't come as a surprise that he condoned infidelity. He had more than likely been cheating on her for years. To him, it was probably as natural as breathing. Why wouldn't he think it was all right to have the trophy wife and then something extra on the side?

"I cannot believe you just said that. Obviously, if you feel the need to stick your dick in any overdone tart, our relationship is over. And for you to think I'm going to be OK with that is utterly mind-boggling." She felt heat rising to her cheeks, and she willed herself to keep it together. Getting emotional was precisely the response he expected.

Richard took a sip of his coffee, his eyes never leaving hers. "While you stand over there, acting all holier-than-thou, I'd like to remind you of a certain chief of police that you have been super cozy with for as long as we've been together."

"What has *that* got to do with anything?" she hissed.

Richard sneered at his wife. She loved playing the martyr, but not this time.

"Remember when I said the key is discretion? Parking your car in the driveway of the conspicuously single chief of police late at night doesn't go unnoticed, especially when he fights off an intruder where a neighbor can see him—and your car in his driveway. Maybe you should have asked me for some pointers before letting that incompetent twat get his dick wet."

Changing her mind, Kate grabbed her mug and hurled it across the kitchen at him. "Fuck you!" she shouted, appalled by his casual cruelty.

He easily dodged the caffeinated missile. "That pathetic bastard's been sniffing around you for as long as you've known each other. I didn't think he'd ever be man enough to try anything more than follow you around with those sad little puppy dog eyes."

"He's more of a man than you could ever hope to be. And my only regret is wasting so much time with you. I should have been with him all along."

"Sure, Kate. Whatever you say. I've got to get ready for work. You need to calm down and think this over."

"I want a divorce. You and I are through. I can't live like this anymore."

"Divorce? Are you fucking kidding me? You fuck some hick cop, and suddenly you're demanding a divorce? Sorry, but that's not how it works. I don't care if you fool around, as long as it's not common knowledge and everything continues as usual."

Was Richard having a stress-induced midlife meltdown? It was the only explanation for his outlandish suggestion. Speaking slowly and enunciating each word, as if speaking to a child, she said, "We are not staying together. I can't stand to be under the same roof as you. I want a divorce. I don't know if this thing with Nick will work out. Maybe it's a phase, but probably not. I love him, and I know he loves me. So do yourself a favor and get the fuck over it. Oh, and one last thing, I already saw a lawyer, so don't even bother trying to hide any more assets."

"Isn't this fucking lovely? Nick fucks my sloppy seconds, and suddenly it's all sunsets and roses. That is the biggest load of bullshit, Kate. I'm going to destroy that little fucker. When I'm through with him, he won't be able to get a job collecting shopping carts."

Kate had been afraid Richard would react this way. He always played to win, regardless of whether he wanted the prize. She wouldn't be responsible for destroying Nick's career, no matter what he'd told her. He loved his job; serving the community gave him purpose and a sense of pride. Regardless of how she felt about him, she couldn't possibly allow Richard and his vindictive actions to destroy an innocent man's career.

"What a nasty fucking bastard you are," she said, turning her back to him and retreating to the bedroom. She twisted the lock on the door. She needed to take a shower to try to clear her mind.

On her way to the bathroom, the bedroom door rattled. Richard pounded furiously on the door. "Unlock the fucking door, you dried-up old bitch!"

Shocked by his venom, she replied, "Sorry, but you'll have to wait." She sounded far more confident than she felt.

He hammered on the door with a clenched fist. "I don't have time to screw around."

Kate flung the robe onto the bed before slipping out of her pajamas. She pulled her hair up into a messy topknot and turned the shower on. She waited for the hot water to come through.

"Let me in, goddamn it!"

"I'm taking a shower. I'll let you in when I've finished. Until then, leave me the hell alone and go read the paper or something." She liked this new, assertive version of herself. If only it had revealed itself earlier in her life, she might have avoided years of dissatisfaction and emptiness. Better late than never. She stepped into the shower, trying to ignore Richard's onslaught. As powerful as the water pressure was, it couldn't cancel out her husband's ranting.

"I get it," he fumed. "You think it's better on the other side. It's new and exciting, and you feel all giddy like a schoolgirl with her first crush. Trust me when I tell you it won't last. We have a good thing here. You don't need to get all crazy on me and throw it away because you finally scratched that itch you've denied all these years."

Kate tried to ignore his tirade. After soaping herself and rinsing off, she climbed out of the shower and wrapped a towel around herself. She walked over to the bedroom door and pressed her hands against it, listening to Richard's pathetic attempts to change her mind.

Hearing the muffled tread of her feet on the other side of the door, Richard continued. "I get it. You feel angry and humiliated, but there's no need to sabotage my business to punish me."

"What are you talking about?"

"Carly told me about what you did the other day. Handing over my money to some loser who couldn't pay his rent? What the hell is up with that?"

"It's called compassion, Richard, something I doubt you're familiar with."

"Don't bullshit me. You were trying to humiliate Carly by overriding her and flouting the rules that I put in place to ensure that you can continue to enjoy the comfortable lifestyle you're so damn accustomed to."

Unable to contain herself, Kate unlocked the door and flung it open angrily. "You are out of your mind if you think I helped that boy to spite Carly or damage your pathetic business. The only reason I loaned him the money was because I felt sorry for him. I didn't think that there was any need to evict someone because they were going to be a few days late paying the rent."

Richard scoffed and pushed past her. He entered the walk-in closet.

Kate continued, unable to stop now; she had finally found her voice. "And as for the 'comfortable lifestyle' you have so graciously provided, you can take it and shove it up your ass, you pompous fucking prick. This house has been nothing but a lonely prison, and I can't wait to be free of it."

Richard removed a shirt from its hanger and whirled around at Kate, his face a dangerous shade of red. "So what? You plan on packing your bags and shacking up with that dickhead cop?"

Kate hadn't even considered that. "Sounds like a great plan. Thanks for the suggestion," she replied.

Richard gawked at her. "I bet that loser didn't even reimburse you," he retorted lamely.

Kate smirked. "Not that it's any concern of yours, but Christian came into the jewelers on Thursday, as promised, and paid me back every cent he borrowed."

She squeezed past him and collected a bra and panties, and selected an outfit for the gym. Kim promised to spend an hour with her at the gym if Kate accompanied her afterward for a leisurely lunch. After her run-in with Richard, she couldn't wait to get to the gym and sweat out some of her anger.

Richard shook his head in defeat. "We'll talk about this later. I can't afford to be late for the open house." He roughly secured the knot on his tie and jammed his arms into his suit jacket. "Did you hear me?" he asked when Kate didn't acknowledge him.

"I heard you, Richard. I just really don't care," Kate called over her shoulder. Richard snatched up his phone from beside the bed and stalked out of the room.

After a grueling workout at the gym earlier in the day, Kate was leisurely sipping on her third glass of wine. She hadn't realized how cathartic it would be to drink a few glasses of sauvignon blanc with someone who genuinely cared about her.

Kim listened to her confession about Nick and the ongoing drama with Richard without judgment, quietly sipping wine between mouthfuls of slightly overcooked salmon. None of it surprised her. "What baffles me," Kim said, "is what took you two so long to get around to it. Anyone with a set of eyes in their head can plainly see the connection you share."

Being able to discuss the situation with someone she trusted helped clarify her stance. Her marriage to Richard was over. He wasn't going to wear her down with his usual bullying tactics or threats of becoming the town pariah. When Kate confessed that she was afraid nobody would want anything to do with her once she left Richard, Kim laughed so raucously that people dining at the nearby tables turned to see what was so damn funny.

"Kate," she said, "people get divorced every damn day. If anything, it'll make you seem more interesting, mysterious, even, especially if they find out you're banging that hot police chief that no red-blooded woman in this town has managed to tie down. Hell, you'll probably fend off brunch invites from those country club bitches. They'll want to find out how good Nick is in the sack."

Kate blushed. Her entire face went beet red all the way down to her chest, which had Kim laughing boisterously once more. She couldn't understand her friend's endless amusement at her embarrassment whenever the conversation turned to sex. Not everyone was as liberated and comfortable with their sexuality as Kim.

It was late afternoon when Kate drove home after spending the day with her best friend. Shaking her head as she pulled into the driveway, Kate wondered what it would be like if she took Kim up on her offer to stay in the spare bedroom at her cottage on the edge of town until she sorted out something more permanent. Undoubtedly, Kim would do her best to loosen her up with wine and cheese platters, undoing all her hard work at the gym.

Still, the offer came as a relief. Kate now had a solid plan and zero excuses to linger any longer than it took to pack a suitcase. Kim headed home to change the sheets on the guest bed, and Kate agreed to meet at her place for a light dinner and some serious Netflix time.

Some wretched dinner was scheduled with one of Richard's pals later that night, but he would be showing up solo unless he brought Carly along. Kate imagined how that would go: tits out, lips pouting, thinking she was somehow going to seduce Clarence Hudson with her crude attempts at flattery and false promises. Clarence was a devout Christian and very devoted to his family. Richard had no hope of brokering a deal over Clarence's parcel of land on the edge of town if the old coot discovered that both Richard and Kate had slept with other people.

She pressed the garage door remote and waited for the door to roll up. Winter had finally set in, so she had spent half a day cleaning out the garage so she could squeeze her car in beside Richard's Mercedes. It was a tight fit and required almost gymnastic flexibility to get in and out of the car, but she didn't want to sit in the driver's seat for five minutes, waiting for the car to thaw out anytime she wanted to drive somewhere.

The car rolled forward into the garage, alongside the newly repaired Mercedes. Grabbing her purse from the passenger seat, Kate tossed her keys inside and stepped out of the car. She shuffled along the narrow gap between the car and wall, careful not to catch herself on the hooks where Richard hung the sporting equipment he insisted on keeping but rarely bothered to use.

When she reached the entrance to the house, she flicked on the light switch and fished inside her purse for the keys. Once inside the house, she placed her purse on the counter and removed her coat and scarf, hanging them on the hooks in the hall. She immediately noticed a cold draft drifting down the hallway. The front door was ajar.

She walked out onto the tiled entryway and down the footpath. Had Richard gone out to the garden? She couldn't imagine why he would bother. It was unlike him to leave the door open, especially with the heating running. She stepped back inside and secured the door behind her. The soles of her sneakers had a thick crust of snow, so she bent down, pulled them off, and set them on the mat by the door.

"Richard, the front door is open," she called out. "Anybody could have walked on in and helped themselves to the television. You know there's been a string of break-ins over at Glenview?" She walked down the hall and through to the kitchen. One of the stools was lying on its side.

"Richard?" she called uncertainly. She heard muffled groans coming from down the hallway.

Unsure of how to proceed, she paused in the hall a few feet from the master bedroom. Would he stoop so low as to bring Carly into their home and have sex with her in their marriage bed?

Her heart raced, but Kate had to give him some credit. He was a cold bastard at times, but bringing another woman into the house and having sex with her? Surely that was beneath him, even after the massive fight they had that morning.

Still, she could hear noises coming from their bedroom.

"Richard?" she called timidly, wanting to let him know she was home so he would stop doing whoever he was with and save her the embarrassment of walking in on them in the act. Bracing herself for the sight of her husband balls deep in his secretary, Kate took a tentative step toward the bedroom.

It was dark in the hallway now that the afternoon was slowly giving way to evening. She stepped into the faded band of light spilling across the carpet from the open bedroom door. The room was empty. Puzzled, she quickly crossed the room and poked her head in the bathroom, but it, too, was empty. As usual, Richard's wet towel lay in a crumpled heap on the tiled floor.

There was a thump from somewhere deeper in the house, and she went in search of the source of the noise. He must be in either the guest bedroom or the study. She had already checked everywhere else in the house.

Was that a muffled cry she just heard? Maybe she had been too quick to assume the worst of her husband. What if he had a heart attack while she was out drinking and having a good time with Kim?

"Richard, where are you?" Panic set in as her mind worked through the morbid possibilities. He could have had a stroke or fallen and hit his head, lying on the floor somewhere, unable to reach his cell to call for help.

She flung open the guest room door, emitting a puff of stale air from the neglected space. The room was empty. A muffled thud came from inside Richard's office opposite the guest room. It sounded like someone kicking against the plush wool carpeting. As she pulled the guest room door closed, she remembered the intruder at Nick's house and felt a twinge of fear. Richard might be a prick, but he was still her husband, and she wasn't about to stand by and let some intruder hurt him. Was she? It was hard to ignore the sudden tightening in her chest and the urge to backtrack down the hallway and pretend she hadn't just heard a wet coughing sound coming from the other side of the door.

Taking hold of the doorknob, she turned it and pushed open the door before she could get cold feet. The burgundy drapes blocked the fading afternoon light. A small lamp on the desk beside his laptop was the only source of illumination. Her eyes followed the crimson splashes crisscrossing the walls before drifting down to her husband, slumped back in the chair behind the behemoth mahogany desk. A stranger straddled him lewdly.

Someone moaned. Whether from pleasure or pain, it was impossible to tell.

Kate's hand clutched the doorknob. She stood motionless in the doorway, silently watching as Richard made a wet gurgling sound. His hands beat weakly at the girl hunched over his body. She swatted them aside like they were nothing more than flies. Then she noticed they were no longer alone.

Kate realized her error. It wasn't a girl at all. Not really.

Twisting to face Kate, the demon grinned, blood and globs of flesh caught in its jagged teeth. It diverted its attention from Kate long enough to rake its claws across Richard's throat. Blood spurted from the wound, dousing the demon and the desk behind it. His slashed windpipe whistled moistly as he took his dying breaths. Blood bubbled between what remained of his lips before bursting with a sickening pop.

Kate had to move, but when she attempted to remove her hand from the doorknob, her body refused to cooperate with her brain.

With Richard dead, the creature turned back to Kate. Its distorted features dripped with blood, and its long, matted hair hung in wet clumps around its face.

"The nosy cop's pretty plaything," it said. "I had to entertain myself while I waited for you." It rolled its dead black eyes in Richard's direction. "He wasn't much fun. He hardly fought at all. No wonder you prefer to fuck that posturing policeman."

"What *are* you?" Kate whispered.

"It doesn't matter what I am. What I'm going to do to the policeman's pretty bitch is the more pertinent question, don't you think?" It slowly lifted itself from Richard's lap.

The prospect of ending up like Richard gave her the fortitude to release her hold on the doorknob, and she spun away, sprinting down the hallway. She didn't dare look back. She reached the kitchen and grabbed her purse, spilling the contents out onto the countertop. Where were her keys? She snatched them up with a trembling hand and turned toward the garage door when she saw the demon barreling down the hallway, its face twisted in a predatory snarl.

Kate ripped the garage door open and was about to step through when the creature launched itself at her. It knocked Kate sideways down the hall toward the front entry. She landed heavily on her left shoulder. Pain, white-hot and almost blinding in its intensity, spread from her shoulder and out across her chest. The creature dived after her, its gore-smeared claws swiping the air where Kate's face had been a second before.

Kate thrust herself back toward the front door, but her feet slipped on the tiles as she tried to keep as much distance as possible between herself and the demonic creature. It snapped and snarled as it crawled after her, its matted hair falling across its distorted face. As it climbed to its feet, Kate scuttled back, passing the solid oak hall table. Reaching out, she grabbed one of the legs and tipped it forward, sending the table crashing over. A table lamp and photo frames containing smiling pictures of Richard and herself during happier times clattered to the floor. The hall table landed at an angle against the opposite wall, momentarily blocking the demon's progress.

The creature laughed at her attempt to thwart its attack. "I'm going to enjoy ripping off your limbs, like plucking the wings off a blowfly. I'll leave a trail of your pretty parts for that interfering cop to find. He'll have to collect you piece by bloody piece." It gripped the hall table and flung it aside. Kate extended her arm and grabbed hold of the lamp that had somehow remained intact despite the fall and held it out in front of her like a shield.

The creature latched onto her ankle and jerked her forward. Kate screamed as the creature dragged her toward its gaping mouth. Picturing Richard's grisly demise, she kicked out with her free foot, and her heel grazed its chin. The blow caused its jaw to snap shut, and she quickly swung the heavy crystal lamp at its head while it was distracted.

"Take that, you murdering fuck!" Kate screamed. Stunned by the impact, the demon loosened its hold on her ankle enough to allow Kate to jerk her foot free. The distraction gave her precious few seconds to get to her feet and yank open the front door. She raced down the steps, along the icy path, and out into the cul-de-sac.

***

Next door, George Maitland was reading the latest crime thriller by his favorite author when he heard an ungodly commotion coming from the Lyttle residence. The wind had died down a few hours earlier, and the afternoon was still and quiet, which allowed the sound to travel between the two houses. Unaccustomed to hearing such a racket from the Lyttle residence, he marked his page in the book and placed it on the table beside his chair along with his reading glasses. Occasionally, he or his wife heard the Lyttle's bickering, but it was infrequent. Mostly the house was a quiet, joyless place, and he found himself pitying the wife. Her husband appeared to be more interested in his job than spending time with her. The man was rarely home. He left early in the morning and returned late in the evening, leaving her to fill her time with whatever she did to stave off the boredom and loneliness. George's wife was fond of scolding him for his musing on the neighbor's private lives. He had far too much time on his hands since retiring. She was probably right, but he'd be damned if he would ever admit as much.

It hadn't taken him long to realize that Richard Lyttle was an arrogant so-and-so interested in peacocking around in his fancy suits and flashy cars and using his wife as arm candy when it suited him. Since the Lyttles had moved into the neighborhood nearly seven years ago, they had spoken only a handful of times, which was okay with George. Having dealt with his share of obnoxious turds during his thirty-odd years of teaching, he wasn't inclined to suffer such company in his private life.

His dislike for Richard didn't stop his wife from sharing the occasional recipe with Mrs. Lyttle over a pot of tea or puttering around in the greenhouse together, admiring the dizzying array of orchids his wife cultivated.

There was most certainly something amiss next door. It sounded like someone was tearing the house apart. He hurried over to the phone on the wall by the grandfather clock and dialed the police. George read the paper. Even if some of the details were exaggerated, the basic facts were indisputable. People in Taylor's End were being attacked and killed, and he felt it was prudent to report the disturbance. He hated to think of Mrs. Lyttle in any trouble and resolved to intervene once he had spoken to someone at the police station.

Fifteen

When the call came in, DeAngelo was counting down the minutes before shift changeover. The day had been long and tedious. On top of performing their usual duties, every available officer was charged with revisiting every piece of evidence connected to the recent killings. Chief Bremner wanted the cases examined with fresh eyes hoping that they would find something they had missed. DeAngelo couldn't blame the chief for wanting to be thorough. Everybody with a badge was desperate to catch the nutbag responsible, but the pressure from the public and the added workload was wearing everyone down, including him.

He answered the phone on the third ring and listened with disinterest as a gentleman on the other end of the line reported a domestic disturbance at his neighbors' house.

"Can you tell me your name, sir?" DeAngelo stabbed at his keyboard with his index fingers and cradled the phone against his ear with his shoulder. "And what exactly is it that you are reporting?" DeAngelo stifled a yawn while he listened to Mr. Maitland's long-winded reply. "What was the address?" he finally managed to ask. "58 Rosemont Court. All right, I'll have someone come and check it out shortly."

Nick Bremner entered the station, having just arrived back in Taylor's End after a mandatory drive over to Cedar Rapids to provide an unofficial report on the investigation into the killings. He was still furious that he had been called away to explain himself, which had taken up the better part of the day. It could have just as easily been a phone call or even an email. Unfortunately, there was no fighting bureaucracy, so he had wasted his precious time sitting around and waiting to be seen, only to be admonished for failing to make any arrests in any of the cases.

Fuming, he'd had no choice but to grit his teeth and take the reprimand. Knowing that he was doing everything he could to find the person responsible for terrorizing his town, it felt like a kick in the guts that his superiors were questioning his ability to get the job done. Next, they would send some suited-up task force to take over the investigations. It wasn't at that point yet, but it was damn close.

He was on his way over to the coffee machine when he overheard DeAngelo taking the domestic disturbance call. Stopping beside the officer's desk, he waited impatiently until DeAngelo ended the call.

"Did I hear you say that domestic is at 58 Rosemont Court?" Bremner asked.

DeAngelo nodded. "Sure was. There's a patrol car over near the high school. I'll send them around now."

"Don't bother. I know the people who live there, so I will go and check it out myself." Bremner looked at his watch. "You still have another forty-five on the clock. Wanna join me?"

DeAngelo stood up and collected his jacket from the back of the chair. Dealing with an irate husband and wife wasn't exactly his ideal way to spend a Saturday afternoon, but it sure as heck beat sitting at his desk, sifting through the paperwork he had already looked over countless times. He studied the chief out of the corner of his eye as they hurried outside to the parking lot.

"You said you know the folks we're going to visit?" he asked as they hopped into Bremner's car.

"That's correct." Bremner started the cruiser and backed out of the space. "Kate Lyttle and her husband, Richard, live there."

DeAngelo looked out the window as they drove away from the station. Bremner put the flashers on, but not the siren.

"Isn't Kate that golfing buddy of yours?" DeAngelo asked. He had heard the rumors involving the chief and the wife of the most prominent realtor in Taylor's End.

"Yeah, that's Kate," Bremner said tightly.

DeAngelo was not about to pry into his boss's sex life, especially when it involved a married woman. His wife would berate him over dinner that night for missing a prime opportunity to discover some sordid details about the alleged affair.

"Rosemont Court sounds familiar, but I can't seem to recall where it is."

Bremner glanced across at him. He was grateful for the deliberate change of conversation. He didn't want to discuss the true nature of his relationship with Kate, and he felt physically sick with worry. His stomach churned violently at the prospect of Richard laying a hand on her. He hadn't thought the douchebag had it in him, but if she had confronted him about the affair—either affair—who knew what he might do?

"It backs onto the Peterson Nature Reserve on the southeast side of town," Bremner said. "We should be there in a minute or two."

"Sure, I know where you're talking about now. Justine's parents lived over that way before they sold their place and moved into one of those fancy villas next to the Glenview Estate. Nice, quiet area, as I recall."

Bremner slowed the cruiser and flicked on the indicator before turning onto Rosemont Court. "I know it was called in as a possible domestic, but we need to be alert to other possibilities."

DeAngelo raised his eyebrows but said nothing. It looked like the pressure was becoming too much for the chief, which would go a long way toward explaining why he was suddenly getting tangled up with a married woman. Nick Bremner was the last person he would have thought would have an affair, let alone with a woman married to someone as high profile as Richard Lyttle. The realtor had clout, and that, coupled with the lack of suspects in Michelle Tanner's assault or the two open homicides, left DeAngelo wondering if Bremner would even have a job next month.

They pulled into the Lyttle's driveway and wasted no time exiting the vehicle. The front door stood wide open—not a good sign when it was only thirty-seven degrees outside.

"I don't feel good about this," Bremner said as he rested his hand on his gun. They cautiously approached the house. DeAngelo pointed at the next door, which was only partially visible behind the huge elm. A pinched face peered out at them from a window framed by frothy lace curtains.

"I'm guessing that's Mr. Maitland, the concerned neighbor who made the call."

"Yep, I assume so," Bremner agreed.

They drew their guns and mounted the steps to the front entry.

"Hello? This is the police. Is everything all right in there?" Bremner called out.

There was no response. Glass crunched underfoot as they entered the house. They stepped over the remains of a broken lamp lying across the front hallway. A narrow timber hall table stood out from the wall at an awkward angle, and DeAngelo motioned at the concentration of blackish-red droplets sprinkled along the floor near the lamp.

Bremner nodded and pointed down the hall. They continued, quickly scanning the expansive kitchen and living room. Nothing. Bremner ducked back into the hallway and continued deeper into the house, DeAngelo close behind him.

Bremner had never gone beyond Kate's kitchen and living room. He had only ever stopped by for a casual visit when Richard was home. He stepped into the master bedroom, taking a moment to observe the private space Kate shared with her husband. His eyes fell on the king-size bed, and he wondered what it would be like to wake up beside her every morning. He would give anything to feel the warmth of her body snuggled against him as they lay together.

The dread building inside him was almost overwhelming. He forced himself out of the bedroom and continued the search, terrified of what he might discover. The prospect of losing her now, when they had finally expressed their feelings, was unbearable. He stopped in the hallway.

"Boss, are you all right?" DeAngelo asked.

"Sorry, I'm fine. See if you can locate the light switch, would you? It's as dark as hell in here."

DeAngelo retraced his steps, feeling around on the wall until he found the switch plate. The hall was suddenly filled with light that dispelled the shadows and the panic growing inside him.

The bathroom and guest room were clear. Where the heck were they?

"What the...," DeAngelo said, stepping beside Bremner in the doorway to the study. Bremner took a second to compose himself before entering the room. He stepped around the oversize desk to check for a pulse. Nothing. All he could hear was the soft patter of blood dripping onto the carpet.

He scanned the room, confused by the complete lack of disorder. Richard Lyttle wasn't a slight man. It was difficult to imagine him doing nothing to fend off his attacker.

"Man, I've never seen so much blood. Why didn't he put up a fight?" DeAngelo asked. "Nothing is amiss in here."

The top three buttons of Richard's shirt were open. Two made sense. Three less so—unless the man was getting undressed. He surveyed the desk and the floor. Sure enough, a tie lay discarded on the floor beside the chair.

"Do you think this is the result of a domestic?" DeAngelo asked faintly.

Bremner glanced over at the officer. "It's unlikely. His fly is open, and one of those fancy silk ties he's so fond of is lying on the floor beside him."

"What about his wife? Is she capable of slitting his throat like that?"

"I think Richard made a fateful decision to hook up with our killer, and Kate interrupted them."

"That would explain the smashed lamp in the hallway," DeAngelo said. "If she walked in on this, she had one hell of a fight on her hands."

"Call it in," Bremner ordered. He retraced his steps down the hallway to the front of the house, where blood and glass littered the tiles. He spied a pair of Kate's sneakers on a mat by the door and crouched down to get a better look. He picked one up. The toe was damp. He placed his hand on the spot where the shoe had rested. Wet. He walked over to the garage door and cracked it open. Both cars were in the garage.

"Her purse is still here," DeAngelo called from the kitchen.

Bremner joined him and looked down in bewilderment at the contents of her purse strewn across the countertop.

"We need to find her," he said, struggling to keep his voice even.

DeAngelo placed a hand on his shoulder. "The second backup arrives, we'll do just that. Until then, let's wait outside. I don't know about you, but I could use some fresh air." He guided Bremner out of the kitchen and down the hall to the front yard, where they waited uneasily for help to arrive.

Sixteen

K ate fled into the reserve at the end of the cul-de-sac, following the narrow path deeper into the forest. It was dark and filled with shadows beneath the canopy of snow-laden branches. Her feet grew numb the farther she dashed into the reserve. In some places, her bare feet sank ankle-deep into the snow; in others, the ground was exposed, allowing twigs and stones to dig painfully into the soles of her feet. She inhaled through her nose and exhaled through her mouth, focusing on the steady rhythm of her breathing to maximize her oxygen uptake. If she gave in to panic, that inhuman thing would catch up, seizing her from behind and drag her to the ground like some predatory beast.

She knew that running deeper into the forest was the worst possible thing she could do. The farther she ran from the relative safety of her neighborhood, the more isolated she became. The more isolated she became, the less chance there was of stumbling across someone who could intervene. But what else could she do?

It didn't matter now. Kate was committed to her current course of action. There could be no turning back. Her only hope was to outrun the dreadful creature hunting her. Silently thanking herself for maintaining her fitness over the years, Kate plowed deeper into the forest. She ducked beneath a low-hanging branch, narrowly avoiding a nasty smack in the face. Feet pounded the forest floor behind her. Kate picked up the pace, wondering how much longer she could continue. Jogging on a treadmill for thirty minutes a day was a far cry from running for her life over uneven terrain with nothing to protect her feet from the elements.

It was the thought of her grizzled remains abandoned in the forest, her pitiful body gnawed by the animals and slowly rotting away, that kept her going when her lungs burned and her legs became slow and heavy. She couldn't give up and let that demon thing rip her to shreds. She would not become yet another corpse splashed across the front page of the newspaper.

A fallen branch tangled around her foot, and she staggered, arms outstretched, to stop from falling. When she looked up, she was no longer on the path, but she forged ahead, too afraid to stop and figure out where she was. She risked a hurried glance over her shoulder. The demon was gone. It should have come as a relief, but now it could be anywhere, ready to spring out and grab her.

The reserve covered hundreds of acres of land on the outskirts of town, stretching from the edge of Glenview Estate and wrapping all the way around the southern side of Taylor's End before terminating at the outer perimeter of the golf course. Nightfall would come much sooner beneath the thick canopy of branches, and if she didn't find her way back to a trail soon, she wouldn't make it out alive. Either Richard's killer would catch up with her, or the cold would finish her off.

In any case, dead was dead. Being taken by the elements might be less painful and traumatizing, but it still ended with her in a casket. Kate wasn't ready to die—not now, not out here, cold and alone. Brushing aside another low-hanging branch, she forced herself to keep moving. She couldn't give up, not yet. She would succumb only when her legs were leaden weights, unable to take another step, and her lungs refused to suck in any more air.

The sharp crack of brittle twigs being trampled somewhere to her left sent her veering in the opposite direction with a startled cry. Thorny undergrowth whipped her face and arms, cutting her cheeks as she ran. Why couldn't she find the goddamn trail? She must have jogged along the trails hundreds of times over the years, finding pleasure in the tranquility beneath the shady canopy. Now, instead of a natural haven, it was a dark and foreboding labyrinth filled with hazards waiting to trip her up or gouge out an eye.

Without warning, she emerged into a clearing the size of a small courtyard. There were picnic tables for weary hikers and a solitary trash can, its contents overflowing onto the ground around it. She could have wept with happiness. Instead, she ran around the closest picnic table and read the faded sign nailed to a tree at the edge of the clearing. It was 1.8 miles back to Rosemont Court or 1.2 miles to the Knox Street exit. It was a no-brainer. She was already running on empty. Every additional step she took could be the difference between finding her way out of the reserve or collapsing under a tree, too exhausted to move or fight.

She was so intent on figuring out which trail to take that she almost missed the hushed tread of footsteps creeping across the carpet of snow covering the clearing. Kate cried out in alarm and shot off down the Knox Street path away from her pursuer. Aware that the hellish creature had gained precious ground and almost had her within its reach, she pushed through the pain, forcing her legs to move despite the lethargy trying to slow her down. Its ragged breathing raised the fine hairs on the back of her neck.

It snatched at her ponytail, wrenching a clump of hair from her head, and Kate shrieked. Clutching at her head, she wept as she tried to outrun the creature, but it was hopeless. Her husband's killer was relentless; its determination outstripped Kate's compromised condition. Its claws swept through the air inches from her back, and she cried out again.

But the third time it lunged at her, Kate wasn't quite quick enough. The creature grabbed hold of her sweatshirt and dragged her back. Kate skittered backward. A rock gouged the arch of her foot, its jagged tip tearing open her delicate skin. Howling in pain, she stumbled sideways, catching herself against a tree trunk. Acting on impulse, she twisted free of her sweatshirt, leaving the demon holding a fistful of clothing, and made one final sprint down the Knox Street path.

The creature stood watching as Kate limped off. It had rarely encountered anyone with such a tenacious will to live. It knew she was hurting; her scent was ripe with fear and exhaustion. But she kept on fighting and running. The woman's infuriatingly quick stride was now a pitiful hobble, but she kept on running anyway. It threw back its head and roared, tossing the sweatshirt aside and setting off after her. No more fucking around. When it caught up with her, there would be no escape—only suffering and death. But death would be a long time coming. The demon would make sure of that.

Kate limped further into the reserve. Her skin prickled from the cold that wrapped itself around her bare torso. She was now topless except for a sports bra, and her bare feet were bleeding. Every cell in her body screamed at her to stop. The burning in her lungs was unbearable. It wouldn't be long before she gave up and collapsed.

Just when she thought it was over and she couldn't take another step, a familiar noise cut through the silence of the forest. For a second, Kate's frazzled mind couldn't place the sound, and then she recognized it: it was a motorbike. And judging by the buzz reverberating through the woods, it was close. It was illegal to ride through the reserve, but that didn't stop kids from doing it anyway.

She listened to the revving of the engine as it tore along the trails and tried to gauge its location. It was difficult to tell since noise echoed through the forest, but she thought it might be on a trail that cut across the path she was on. Kate limped toward the sound.

Hope bloomed in her chest.

The engine of the motorbike idled. Please, God, don't let it leave without me; Kate prayed to whatever god was listening. Then a hellish bellow ripped through the forest from the direction of the clearing, and an explosion of startled birds erupted from the trees. Picturing the creature's dead black eyes and needle teeth, Kate veered off the path, using her good arm to shield her face from the low-hanging branches.

Christian eased off the throttle and slowed the bike. It was getting late, and visibility was poor, not to mention it was cold as fuck. He had gone out for a quick ride to blow off steam and clear his head after a shit day at work. Plus, his roommate had asked for some alone time. His girlfriend was dropping around for a quickie.

Christian removed his helmet and roughed up his sweaty hair. He took his cell phone from his pocket to check the time. They should be decent by now; he had given them longer than he had agreed. He took a moment to take in the harsh beauty of the reserve during winter. The stillness was welcome after a hectic shift at the hospital.

It didn't last long.

A violent screech cut through the tranquility and the idling engine of his bike. He camped out in the woods often enough to know that whatever had emitted that primal howl wasn't native to the reserve. He had never heard anything like it. And that wasn't all. Something was coming, crashing through the undergrowth, headed straight for him.

He nervously swallowed as he considered the violence that had struck Taylor's End lately. Maybe it hadn't such been a great idea to ride in the woods alone right before nightfall. He switched on his bike's headlight and jammed his helmet down on his head, preparing for a hasty retreat. Balancing the bike so he could quickly flick the kickstand up with his boot, he watched the trees intently.

A half-naked woman emerged from between a stand of trees, stumbling over a fallen branch and limping in his direction.

"What the fuck?" he exclaimed in astonishment as she approached him. She cradled her left arm and favored the opposite foot. Aside from her obvious lack of clothing, she was also barefoot. Scratches, some of which had split and bled, crisscrossed her face and arms.

He studied her pale face and flushed cheeks, marred by bruises, scratches, and her huge, frantic eyes. Holy shit. He recognized her. It was the woman from the real estate office, the one who had stood up for him and helped him out when he was about to lose the apartment: Kate Lyttle. Why was she out here like this?

Without stopping to explain herself, she swung her leg over his bike and climbed onto the seat behind him, wrapping her arms tight around his waist.

"Go!" she cried in a voice hoarse from exertion.

Stunned by Kate's unexpected appearance, Christian remained unmoving.

"What are you waiting for? We have to get out of here right now!" she sobbed. Unsettled by the noise he had heard in the woods and the fear in Kate's voice, Christian knocked the kickstand up and turned to reassure her. "It's going to be alright. I'll get you out of here."

They weren't alone. Someone else was coming. Probably the person responsible for Kate's injuries. Something broke from the trees where Kate had emerged a minute earlier, barreling toward them with a frightening intensity. Daylight had almost completely faded into night, and the woods cast strange shadows that distorted its features, turning the benign into something sinister. Kate loosened her grip around his waist to slap his shoulder, urging him to go. He threw the bike in gear and squeezed the throttle.

The bike surged forward. Its rear wheel spitting dirt and pebbles as they raced off. Christian didn't know what to make of the thing he glimpsed over Kate's shoulder. Hunger and hate twisted its features into something inhuman.

Kate pressed herself hard against him, her body trembling uncontrollably, her arms locked tight around his waist. Leaning low over the handlebars, he guided the bike along the narrow path lit by his single headlight.

It wasn't until they neared the Knox Street entrance that he dared slow the bike. He stopped once he reached the asphalt lit by the reassuring glow of the streetlights. Both Christian and Kate turned to look back at the stretch of woods behind them.

They saw nothing more sinister than the shadowy outline of the reserve in the distance. Kate's body relaxed against him, and Christian gently loosened her hands from around his waist so he could climb off the bike. Mindful of her injuries, he gently lifted her from the back of the motorbike and supported her until he was convinced that she wouldn't collapse onto the road at his feet. Aware that Kate must be dangerously close to hypothermia, he unzipped his jacket and offered it to her. She accepted gratefully. Her body trembled violently, and her fingers were so numb that she almost dropped the jacket. Seeing her struggle, Christian stepped in and helped her into it, easing it over her dislocated shoulder as gently as he could. She whimpered, and he apologized. With one quick motion, he zipped it up. It was at least three sizes too big, but it was the best he could do. He removed his helmet, and Kate fell against him sobbing in relief.

"Christian, I can't believe it's you."

"Yeah, it's a crazy coincidence," he agreed, wrapping his arms around her.

She pressed her face against the warmth of his chest. "You saved my life. I didn't think I was going to make it. It was so cold, and I couldn't keep running, I—"

"Shhh. Whatever happened, you're safe now." He gently pushed her away from him so he could look at her. "You need to take a deep breath before you hyperventilate." She nodded and concentrated on her breathing. "We need to get you to the hospital. I can call the paramedics, or if you prefer, I can take you there myself. What do you want to do?"

Kate shook her head. All the color had drained from her cheeks, and her lips were blue. "I have to go back to the house. Richard's still there. I almost forgot about him. How could I do that? How could I ever forget him? What sort of person would do that?"

Christian looked at her in confusion and took her hand in his. "We can call your husband when you get to the hospital, and he can meet us there." Her incoherent rambling must be a sign of shock setting in.

She looked up at him, blinking back tears. "You don't understand. The thing that was chasing me through the woods? It attacked Richard before it came after me. And I know he..."

"What?" Christian asked after a long silence.

"He's probably dead, but I still need to get help. I should have run down the street instead of into the reserve. That was stupid. Somebody would have seen me and called the police. They might have got to Richard in time."

"I'm sorry, Kate," he said, "but I need you to climb back on the bike so we can get you medical attention. You might be going into shock, so the sooner we leave, the better. And honestly, I want to get the fuck away from that place."

He helped her up onto the bike and climbed on in front of her. Relieved when she wrapped her arms around him once more. He didn't fully understand what had happened back in the woods, but Kate was lucky that he had decided to take the bike out for a quick ride that night. That thing had been hot on her tail and would have run her down if he hadn't stopped to take a breather.

He started the bike and rode down the street. He raced past shadows that stretched toward them, hiding horrors he dared not contemplate. Born and bred here, he had always felt that Taylor's End was so familiar and predictable. Just another nothing and nowhere town like countless others. Now, as he sped down the road, a frightened and damaged woman he hardly knew clinging to him like he was her savior, the darkened streets looked menacing and perilous.

Seventeen

B remner walked out into the front yard of 58 Rosemont Court. He needed a few minutes outside in the fresh air to help clear his head. The smell of blood and emptied bowels was becoming too much. He was sending himself crazy with worry contemplating what might have happened to Kate if she had been home when Richard was killed. Everything pointed in that direction. Her car was in the garage. The contents of her purse were strewn across the kitchen counter. And then there were the footprints in the snow leading away from the house and into the reserve.

He knew that Kate had been chased into the woods. Two sets of footprints were visible in the inch and a half of snow blanketing the front yard. They disappeared at the edge of the lawn, presumably where she stepped down onto the road, only to reappear at the entrance to the reserve. He bet his life that Kate was pursued into the woods by the same individual that had slaughtered her husband. He had sent four of his officers into the reserve to search for her while he stood around feeling completely useless.

The waiting was unbearable. Bremner paced back and forth alongside the coroner's van parked in the driveway. The guys responsible for transporting the body to the morgue stood around smoking cigarette after cigarette while they waited to move the remains. If they kept smoking at such a prodigious rate, Bremner thought, it wouldn't be long before one of them took a horizontal ride in the back of the van.

His cell phone rang. "Hello?" he answered.

"Chief, Kate Lyttle has shown up at the hospital with some young guy that found her running through the reserve."

Listening attentively, he walked out into the street while he processed what he was hearing. "Are you sure?"

Officer Betts replied, "Yes. We don't have any details about the extent of her injuries yet, but she is conscious and was asking about her husband."

"OK. I'll be there shortly." Pocketing his phone, Bremner spoke into the radio on his jacket. "Kate Lyttle is at the hospital. I repeat, Kate Lyttle is alive. I'm calling the search off. Anyone who is searching the woods, please make your way back to Rosemont Court for further instructions."

His body sagged with relief as the news sank in. All this time, he was mentally preparing himself for the moment he would find Kate dead in the woods, her body ravaged like her husband's and the bodies of the victims before him. But she had eluded the attacker, and she was alive and safe only a short drive from where he now stood.

He took a minute to compose himself before walking over to the guys waiting to retrieve the body. "Can I get one of you guys to move the van for me?"

"Sure thing. You nearly finished with the body?" the older of the two asked. Bremner shook his head. "It will probably be another half an hour or so." They nodded dolefully, and the younger one stubbed out his cigarette before climbing into the van and reversing it out into the street.

DeAngelo appeared on the front steps, and Joe trailed after him. The young officer's face was the color of cottage cheese.

"Are you heading across to the hospital now?" DeAngelo asked.

Bremner opened the door to his cruiser and nodded. "I am. Kate's injured, but she can talk. I want to see what sort of state she's in and ask her a few questions while everything is still fresh in her mind. The guy that found her in the woods is waiting for me too. Can you take care of things here while I'm gone?"

"Yeah, no problem. We should be ready to wrap it up within the hour. What do you want me to do with the guys when they return from the woods?"

"I want every available officer out patrolling the streets. Whoever did this could still be trying to make their way home. If they are, I want them found and apprehended." Feeling a stab of sympathy for the rookie, Bremner waved him over. "Joe, get your ass in the car. You're coming with me."

Bremner didn't say a word on the drive over. His eyes focused straight ahead as he navigated the icy streets. The cruiser had barely rolled to a stop under the annex to the emergency entrance before he leaped out and ran inside.

"I need to see Kate Lyttle," he informed the nurse at the patient intake desk. "Right now."

The nurse was flustered by Bremner's arrival. "I'm sorry," she stammered, "but you will have to wait. She's being treated by the doctor at the moment."

Bremner glared at her and crossed the waiting area, heading for the corridor and the treatment rooms.

"Sir, please stop," the nurse said, running out after him. "I cannot allow you to go in there." Joe trailed after the pair, keeping out of the chief's way.

Nick Bremner passed the first room, which was empty, and proceeded to the next. He gave a short, sharp knock before opening the door.

Behind him, the nurse gasped. "What do you think you are doing?"

"Kate?"

Across the room, Kate raised her head at the sound of her name. She sat on the examination bed, a blanket wrapped around her shivering body. She smiled weakly.

Ignoring the nurse's outraged protests, Bremner crossed the room and took her hand in his. "I'm so glad to see you." He leaned down and kissed her. Behind them, Joe gawked at the open display of affection. After closely looking her over for injuries, Bremner turned to the nurse, who had stopped in the doorway. "Where is the doctor? I thought you said she was receiving treatment." He heard the harsh edge to his voice but was powerless to contain it. Seeing Kate hurt and vulnerable made him act irrationally. At a time when he needed a clear head, all he could think about was keeping her safe and exacting a form of revenge that did not sit comfortably with his role as chief of police.

Kate reached out and touched his arm. "Nick, I'm all right. The doctor stepped out of the room for a moment. He will be back soon. Please, just relax."

She was right. He needed to take it down a notch. Kate had survived her ordeal. Nothing constructive would come of him lashing out at innocent people.

"I'm sorry," he said. "I didn't mean to sound so curt."

The nurse nodded and stepped aside for Dr. Marmont and the nurse assisting him as they entered the room.

"I'll take it from here, Theresa," the doctor said. "Please return to the intake desk and make sure nobody is running amok out in the waiting area." She gave Bremner a dirty look before turning her back to them and exiting the room. Dr. Marmont turned his attention to the two policemen crowding the treatment room. "Chief Bremner, I can't say I'm entirely surprised to see you here, although it is rather unorthodox to barge in while a patient is receiving treatment, wouldn't you agree?"

Heat rushed to Bremner's cheeks. "I know the patient," he explained lamely.

Dr. Marmont glanced over the top of his glasses at Joe, "And you brought backup for the occasion."

Bremner cracked a smile, grateful to the doctor for lightening the mood in the room. "That's Joe Smith, my newest recruit. He's ruthlessly ambitious. By this time next year, he'll probably have my job, and you will be reprimanding Joe instead of me." Joe's mouth dropped open, mortified by the suggestion.

Kate giggled at the young man's horrified expression. "He's joking with you. Stick around long enough, and you'll learn to ignore it."

"I understand your concern," the doctor said to Bremner, "but I do need to attend Mrs. Lyttle now. Perhaps you could speak to her after we've reset her shoulder and cleaned up her wounds."

"Reset her shoulder?" Bremner asked.

"I've got a dislocated shoulder," Kate said, "but Dr. Marmont assures me he can pop it back in. I'll be back to normal in no time."

Dr. Marmont motioned for the nurse to pull the privacy curtain across. "Chief Bremner, Joe, I must insist that you both leave the room while I treat Mrs. Lyttle. I'll let you know the minute I'm finished. Perhaps you could talk to Christian while you're waiting. I believe he's waiting in the staff room. If you go and ask Theresa *nicely,* I'm certain she would be happy to show you the way."

"Why would he be in the staff room?" Joe asked.

"Good question," Bremner said.

"Christian is an orderly here at the hospital," Dr. Marmont explained. "Now, I won't tell you again. Out." He shooed them away and closed the door behind them.

"Now what?" Joe asked. Relieved to discover that Kate was going to be okay, Bremner clapped Joe on the shoulder. "Now we go and find out what the hell happened to her out in the woods."

***

The following day Christian woke to the sound of his phone ringing. Reaching out, he felt beside the bed for the phone, but it wasn't there. He must have knocked it from the nightstand while he was sleeping. Too tired to bother searching for it, he allowed it to ring out and covered his head with a pillow. When the phone started ringing again, he forced his eyes open with a groan. Throwing the pillow aside, he reached over the edge of the bed and felt around on the floor. His fingers found the cord to the charger and traced their way to the phone lying under the bed among the fluff balls and empty water bottles. Picking it up, he answered on the final ring.

"Hello?" he mumbled grumpily, his voice thick with sleep.

"Hey, man. Did I wake you?" Jeb asked. His gleeful lack of remorse was apparent in his voice.

"What time is it?" Christian rubbed his eyes with his free hand, wishing he was still asleep.

"It's nearly ten. Kind of early for a Sunday morning, but with Grandad out of commission, I've been getting up earlier to get his chores done. And if I can't sleep in, why the fuck should you?" He chuckled, pleased with himself.

"You can be a real asshole. Has anyone ever told you that?"

"Frequently. I'm starting to develop a complex about it. But seriously, I called to ask if you wanted to meet at the diner for a late breakfast? I know I was supposed to come over the other night, but things have been super hectic around here. What do you say?"

It didn't take long for Christian to consider the offer. He was awake now, and he didn't need to check the refrigerator's contents to know what it contained: sweet fuck all. Dale hadn't bought the groceries yet, so the kitchen was a wasteland of moldy takeout containers and stale bread too far gone to even use as toast. "Yeah, I'm in. I could use a decent meal. Are you already there?"

"Nope. I'm about to head into town. I can be there in ten."

"Make it twenty. I need to run through the shower first," Christian said, sniffing his armpits. If he showed up to the diner stinking like body odor, Anna would call him out on it, regardless of who was within earshot.

Christian arrived at the diner thirty minutes later and made his way over to the booth where Jeb was sitting, greedily poring over the menu. Christian slipped into the seat opposite him and placed his helmet on the padded bench against the wall. He dropped his phone, wallet, and keys on the table in front of him. "Like you don't already know what you are gonna order."

Jeb switched on his cell phone and checked the time. "Twenty minutes? Try thirty, asshole."

Christian grinned. "Yeah yeah, I'm running a few minutes late. You could have ordered for me."

Jeb shrugged. "I can never remember how you like your eggs." He looked around for the waitress and waited while she poured a customer his coffee before beckoning her over. "I'll have the Big Breakfast, with extra crispy bacon, fried eggs, and extra hash browns. And I'll take a refill on my coffee when you get a chance. Thanks."

She made a note of Jeb's order before turning to Christian with a smile. Her teeth were cracked and yellow from neglect. In places, the beginning of rot was evident near her gums. Should he tell her to lay off the pipe before she ended up with meth mouth? Why did Anna keep this girl around? Even a blind man could see she was a hopeless tweaker.

"I'll have the same, but make my eggs—"

"Scrambled," she said. "Did you want a coffee with that?"

"Sure. That would be great."

Jeb waited until she left with their order. "She *really* has it bad for you. Why don't you fuck her already? I've heard those meth heads fuck like crazy."

"One: there is a reason why you are permanently single. Two: tweakers aren't my thing. And three—"

"You already have a boner for that scrawny chick I've heard about but have yet to see in real life."

"Whatever, she's real. If you don't believe me, ask Anna. We've met here a couple of times."

"All right, I believe you." Jeb raised his hands in mock surrender. "Anyway, I tried calling you last night, but it kept going to voicemail. Were you two hooking up or something?"

The waitress returned with the coffee pot and a mug for Christian. She filled both mugs before retreating. Once she was occupied taking someone else's order, Christian sank back against the backrest and sighed. "I wish I'd spent the night banging Ella. Instead, I was practically dragged down to the police station and questioned for hours. I found that real estate douche's wife running half-naked through the woods. She was pretty banged up, so I took her to the hospital, and the next thing I knew, the chief of police was going Godzilla on me. Fun times."

"What?" Jeb scoffed, half choking on a mouthful of coffee.

"True story. The cops think the killer terrorizing Taylor's End was hunting her down after she walked in on them slashing her husband to bits."

"Fuck. That's some heavy shit," Jeb murmured. "But at least she survived. I wish I'd been able to help Andrea. I was right there, and I didn't have a clue there was some sicko waiting around to kill her."

Sensing the sudden change in Jeb's mood, Christian attempted to alleviate his friend's misplaced sense of guilt. "You need to stop beating yourself up over Andrea. What happened to her had nothing to do with you."

The waitress brought over their orders and lingered at the table, fussing over the ketchup and hot sauce bottles until Christian motioned for her to leave. Jeb picked up a piece of bacon and took a bite. "I know. It's easier said than done, though. There's so much shit going wrong lately that it's hard not to get dragged down by it all."

Christian shoveled eggs onto his fork. "Tell me about it. The cops were all over me last night. Half the time, they were acting like I was the killer; then they gave up on that idea and instead grilled me about what I'd seen. But I saw Kate's attacker for only a second, and it was damn near dark. It might have been a female, but it could have easily been a skinny guy with long hair. I couldn't give them much of a description. It took three hours of questioning for the cops to figure it out."

"That's bullshit."

Christian shrugged it off. "Anyway, what's been happening out your way?"

Jeb jammed a hash brown into his mouth and chewed, taking his time with the golden fried potato before replying, "It's pretty fucked up, man. Tom doesn't eat unless I remind him to, and he hardly sleeps. When he does get some sleep, he often wakes up screaming about some girl. I don't have a clue who he's referring to. Maybe she's someone from his past or something. He hasn't stepped outside the house since they released him from the hospital. It probably doesn't help that Rosie is gone."

"Killing Rosie was low. It's bad enough that some bastard beat up your grandad. But to kill his dog too? That is some twisted shit."

"I know, right? Who does something like that?"

"I hate to bring it up—" Christian put his fork down and looked across the table at his friend. "But have you considered getting him more help than you can give him? I'm no expert, but it sounds like he might need to be placed in a care facility."

"I don't think I could do that to him. The only way he will leave the farm is if he is taken away in a pine box."

"Jeez, it sucks to be you, man. Maybe he needs some antidepressants or something? Can you at least get him to see his regular doctor?"

Jeb shook his head and glumly peered down into his mug. "You know how stubborn the old coot is. I've been trying to convince him to talk to someone, but he refuses even to consider the idea."

Christian grimaced. Tom had always been such a robust man, out in the weather, working the farm all year round. It was difficult to imagine him as the scared and frail old man that Jeb described. "I can come out to the farm and try to convince him to get a checkup if you think it will help. I'd hate for him to end up getting sick because he was too pigheaded to see a doctor."

"I don't know if it will make any difference, but it's worth a try," Jeb replied. He sipped his coffee thoughtfully. "I wonder if he will ever return to his old self. He raised me without ever once complaining, although I must have been a pain in the ass to take care of at times. He's always been so strong-willed and got on with life as best he could regardless of the setbacks."

"Don't forget, his potty-mouth taught us just about all the best cuss words we know," Christian added.

"Yeah fucking right," Jeb agreed with a smile, which set them both laughing.

Being a dedicated workaholic, Anna stood behind the counter, refilling the salt and pepper shakers while watching over the diner. It probably hadn't been necessary to come into work today. There was enough staff to keep the place running smoothly, but she wasn't the type 0f person to sit around the house idly. After she wiped and replenished all the salt shakers, she poured herself a cup of coffee and sweetened it with a generous amount of sugar. With coffee in hand, she collected a copy of the paper, walked around the other side of the counter, and took a seat at one of the stools. It felt good to be off her feet for a bit. It was the first break she had had since coming in at six to prep for opening. A short coffee break was in order.

No sooner had she spread the paper out in front of her than the bell over the door jingled, and a pair of police officers entered the diner, their uniforms almost as crumpled as their worn-out faces. Anna stifled a yawn and refolded the newspaper before taking a slug of her coffee. The paper could wait. Judging by their demeanor, the officers wouldn't last much longer without a substantial caffeine injection.

Anna waited for the pair to settle themselves on a couple of stools and walked over with a freshly brewed pot of coffee.

"Rough night, huh?" Anna casually inquired.

"The worst," Betts agreed. "You should probably leave the coffee pot here. We'll be needing it." Betts, a plump blonde in her late twenties, smiled bleakly. It was probably the worst-kept secret in Taylor's End that she and the man seated beside her were in a relationship and had been seeing each other for over two years. There was a running bet as to when the couple would finally go public and make it official. Anna suspected that the fear of repercussions in the workplace kept them from being out in the open.

"Can we grab a couple of cheeseburgers and some onion rings, too?" her partner added. He took a sip of the wickedly strong brew. Anna took the order out to the kitchen and brought over cutlery and napkins. She retreated a respectful distance and set to work polishing the water spots from a tub of cutlery that had gone through the dishwasher. She couldn't help overhearing their hushed exchange as they waited for their meals.

Betts listened as Larry, one of the first to respond at the Lyttle house the previous evening, told her what he saw. "It was a real shit show," Larry admitted, and looked at her intently, "Whoever did it, they are seriously messed up—like, Ted Bundy messed up." Betts took a risk and placed a hand on her lover's knee, squeezing it gently in a show of support. The contact surprised him, and he put his hand over hers. "Apparently, the guy's wife walked in on the killer while they were murdering her husband. She claims she smashed a lamp over their head in the proceeding struggle." He paused to swallow another mouthful of coffee. "So we're hoping the killer will have some distinguishable facial injuries." She pieced much of it together from the radio chatter she heard while on duty at the station, but hearing a firsthand account of the crime added another dimension to what she already knew. It also explained why the chief had gone so hard on the boy who had found the victim's wife. Everyone at the station knew he was banging the newly widowed Kate Lyttle, and it must be tearing him up inside knowing her attacker was still on the loose.

"It would be helpful to have something concrete to look for," Betts said. "So far, we've been searching for a killer we don't understand at all. Is it true that the killer might be a woman?"

Her partner shrugged. "Mrs. Lyttle and the kid who rescued her seem to think it could be female, but neither could say it with any certainty. For now, I think Chief Bremner wants to go after anyone with any visible injuries to the face. He doesn't want to rule anyone out because of their gender. If they have cuts or grazes, he wants them brought down to the station."

"It's a small town. Surely it won't be too difficult to find them now. Not if the killer truly was smashed over the head with a lamp base."

"The chief is hopeful that we are closing in on them. He was so freaked out last night when Mrs. Lyttle was missing. I felt bad for the guy. If that had been you . . ."

Betts gave his knee another squeeze. "I heard he kissed her at the hospital. Right in front of Joe."

The bell rang in the kitchen, and Anna left to collect their orders. She returned shortly and slid the burgers in front of the couple. "If you're still hungry after you get through that, there is a slice of pie for each of you. On the house." She refilled their coffee and popped a bottle of ketchup on the counter.

Betts smiled gratefully. "Thanks, Anna. We sure do appreciate your generosity."

"Nonsense, it's the least I can do. You folk were up all night, trying to catch a killer, while the rest of us were tucked in bed." Anna gave them one of her legendary smiles before walking out the back to clear her head and organize her thoughts.

She had never cared much for Richard Lyttle. He had come into the diner often enough over the years, but she never warmed to him. His wife was a different story. Kate Lyttle was a regular at Anna's Eat-In, always eager for coffee, pie, and a good chat—all three of which Anna cheerfully provided. Kate never had a bad word to say about anyone. No matter what was going on behind closed doors, she always found the good in life.

Despite how much their union baffled her, Anna was horrified by Richard's murder. She couldn't begin to imagine the trauma that Kate had experienced. Finding the killer with her husband, then hunted through the woods like an animal? It was too awful to contemplate. She made a mental note to find out where Kate was staying and drop by with a wedge of blueberry pie.

First, she needed to tell someone about the girl she had seen last night. It was unlikely to amount to anything, but she felt obligated to report it anyway, considering what had happened yesterday. If she hadn't overheard the two off-duty cops talking just now, she might not have given it any further thought. No, that wasn't true. She would have told someone eventually. It just might have been pushed down her to-do list for a day or two. Sleep had been a long time coming last night as she lay in bed, replaying events from earlier in the evening and worrying about what she had seen. Had she seen anything worth being concerned about at all? She repeated the thought pattern until exhaustion eventually won out, and she fell into a fitful, uneasy sleep.

As was her habit, Anna had spent all that Saturday at the diner, intending to enjoy a relaxing evening at home with a bottle of merlot, some comfort food. Preferably something that involved fried meat with a side of potatoes—and a couple of DVDs she had been meaning to watch. Everyone kept telling her she needed to move with the times and get herself a Netflix subscription, but it seemed like a waste of money. She rarely had time to sit down and spend a few hours doing nothing.

Anna's good friend Fred Parsons was sick with the flu, so she had whipped up a thermos of chicken and vegetable soup for him. She hated the idea of him wallowing in self-pity, too sick and miserable to fix himself anything to eat, so she decided to drop by and check how he was. He lived alone on Grants Parade, wandering around in a house much too big for his needs. His wife had passed away from breast cancer last spring, mere months after the diagnosis. Anna had done what she could to bolster his spirits over the last year, but a friend was no substitute for a wife who had been by his side for over twenty years. It stung to see Fred hurting so much. Anna had been good friends with the couple, and she understood how lost he must feel without her.

Moments after she turned onto Grants Parade, the headlights shone on a disheveled young woman running down the middle of the street toward her. When the lights caught her in their glare, she threw her arm up to shield her eyes, concealing her face from view. Although Anna didn't get a good look at her face, there was something familiar about her long untidy hair and tattered jeans. The girl ducked in between two parked cars and kept running down the sidewalk, the shadows of the night obscuring her identity. In that brief couple of seconds, Anna thought she had seen blood splattered across her face.

At the time, she had put it down to a combination of exhaustion and the effects of light and shadow playing games with her imagination. Still, imagination or not, Anna briefly contemplated pulling the car over and running after the girl to check if she was all right. Thoughts of a killer prowling the streets of Taylor's End had kept her foot planted firmly on the accelerator.

Anna buttoned her tattered jacket and grabbed her purse and car keys. She popped into the kitchen and told the cook, "I'm heading out for a bit. I'll be back before the lunch rush."

"We'll be fine."

"I have my cell phone if you need to call me."

Paul had been cooking weekends at Anna's Eat-In for over two years. He flipped some pancakes and said, "Go. I think we can manage without you for an hour or so." Anna nodded and left him to tend the hotplate. She felt a bit foolish when she pulled into a parking spot outside the police station and waddled into the building. The officer at the front desk tore his eyes away from the sports section of the paper.

"Hello, my name is Anna Petrov. I'm here to report something suspicious I saw last night. It might have something to do with the murder of Richard Lyttle."

That got the officer's attention. "You have information regarding the Richard Lyttle homicide?" he asked.

Anna nodded uncertainly. "I'm not sure. It might be relevant; it might not. I thought I should report it anyway."

"Come with me. Chief Bremner will want to speak to you personally."

He led her through the station to Bremner's office. He knocked briskly on the door and waited for Bremner to holler before opening the door.

"Anna Petrov to see you. She thinks she may have information regarding last night's homicide."

Bremner stood up and walked around his desk, ushering Anna into the office. The officer gave Bremner a brief nod before returning to the front desk.

"Anna, what brings you to the station? Usually, I'm on your turf."

"Elbows deep in fries and a chicken fillet burger, extra mayo, if I remember correctly."

"You know me too well. I'm sorry I haven't been in lately, but I've been flat out here."

Anna held her hands up. "Of course. I can't imagine what it must be like, trying to track down the lunatic responsible for those murders. I've never seen Taylor's End like this. There's tension and a sense of distrust that I haven't seen before. It makes me so sad. I can only hope the town returns to normal once the killer is locked up and people can begin to feel safe again."

Bremner motioned for Anna to take a seat. He sat on the edge of his desk and folded his arms across his chest. "I know the community is frustrated by the lack of any solid suspects, but I assure you, we are working hard to find the perpetrator."

"Maybe I can help you with that," Anna said.

"How so?"

"Last night, I was driving along Grants Parade when I saw a young woman running down the street."

"OK, how does that relate to the Richard Lyttle murder?" he asked.

"I can't be sure, but I think she had blood on her."

Bremner sat up straight. "Grants Parade? That's only three or four blocks from Rosemont Court." He stood up and walked across to a map of Taylor's End pinned to the wall and double-checked. Sure enough, it was close to the murder scene. He leveled his gaze at Anna. "Can you describe her to me? Did you recognize her from the diner?"

Anna held his gaze, wishing she had more to give him than vague descriptions that could apply to anyone in town. "She had long dark hair and was wearing ripped jeans and boots. I didn't get a decent look at her face. She put her arm up to shield her eyes from my headlights."

"So she isn't someone you know?"

She wrung her hands in her lap. "Wait! I thought she was familiar. I think it was the same girl who showed up at the diner for the first time four or five weeks ago. I've seen her with Christian Johnson a couple of times."

"I don't suppose you know where I could find her?" Bremner asked eagerly.

"You could try Webster's Boarding House. Christian may have mentioned she was staying there, but I can't be certain, though."

Bremner retrieved a notepad from his desk and scribbled down everything Anna had told him. "What is Christian's relationship with this girl?"

Anna recognized Bremner's suspicion for what it was. Unwilling to elaborate for fear of unwittingly dragging Christian into the police investigation, she simply replied, "As far as I know, he had lunch with her a couple of times. He was only trying to be friendly."

"Of course. You have been very helpful, Anna. I'm so glad you came and talked to me." Bremner smiled. It was possibly the first genuine lead he had. It also provided a potential link to his intruder the other week. Containing his enthusiasm, he led her to Chandler's desk and instructed the officer to take her statement.

Eighteen

Sophie Webster woke later than usual on Sunday morning. She was slow to shake off her sleepiness, her head thick and fuzzy. Her limbs felt heavy and unresponsive. It was apparent by the daylight flooding the room that most of the morning had passed. It was unlike her to lie around in bed when there were chores to be done.

As she rolled onto her side, her body screamed in protest. Gritting her teeth, she took a shallow breath and eased herself into a sitting position. Her body felt like a buffalo had trampled it. She gingerly swung her legs out of bed, feeling around the floor with her bare feet until she found her slippers. She slid her feet inside the ratty footwear that Nathan had given her for Christmas one year.

Her skull felt three sizes too small for her brain. Her entire head throbbed. The skin across her face was tight and swollen, her left eye puffy and sore. Her chest and shoulders felt even worse than her head if that was even possible. She unbuttoned her shirt and examined her breasts. Ugly purple bruising smudged much of her chest and ribs.

Too sore and sorry for herself to even muster up a groan, Sophie blinked away a tear and rebuttoned her shirt, the same one she had worn the previous night. When would she learn to keep her head down and her mouth shut? Nearly twenty years of marriage should have taught her a thing or two about what made her husband tick. It was a mistake to think he would back down if she dared to stand up for herself. All it did was antagonize him.

She stood up and waited for the bout of dizziness to subside. She pressed one hand against the wall for support and thought about the events of the previous night. Connor had been inconsolable since Todd's murder. Alternating between furious rages reminiscent of his father's and periods of maudlin introversion that she couldn't breach no matter how hard she tried.

Only wanting to do something to lift her son's mood, Sophie had given the boys twenty dollars each and suggested they catch an early movie. A few hours at the theatre, while dinner was cooking, might cheer them up, especially Connor. He had never spent so much time at home. Most of the time, he was practically impossible to track down. Since Todd's funeral, all he seemed to do was sit around playing video games.

Not thinking, she had given Nathan the money right there in the kitchen, taking the bills from her purse, which was sitting on the end of the bench. Jim must have overheard the exchange and taken offense to her giving the boys a treat because he jumped up, snatched the money out of Nathan's hand, and shoved him aside. Sophie watched her youngest son stumble back into the living room, catching himself on one of the chairs. He regained his balance and looked on helplessly.

They both knew how this would play out. The situation was all too familiar, and Sophie didn't want Jim turning his attention to her son. She discreetly waved him away while she held her husband's attention. Her hand was still firmly wrapped around the kitchen knife she had used to slice carrots.

"Put that fucking knife down, woman," he growled, curling his hands into tight fists at his sides.

She shook her head and held the knife out in front of her. "No. Not this time, Jim." The knife trembled in her hand, but she stood firm. He had no right to lash out because she wanted to give the boys some money to see a movie. "Get away from me. I mean it, Jim. Stay back."

He did not hesitate for a second, "You don't have the fucking guts to use that knife on me," he smirked. She had proved him wrong. In the brief struggle that ensued, Sophie maintained her grip on the knife and cut his forearm. He grabbed hold of her and bent her arm back until she released the handle. The knife clattered to the floor.

"You're going to pay for that, bitch," he snarled. And she did.

After that, events got blurry. Jim punched and kicked her until she was curled up on the kitchen floor. He screamed over and over how she had no right to spend his money on those sniveling brats. She hoped for a reprieve from the blows once she was on the floor, but she was out of luck. Her vulnerability just made it easier for him to lay the boot in, which he did with ruthless accuracy. She must have lost consciousness soon after because the next thing she knew, she was waking up in bed the following morning.

Sophie stood propped up against the wall for longer than necessary, too ashamed to go out and face her boys. Eventually, the prospect of some aspirin and a soothing cup of tea sent her hobbling out into the kitchen.

Any evidence of last night's altercation was carefully mopped up, and Nathan stood at the stove with a spatula. Watching the pan as he cooked up a batch of scrambled eggs, he glanced back at her and pointed to a steaming mug of tea brewing next to the fruit bowl. "We heard you get up," he said, "and thought you might like some breakfast."

She tried to smile, but it hurt too much. "That sounds lovely. I might sit down for a minute or two if that's OK." She took the tea and joined Connor at the dining table, wincing as she lowered herself onto the chair.

Connor studied her cuts and bruises from across the table. He sniffed and asked, "When does this end? I remember when I was a little kid how all my friends would say how pretty you were. Now, you've taken so many beatings that no one would think you are the same person. It's sickening."

"Connor, give it a rest, all right?" Nathan said. "Mom, your eggs are ready. Do you want one piece of toast or two?"

Connor pushed his chair back and walked away, only to return with a glass of water and some aspirin a minute later. "Here. They probably won't make a dent in the pain. I can arrange for someone to take you to the hospital so you can get something stronger if you want."

Nathan brought over a plate of eggs and placed them on the table in front of her. She thanked him and swallowed the aspirin with a mouthful of water. "I'll be fine."

"I think you should let Connor take you," Nathan said.

"The old man did a real number on you. We had to carry you to bed last night, and you didn't budge. You were out cold. He might have done some serious damage."

Sophie scooped eggs onto her fork and made a show of eating them. One of her teeth felt loose in her mouth. She ran her tongue around her mouth, assessing the damage. "Maybe we could go later today. I'll wait and see how I'm feeling a bit later."

"We should go now, while Jim is still passed out in his office." Connor urged.

"Later, I promise. I'd like to eat my breakfast and take a shower first."

Connor looked at her sourly and shrugged. She wouldn't go to the hospital. There would be too many questions.

She slowly ate the breakfast that Nathan had cooked her, knowing that his feelings would be hurt if she pushed the plate aside untouched. She studied the boys while she chewed and a deep sadness crept over her. She had failed them as a mother. To have raised them in such a hateful and violent household was unforgivable. They should have never witnessed their mom being bashed senseless, nor should they have been on the receiving end of their father's temper when she was unable to divert his attention.

Nathan looked across at her, unable to hide his concern. "Mom, why are you crying? Are you OK?"

Connor put his fork down and rolled his eyes at his brother. "Are you fucking stupid? No, she isn't OK. Jesus, man, you should try thinking before you open that idiot mouth of yours."

"Boys, that's enough," she said. Please don't fight today." Both Connor and Nathan looked down at their plates, ashamed. Sophie slid out from her chair and picked up her plate. "Thanks for a lovely breakfast, Nathan. I'm going to take a shower before I get into today's chores. Do you boys mind cleaning up the breakfast dishes?"

"Can you manage the chores?" Connor asked.

"I'll do what I can," Sophie said. "Some things might have to wait until tomorrow."

"If you need help with anything, just call out."

"Thanks, Connor. I'll see how I go." She placed her plate and empty mug in the sink and shuffled off to the bathroom to freshen up.

After she locked the door behind her, Sophie ran the shower and peeled off yesterday's clothes, using the towel rail for support while she undressed. The hot water soothed the aches and pains crippling her body, dissolving some of the tension tightening her shoulders. She stayed in the shower long after she had soaped her body clean.

Once she toweled herself dry, Sophie wiped the condensation from the mirror above the sink and examined her reflection. It was little wonder the boys avoided making eye contact with her during breakfast. With a swollen black eye and lips so puffy it looked like she had experienced a life-threatening allergic reaction, she was barely recognizable. Connor was right. There was no hint of the pretty young woman she had once been. All she saw in the mirror was a sad, worn-out shell of a person.

Staying with Jim had been the worst mistake of her life.

Turning away from her reflection, Sophie went and found some soft, fleecy sweatpants to wear and a roomy cardigan that was easy to pull on without stretching too much. Shoes took more effort. Bending over to put her sneakers on hurt her ribs. Persevering, she laced them up without calling the boys for assistance.

Sunday mornings were spent tidying the apartment and scrubbing the guest bathrooms up on the second floor. Today, they would have to make do with some fresh bars of soap and a pack of toilet rolls. After taking a six-pack of toilet paper and a box of lavender-scented soap from the supply closet, she climbed the stairs to the second floor, pausing at the top to take a moment to recover from the exertion. She stopped outside the men's bathroom and lightly tapped on the door.

"Just a minute," a voice called out from inside the bathroom.

Thirty seconds later, the door opened, and Thomas Wilson poked his head out shyly, his shaving kit tucked under his arm and his face freshly shaved.

"Good morning, Sophie. How are you?" he asked before he noticed her battered face. It wasn't the first time he had seen the shocking result of Jim Webster's handiwork, but it was easily the worst. This time, the horrid man had gone too far. Sophie needed recuperation in a hospital bed, not chores.

"Hello, Thomas," she replied, with more cheer than she felt. "I'm restocking the bathrooms. I don't want anyone running out of toilet paper. I might not get a chance to clean in there today, but I promise I'll give them a thorough clean tomorrow."

"Sure. I think we'll get by another day or so. It's not too grubby in there anyway." Thomas excused himself and retreated to his room, leaving Sophie to herself.

She stacked the new toilet rolls on the narrow shelf above the toilet and tried to ignore the grimy ring around the bath. As much as she wanted to clean it, there was no way she could physically get down on her hands and knees to scrub the bathtub. One of the boys would have to clean it for her, but it would probably end up looking much the same as it did now. Turning her back to the mess, Sophie exited the room and walked next door to the ladies' bathroom.

The door stood slightly ajar. Assuming the bathroom was empty, Sophie didn't bother to knock. After all, a young woman wouldn't use the amenities in a house full of strangers without locking the door. She stepped into the cramped bathroom with its outdated tiles and rust-stained bath surrounded by a flimsy dollar-shop shower curtain.

Ella stood over the vanity with her back to the door.

"Oh, Ella, I'm sorry. I didn't realize you were in here," Sophie said. While it appeared to be Ella from behind, the visage reflected in the age-spotted mirror above the sink was unlike anything Sophie had ever encountered before.

It plucked at a shard of glass embedded in its cheek with thick, pointed claws, dropping the sliver of glass into the bloody sink, where it landed with a musical tinkle. It raised its ugly head when it noticed Sophie standing in the background and slowly turned to face her.

The rolls of toilet paper tumbled to the floor, and the bars of soap landed with a thud at her feet. She took a trembling step away from the demon and bumped into the edge of the door. It swung shut behind her, closing with a loud click. She made the sign of the cross and shuddered, groping blindly for the doorknob. She pulled the door open behind her as the creature lunged at her with a snarl. Thick blackish blood oozed from the wound in its cheek, and its dead black eyes narrowed into furious slits. Its arm shot out and slammed the door shut.

The creature pressed its hands against the door on either side of Sophie's head, trapping her. Leaning in close, it sniffed around her face with its long, aquiline nose. "You smell like a used-up whore. A few beatings too many past her prime." It smirked coldly.

She recoiled from its rotten breath. The stink of dead things clogged her nose, and she had to fight back the urge to retch. "Please let me go," she begged. "I should have knocked. If you let me leave, I won't tell anyone what I saw."

The demon stared at her as it dragged its claws along the door, leaving deep gouges in the wood. Sophie watched in mounting horror as its claws hovered close to her cheek, flexing so close that the tips brushed her face, etching bloody grooves into her skin.

"You're not going to be around to tell anyone what you saw," the creature said, hooking a thick yellow claw in front of her face in a scooping motion.

Her chest hitched, and she shrank against the door, muttering a prayer as tears streamed down her cheeks.

"God can't save you," it growled. "Nobody can." It forced its fingers into her eye socket and scooped out her eyeball, crushing it to jelly in its fist. Sophie screamed and clutched at her face, blood and fluid spilling from the ugly hole where her eye had been a moment before. The creature brushed her hand aside and, clutching her skull, closed its mouth over her empty eye socket, greedily sucking the fluid from the wound. Its mouth made awful slurping sounds as its tongue probed the raw cavity, and Sophie's body twitched and writhed as it pinned her against the door.

Years of silent suffering were finally shattered by a long, drawn-out shriek that could be heard throughout the house. She flailed against the murderous creature, beating at it ineffectually as it sucked the wound in her head. The demon pulled away from her bleeding face and whispered close to her ear. "You taste as weak and pathetic as you sound. I'm going to put an end to your wretched existence now, and then I'm going downstairs to kill your children. And it's all because you didn't think to knock before busting in with your cheap soap and toilet paper."

"Please don't kill my boys," she begged, looking up at the monstrous creature with her one remaining eye.

Its lips split into a nasty grin. "I won't just kill them. That would be such a dreadful waste. I'll eat them too. A nibble here and there. Then I'll rip their white-trash hearts out while they watch." It wrapped its fingers around her throat, digging its claws deep into her flesh. She screamed for mercy, and with a violent twist, it snapped her neck. Sophie went limp, and her body slumped against the demon before it released its grip on her. She collapsed onto the tiles behind the door.

Nineteen

Connor froze when he heard his mother cry out. The moment he had dreaded for weeks had finally arrived. He placed his glass of juice down on the dining table and gazed up at the ceiling uneasily.

Jim was in the kitchen slapping together a pastrami sandwich when he heard it. "What the fuck is that woman doing now? I bet she's spotted an itty-bitty spider in the bathtub or something." He took a bite of his sandwich before throwing the remaining slices of meat back in the refrigerator. "I'll have to go up there and get rid of the damn thing. Otherwise, she's gonna scream all fucking day," he grumbled.

Outside, Rebel started barking furiously. Connor watched as his father opened the door to the apartment and stepped out into the communal area of the boarding house, munching on the sandwich as he went. He should say something, give the old man a fighting chance, but he couldn't formulate any words. Instead, he stood mutely as his father stopped beside the banister and called up the stairs. "Hey, Sophie, is everything all right up there?"

When there was no response, Jim started up the staircase. The creaky stairs groaned beneath his weight.

Connor couldn't stand by and allow the demon to butcher anyone else. He shook off the inertia holding him in place, but before he charged upstairs, he had to ensure that Nathan was safe. He ran down the short hallway to his brother's door and flung it open, bursting into the room like a madman. He yanked the headphones from over his brother's ears and tossed them on the floor.

"Hey, man, what the fuck?" Nathan said.

Already gripped by panic, Connor practically screamed down into his brother's face. "Shut up and listen. You need to get out of the house right now. Grab your coat and run down to Mrs. Chapman's place. When you get there, ask if you can wait inside until the police arrive."

Nathan wriggled and twisted his way out of the beanbag in front of the stereo system and stood up. "Are you fucking kidding me? Are you on a bad trip again? Is that what this is all about?"

Acutely aware of the time ticking away, Connor grabbed Nathan by the shoulders and shoved him toward the door.

"Ouch. Get your hands off me. I swear you've lost it," his brother complained.

"Listen, you have to get your ass out of here. Don't argue. Don't ask questions. There isn't time."

"Why do I have to go outside? It's freezing out there."

"Shut up and do as I say," Connor snapped. He thrust his cell phone into Nathan's hand. "Call 911 once you're safely away from the house."

Nathan removed his coat from the hook on the back of his bedroom door and jammed his arms into the sleeves.

Connor was about to lead his brother out of the house through the front door but decided against it. It was too risky taking his brother through the rest of the house, not when the demon could already be downstairs, skulking around in the shadows, waiting for them to try to escape. He hurried over to the window and grappled with the latch, which was stiff and uncooperative. "Fuckin' open, you cocksucker!" he cursed angrily. Nathan flinched at his brother's outburst and stepped in and rattled the latch before sliding the window open. "Climb out the window and go straight out to the street," Connor said. "Whatever you do, don't stop until you're safe inside Mrs. Chapman's place."

Nathan swung a leg out of the open window, gritting his teeth against the cold. "What are you going to do now?" he asked as he maneuvered his body out of the window, clutching the frame so he could lower his legs down to the ground below.

"Don't worry about me. Just go. And don't forget to call the cops." He watched Nathan drop out onto the ground below the window and motioned for him to get the hell out of there. With a worried shake of his head, Nathan disappeared down the icy walk alongside the house.

Now that his brother was safely out of the boarding house, Connor faced the daunting prospect of going upstairs and facing the demonic creature that had almost certainly killed Todd. Fear froze him in place until he reminded himself that his mom could still be alive up there. He couldn't stand around holding his dick while his mom was alone and utterly defenseless with that thing.

If he was going upstairs to confront the demon, he couldn't do so empty-handed. Without a weapon, he would be impotent against such a murderous creature. Even armed, he didn't like his chances against it. But the probability of being torn to shreds wasn't enough to deter him. Short on time and ideas, he ran into the kitchen to find a suitable weapon. The humble kitchen was a treasure trove of potential implements. It was a matter of finding something that he could wield without posing too much risk to himself. After his mom's disastrous attempt at fending off his shit-for-brains father with a knife the previous night, he wasn't keen on trying his luck with a blade. It was too easy to have things go wrong.

Connor wrenched open the top drawer in the kitchen and almost laughed at the collection of knives, forks, and spoons neatly separated by the cutlery divider. Hell yeah, he'd march upstairs armed with a fucking teaspoon! He slammed the cutlery drawer closed and pulled out the drawer beneath it. Without meaning to, he accidentally yanked the entire drawer out, spilling cooking utensils all over the floor. Tossing the empty drawer aside, he knelt on the linoleum and rifled through the various implements scattered on the floor. His hand wrapped around the handle of the meat tenderizer. Its weight reassured him. Yep, that would do nicely. Feeling slightly more confident, he collected a second weapon from amongst the collection of utensils at his feet. Smiling grimly, he picked up a carving fork and kicked aside a spatula on his way out of the kitchen.

As Jim made his way upstairs, he regretted those last couple of beers he had drunk the previous night. As he grew older, it was getting harder to recover from a night of boozing. The lousy hangover the next day was hardly worth the extra beer or two, even though they always seemed like a great idea when he was too plastered to know better. He took another bite of the pastrami sandwich, hoping that some food would help settle his stomach.

He could never understand why the silly bitch always got so worked up over a harmless arachnid. Luckily for Sophie, he was too hungover to make an issue out of it. At the top of the stairs, he stuffed the last of the sandwich in his mouth before wiping his fingers on the front of his pants, which were spotted with grease from last night's fried chicken. His stomach roiled, the bread dough and processed meat aggravating his delicate constitution. He paused and fought against the urge to vomit. After a few moments, his stomach settled enough to allow him to continue across the landing to the bathrooms.

Something was seriously amiss. Blood oozed from under the door and dribbled over the tiled lip onto the scuffed floorboards in the hallway.

Jim paused outside the bathroom, staring down at the small, irregularly shaped puddle of blood forming at his feet. What the fuck was going on? He crouched down with considerable effort to examine the pooling blood. Had Sophie slipped and cracked her head on the tiles? Or had one of the residents flipped their lid and taken a razor to their wrists? He knew that Thomas Wilson was teetering precariously close to the edge and had been ever since he lost his job three months ago. Maybe the miserable fucker had finally had enough and decided to snuff himself. It was a reasonable enough theory, but why would Thomas kill himself in the female bathroom?

"Sophie, are you in there?" he asked timidly, appalled by the trepidation he felt. He was a man, for fuck's sake. It was time to quit acting like a quivering pussy and find out what the hell was going on. Grasping the doorknob unsteadily, Jim turned the handle and pushed. The doorknob twisted in his hand, but the door remained firmly closed. "Sophie, what's going on in there? Something is blocking the frigging door."

He dropped his shoulder and threw his weight against the door, and it opened a crack. A second, more forceful shove opened it wide enough to allow him to squeeze through. He sucked in his gut and forced his body through the narrow gap between the door and frame. Dropping to his knees, Jim reached down to touch his wife, who lay behind the door. Her face was turned toward the tiles at an impossible angle. Her mouth hung slack, and there was a glistening red hole where her left eye should have been.

Jim gagged, tasting bitter vomit at the back of his throat. He swallowed it down, unable to tear his eyes away from her ruined face. The knowledge that he was responsible for many of her injuries filled him with a deep sense of shame. Grief and disbelief erupted from him in a mournful wail, and he scooped her into his arms. "Sophie? Wake up. Come on, you gotta wake up." He shook her shoulders, and her head lolled unnaturally. "No. The fuckin' cops will pin this on me for sure," he sobbed.

It was the first time Jim Webster had cried since he was a small child. Although he knew his tears were useless, he couldn't stop. Crying wouldn't bring his wife back, nor could it absolve him of the shitty way he had treated her throughout their marriage.

Overcome with emotion, the possibility that he might be in danger never entered Jim's mind. It wasn't until he heard the rustling of the cheap plastic shower curtain that he tore his attention away from his wife's body and peered behind him.

He moved fast for such a large man at least a decade past his prime. A lack of fitness and too much alcohol hadn't dulled his reflexes. Jim thrust his wife's body aside and got to his feet. He flung open the door and bolted out of the room. His heel landed in the puddle of blood outside the bathroom, and his leg started to slide out from under him.

Back in the bathroom, the demon emitted a chilling screech that bounced off the tiled walls of the cramped room. The acoustics were astounding. Jim clutched at his ears to dull the piercing sound as he regained his balance. The creature tore the shower curtain from the plastic rings and sprang out of the bathtub, bounding over Sophie's body and out the door. Flecks of foamy red spittle flew from its gaping mouth as it charged toward Jim. It crashed into him on the landing, wrapping its powerful arms around his middle and tackling him to the floor. The force of the fall shook the entire second floor, causing a faded print hanging at the top of the stairs to jump off from its hook. The glass in the frame shattered on impact when it dropped to the floor. Jim lay beneath the demon, gasping for air. Each breath felt like he was trying to inhale with a pillow jammed over his face. Even more alarming was the ugly motherfucker pinning him to the floor. The demon's gore-smeared face was perched less than ten inches from his own. A long tendril of bloody drool dangled from its mouth. He watched as the string of saliva detached from its curled lip and plopped onto his cheek. He yelled in revulsion and shoved with both hands against the creature's chest.

The creature wasn't easily dislodged. Straddling his substantial belly, it squeezed his sides with its powerful thighs, reached forward, and raked its claws across his stubbled cheek. Blood welled in the deep furrows, and he howled in pain.

"You fucking whore! I'm gonna kill you!"

It shook its head and sneered down at him as it dug its fingers into the fleshy meat covering his ribs. He grabbed hold of its forearm and tried to loosen its grip, but the demon clung to him with the tenacity of a bloodthirsty leech.

"Get the fuck off me!" he cried. He punched at it with clenched fists. It barely seemed to notice the blows, and Jim briefly wondered if it even felt pain. It struck the side of his head with the back of its hand. Jim groaned, blinking away the darkness that clouded his vision. Through the woozy haze, he realized that despite outweighing the hellish creature by at least a hundred pounds, it was monumentally stronger than him. Attempting to overpower it was futile. Behind them, Reggie Billets, still rotten drunk from the night before, opened his bedroom door and yelled, "Shut the hell up, I'm trying to sleep," before slamming it shut.

Thinking about Sophie lying dead in the bathroom, Jim unleashed a primal roar and screamed, "How do you like this, motherfucker?" He reached up and jammed his thumb into the demon's eye, driving it all the way up to his second joint. Hot, gummy eye juice dribbled down his hairy wrist as he twisted his thumb around in the gooey hole. The creature immediately released its grip on him and flung itself back. Its ruined eye made a wet sucking noise as it pulled free. It probed its face, feeling the mangled remains of the eyeball that now dangled partway down its cheek. A growl rumbled deep in its throat. It drew back its lips to expose the full horror of its predatory mouth.

Jim shrank away from the furious creature, rolling onto his side and up onto his knees. He crawled across the landing toward the stairs and used the banister to pull himself to his feet. Clinging to the handrail, Jim edged his way closer to the stairs, one unsteady step at a time. Still feeling woozy from the blow to his head, Jim cursed his wobbly legs. Each step felt like he was wading through quicksand. The top of the staircase looked impossibly far away. He inched himself closer with frustrating slowness.

A door opened along the narrow passage behind them, and Thomas Wilson timidly poked his head through the gap. He saw the rotten bastard that owned the place out on the landing with someone. It vaguely resembled the girl staying up in the attic room—except it couldn't be her. Jim Webster didn't seem to care if anyone in the boarding house knew he beat his family, but Thomas had yet to see the man physically attack any of the residents. If he raised his fists to a paying guest, there was a strong possibility some of the residents would leave. Jim was too tight-fisted to allow that to happen. And yet, from behind, the person he was wrestling with shared an uncanny resemblance to the girl upstairs. Thomas Wilson watched as Jim struggled to get out from under the girl. Someone as big and powerfully built as Jim Webster should have had no trouble flicking her aside.

While he watched the pair struggle, Ella twisted her neck around to scowl at him. Thomas recoiled. He slammed his bedroom door shut and drew the bolt across. He dropped to his belly and wriggled under the bed, burrowing deep beneath the sagging mattress, where he curled up with the dust bunnies and cum-stained soft porn magazines scattered across the floor. Not so long ago, Thomas had been on the verge of suicide. Now, faced with the reality of death, he recognized a desire to live burning deep within him.

He would stay put until the shitstorm raging out on the landing was over. Jim Webster was a big man, and he was proficient with his fists. He could take care of himself. And if not, so what? Thomas had seen the appalling bruises the bastard had given his wife and kids. Whatever was happening out on the landing, the abusive prick had it coming.

When Jim finally reached the top of the stairs, he felt a momentary sense of relief, escaping the clutches of the monstrosity. He carefully descended the first two stairs, plotting what he would do to the evil fucker when he reached his office and retrieved the handgun. He was going to empty the entire clip into the bitch's face.

His furious optimism was short-lived. A hand dropped onto his shoulder and hauled him back up onto the landing. He teetered over the edge of the stairs. He was so close to the creature now that he could see the pores on its suppurating face. He balled his hand into a fist and drove it as hard as he could into the creature's abdomen.

Such a powerful jab would have dropped anybody else, but the demon barely flinched. Its mouth twisted into an ugly sneer as it tightened its grip on his shoulder, and quick as a viper, it drew back its free arm and plunged its hand into the soft white mound of his belly. Its thickened, yellow talons carved through the generous layer of blubber padding his hairy middle before slicing into the muscle beneath.

Jim's eyes bulged, and his mouth dropped open in an agonized scream. Blood, thick and dark as syrup, bubbled over his bottom lip. The creature's fist closed around the slippery coils of intestines and ripped them out of his body. Jim looked down in disbelief at the steaming loops of guts dangling from the ragged hole in his belly and mumbled incoherently. He attempted to scoop up his intestines and stuff them back inside his body, but they were far too slippery and unwieldy.

The demon chuckled darkly as Jim endeavored to return his entrails to their rightful place. It reached down and snatched a loop of intestines out of his hand. "I win, you filthy fucking maggot." It shoved him over the edge of the landing with its free hand, a nasty grin twisting up the corners of its mouth. His body sailed through the air before slamming against the stairs. He let out a single yell, and the back of his head hit the hardwood tread, shattering his skull with a sickening crack. The downward momentum sent him tumbling down the remaining steps in a jumble of flaccid limbs, his body cartwheeling over and over until he came to rest at the base of the staircase.

Twenty

Connor paused at the base of the stairs where his father lay. His exposed viscera hung from his belly. A halo of blood spread around his head. Only moments before, he had heard his father cry out the same way he or his brother did when they were on the receiving end of one of the old man's thrashings. As he looked down at his father's pitiful body, Connor felt no pleasure in the suffering his father had endured.

Hoping for the element of surprise, he stepped around Jim's body and tiptoed up the stairs. Halfway up, a floorboard creaked under his weight. Connor froze. When nothing happened, he continued his ascent, his palms slick with sweat as he gripped the handles of his makeshift weapons. Looking down, Connor felt inadequately armed against what was waiting for him upstairs. If the demon creature had disposed of his father so easily, what hope did he have of defeating it? His mother must surely be dead too. She had probably been dead the entire time he was trying to send his brother to safety. His search for the demon had ceased to be a rescue mission and was now a suicidal act of revenge. While he wasn't willing to die to avenge his father, Connor had a score to settle on behalf of Todd and his mom.

As he reached the top of the staircase, he navigated around the blood splattered across the floor and edged his way toward the bathrooms. He nudged the door to the men's bathroom with the toe of his sneaker, both hands poised for action. The door swung open, and he sagged with relief when it revealed an empty room.

He hesitated outside the other bathroom, knowing that his mother would be dead inside. For most of his life, Connor had lived in fear of one day finding his mom dead after a beating that Jim had taken too far. Often, as he lay in bed, listening to his father lashing out at his mom for whatever trifling thing had set him off, he worried that she might not be there to make him breakfast when he woke up in the morning. Now, it appeared as though that day had finally arrived. He would have to face the sobering reality that the only person who had ever loved him unconditionally was gone. She was not taken from him by the tyrannical bastard who ruled their lives but by a demonic being that Connor had known about for weeks. He had allowed it to live under their roof without warning his family of the danger. Guilt choked him. How many times had he hated his mom for being so weak and pathetic? How many times had he cursed her for not being brave enough to stand up to the aggressive fuck and leave with her children? As he stood on the other side of the partially open door, looking down at the red smears marring the tiles, Connor wondered how he could have been so simplistic. It was unfair to think that it was easy to pack up her boys and flee her husband. No way would his father allow her to do such a thing. He would just as soon point a shotgun to their heads and pull the trigger.

He was wasting precious time. Connor cautiously poked his head into the bathroom, half expecting the demon to launch itself at his face. Nothing reached out to attack him. The room was empty except for his mom, lying dead a few feet away from the door. He stifled a sob, refusing to look too closely, afraid that if he did so, he would lose his shit completely.

Turning his back on the wretched conclusion to his mom's miserable life, Connor gave the hallway a cursory inspection before continuing over to the base of the attic stairs. The steep, narrow staircase was unnerving under normal circumstances, but now, with a demonic killer on the loose, they filled him with dread. He flipped the switch on the wall, hoping that the bare light bulb dangling from a cord midway up would dispel the shadows.

But the staircase remained shrouded in darkness. Like it or not, he would have to make his way up to the attic room with limited visibility. He adjusted his grip on the meat tenderizer and took a tentative step toward the demon's room. As he climbed the stairs, he wondered if Nathan had followed his instructions and sought refuge at Mrs. Chapman's. He had no idea who would take care of his little brother if the demon nailed his ass, but it was too late to worry about that now.

A door opened somewhere behind him. Maybe it was nothing more than a wall shifting or even the plumbing reacting to the fluctuating temperature, but Connor didn't think so. Although it was likely that some of the other residents were at home, who would dare venture out of their room after hell was unleashed a few short yards away? He had checked both bathrooms, so where the hell had the damn thing been hiding? Surely it hadn't found its way into one of the resident's rooms. None of the bedroom doors were open when he checked the hallway. Despite the tenants having absolutely nothing worth pinching, they usually kept their doors locked, for they all lived with the paranoia reserved for strangers forced to live under the one roof.

So, where the fuck was it hiding?

The only other place with a door on the second floor was the cupboard under the attic stairs that housed the water heater. It was a tight squeeze, but it was possible. Connor silently berated himself for neglecting to check under the stairs. That one moment of stupidity would probably cost him his life. Trapped partway up the narrow staircase, he could continue up and hope the attic room was unlocked, or turn around, face whatever was coming for him, and fight like a motherfucker.

He chose to fight like a motherfucker.

He jammed the carving fork in the waistband of his jeans and spun around with the metal meat mallet raised defensively in front of his torso. The demon raked at his face with a powerful swipe of its razor-tipped claws.

He nimbly ducked to the side, feeling the whoosh of the creature's clawed fingertips passing only millimeters from his face. Connor retreated beyond its range, but his heel caught the step behind him, forcing him to steady himself against the tongue-and-groove paneling. Pouncing while he was vulnerable, the demon closed the distance between them and swung at him a second time. Trapped between the walls of the staircase, Connor had no room to maneuver out of its path. It struck him across the same ear it had savaged during their previous altercation, splitting open the scabbed-over wound. Connor staggered against the wall, cupping a hand to his bleeding and mangled ear. It felt like someone had jammed a burning flare into it. He knew he had to do something and fast. Otherwise, he was going to be dog food just like his old man.

Before he could overthink it, Connor raised the mallet over his head and drove it down as hard as he could. The heavy utensil smashed against the top of the demon's head, splitting its scalp and shattering the bone beneath. It staggered onto the landing, beyond the of range of the mallet, and clutched at the gash bleeding profusely beneath the tangled hair hanging across its face.

Faced with no option but to follow the demon down onto the landing, Connor held the meat tenderizer aloft and, feeling like a total wanker, barged past the bleeding creature, yelling and swearing the entire time. He hoped he would seem a whole lot scarier if he were making a shitload of noise while swinging the metal tenderizer back and forth.

It almost worked.

The demon had other plans. Despite the blood cascading down its face, the creature snatched the hood of Connor's sweatshirt as he bolted past. It spun him around and threw him at the wall with enough force to put a hole in the plaster. He lost his grip on the meat tenderizer, and it clattered to the floor. The creature kicked it out of reach with a snarl and belted him in the face. Connor's head snapped back. Something small and hard and sharp lodged in his throat. He coughed and spat out a fragment of tooth along with a mouthful of blood. He had been on the receiving end of enough floggings to learn that if you wanted to walk away in one piece, you had to get out of the way. When the demon swung at him again, he was already darting to the left. Its claws raked across his chest, shredding his hoodie and the T-shirt underneath. It hurt like fuck.

Once he was beyond the creature's reach, he felt his chest, assessing the damage. There was plenty of blood seeping through the layers of clothing, but it appeared to be superficial. His nipples were still attached, and he might need a few stitches if he survived the encounter. The nipples were a big deal. A quarter-inch higher, and he could have kissed those babies goodbye. As it was, thanks to the six-inch gashes marring his pecs, he wasn't going to win any Mr. Universe contests.

Connor spotted the demon lunging too late. It tackled him around the waist and drove him across the landing. His body smashed into the balustrade overlooking the ground floor below.

The railing groaned and creaked under the burden thrust upon it. Connor grabbed hold of the banister to stop himself from flipping over the edge. His back arched over the waist-high wooden rail, threatening to send them both crashing to the ground floor. Unable to support their weight any longer, the wooden posts cracked and splintered, tearing free of their anchor points. The banister pitched forward, and Connor cried out in alarm. Pinned beneath the demon, he could only close his eyes and wait for the inevitable.

But the fall never came. In an uncharacteristic act of courage, Thomas Wilson came screaming down the hallway, wielding an aluminum baseball bat like it was a five-foot-long flaming sword.

"Let the kid go!" he yelled as he ran at the pair hanging over the edge of the landing. He swung the bat in a wide arc and smashed it down on the back of the demon's skull. The blow left a sizable dent in the aluminum bat.

The creature slumped forward, crushing Connor beneath its weight. Thomas dropped the bat and reached beneath the unconscious creature to grab hold of Connor's arm. He huffed and grunted as he dragged the boy free, and once Connor was a safe distance from the edge of the landing, they turned to watch the banister finally give way, tipping the demon over the side. Both Connor and Thomas held their breath as the creature dropped from sight.

Regaining consciousness as it plunged to the ground floor, the demon reached up and clutched the landing. The railing fell away beneath it. The creature clung to the floor one-handed and, with a savage grunt, swung its legs back up onto the landing. It slowly climbed to its feet, the repeated blows to its head finally beginning to impair its relentless savagery. The demon spotted the pair cowering against the wall opposite and unfurled its body to its full height, ignoring the blood cascading down its disfigured face.

Jumping to his feet, Connor wrenched Thomas up off the floor and shoved him toward the hallway. "Quick, you need to get the fuck out of here." Thomas didn't argue the point. He had abandoned the baseball bat when he pulled Connor back onto the landing, and he wasn't foolish enough to try and stand his ground empty-handed. Thomas swallowed. He had never attempted to intervene when Jim beat the living crap out of his family. Why had he decided to step in and help the boy out now? That one rash decision to play the hero now looked like it was about to take a hefty bite out of his pudgy old ass.

Thomas looked helplessly from Connor to the partially open door to his bedroom down the hallway, which was blocked off by the demon. "Forget trying to reach your room," Connor whispered. "You'll never make it."

The demon watched the older man grimly assess his chances and sniggered as the crushing realization that he was doomed crumpled Thomas's features.

"Bravery doesn't suit you, old man," it said. "You should have stayed locked away in your bedroom like the spineless swine that you are. Now I'm compelled to kill you. I can't promise it will be quick, but I can promise you it will be painful."

The color drained from Thomas Wilson's face, and he shrank against the wall. The demon took a lazy step toward them.

Connor seized Thomas by the arm and said, "Make a run for one of the bathrooms."

Thomas shook his head. "It's too far. I'll never make it."

"You've gotta try. I'll do what I can to distract it," Connor said. He shoved him away from the wall. Thomas took a few tentative steps across the landing, his eyes locked on the open doorway to the bathroom. His confidence grew with each step, and he truly believed he would make it.

Then his foot caught on the meat tenderizer, and he fell forward.

He hit the floor hard, and he bit through the tip of his tongue. He barely had time to register the pain before the demon sprang forward and latched onto his back, sending them both sliding across the floor and away from the bathroom. Thomas bucked beneath the weight of the creature, but the demon held tight and sank its teeth into the meat between his shoulder blades. It tore away a sizable chunk of flesh. Chewing messily, it turned its head in Connor's direction, daring the boy to intervene.

Desperate to save the man who had risked his own life to help him, Connor ran over to the writhing pair, snatching up the metal tenderizer as he went. With more courage than he felt, Connor raised the mallet and swung it at the demon. It missed its target, swinging wide of the creature's head. Jaws dripping, the demon abandoned the struggling man beneath it and went after Connor instead.

Thomas crawled across the floorboards to the nearest bathroom and pushed his way inside, slamming the door shut behind him. He reached up and slid the bolt across before slumping down, his eyes falling on Sophie's ravaged body. Even with the deep throbbing pain spreading across his back, Thomas felt profoundly sorry for Sophie. The poor woman didn't deserve this. Unable to help her in life, he did what little he could for her in death. He removed the fresh hand towel from the hook beside the sink and gently draped it over her face before crawling across the tiles to the bathtub. He climbed into the empty tub, pulled the shower curtain across, and hugged his knees to his chest.

Out on the landing, Connor hit the stairs running. The creature was close behind. He could hear its heavy footsteps closing the distance between them. He bounded down the stairs two at a time, using the banister to keep from falling. A third of the way down, the demon finally caught up with him. Its claws nicked the back of his neck. He ducked his head, tipping his torso too far over his feet and throwing himself off-balance. Losing his grip on the banister, Connor pitched forward, twisting his body as he fell to avoid smacking face first onto the stairs below. His right shoulder took the brunt of the initial impact, and his body tumbled down the stairs. He blinked away the double vision and slowly rose to his elbows. Every part of his body protested at having to move, but he scrambled to his feet. None of his bones were broken. He gazed up at the stairs, expecting to see the demon coming down after him, but it was no longer there. Where the fuck had it gone?

The carving fork, his paltry backup weapon, lay on the floor a few feet from where he landed. It was a wonder he hadn't accidentally stabbed himself with it when he fell down the stairs. He bent down to pick it up, black spots forming in front of his eyes as he did so. He righted himself and rested against the wall until the bout of dizziness subsided.

Once he felt confident that he could walk in a straight line without falling on his face, he scanned the landing up on the second floor for any sign of the creature. If it had retreated up the stairs after failing to capture him, then it was trying to stay out of sight. Could it have fled the house altogether? While the demon could have easily slipped by him during his clumsy descent, it seemed like a stretch to think it would risk heading out into the street in plain sight with its head split open and bleeding all over the place. Besides, Connor doubted it would leave without first making sure it had well and truly smoked his ass.

Should he haul ass out the front door and look for Nathan? Or should he hunt that flesh-eating motherfucker and put it down once and for all? He was deeply conflicted. Part of him wanted retribution for what it did to Todd and his mom. While the idea of revenge was extremely enticing, he didn't hold much hope of coming out of a second encounter, still breathing.

The only viable choice was to try and get out of the house alive.

He pushed off from the wall. The faint warbling of approaching sirens reached his ears. Hurry the fuck up and get here already, he thought. Maybe it was too much to hope the cops would intervene in time. He crept across the faded, threadbare rug, his eyes seeking out every darkened nook.

As he edged his way down the hall, he saw a shadow hunched beside the hallstand. With raw and frazzled nerves, Connor charged at it, lashing out with feet and fists. The antique Hoover toppled over, and he realized his error. Chuckling at his crazy outburst, he wiped the sweat from his face with his sleeve. Thankfully, nobody witnessed him beating the shit out of a vacuum.

Keeping his eyes on the communal living space, Connor clung to the wall to his right, easing his way closer to the front door. Light filtered through the narrow rectangular panes of glass on either side of the door. In less than a minute, he would twist the deadbolt and jerk the door open. A few seconds after that, he would be out on the street, where the demon wouldn't dare follow. He would be safe.

When he finally reached the front entry, he turned the deadbolt and opened the front door. Harsh midday sunlight spilled across the grubby hall runner. He blinked rapidly as his eyes adjusted to the light. The sirens were close now, only a few blocks away by the sound of it.

With one foot already across the threshold, it would have been easy to ignore the tinkle of breaking glass coming from somewhere in the apartment behind him and continue outside to wait for the police. Between the whooping sirens and Rebel's manic barking, he wasn't sure he heard anything at all. Likely it was a ploy to lure him back into the house so the demon could ambush him and tear out his heart. Too bad it wasn't going to work this time.

But then a dreadful thought crossed his mind, and his hand dropped from the door. He stepped back over the threshold and looked down the hallway at his family's apartment, the door still ajar.

If Nathan had defied him and returned to the house, he had to go back inside. Sure, the cops were just around the corner, but he wasn't about to stand around and do nothing.

Retracing his steps, Connor hurried back along the hallway. He paused briefly beside the staircase, his eyes drawn to the body of the man who had terrorized him for much of his life. The prospect of becoming a lifeless meat sack like Jim, before he had a chance to see the world or fall madly in love with a girl way out of his league, filled him with profound sorrow. It was almost enough to turn him around and send him back the way he came.

Then he heard the crunch of broken glass underfoot, which strengthened his waning resolve. "Nathan?" he called softly, not wanting to draw the demon's attention. "Nathan? Is that you? I told you to get the fuck outta here." Holding the wooden handle of the carving fork in a death grip, Connor slipped inside his apartment. His attention was immediately drawn to the twinkling chips and slivers of crystal that had once been his mom's favorite vase. Her mother had passed it down to her just before she died from the big *C* when he was still in diapers.

How heartbroken she would be when she discovered it smashed to pieces—and then his brain caught up to reality. She wouldn't be getting upset about anything anymore because she was dead in the bathroom upstairs.

The door to the apartment slammed shut behind him. Connor whirled around and saw the demon blocking his exit. He took an uncertain step back, his butt brushing against the back of the sofa. Before he could retreat beyond its range, the creature lashed out. Its talons raked crimson furrows across his cheek. The blow sent him toppling over the back of the sofa, and he landed among the frilly cushions. He cupped the side of his face with his free hand, blood streaming between his fingers. Tears filled his eyes, blurring his vision before spilling down his cheeks and mixing with the blood and snot coating his lower face. He wiped the tears from his eyes and spotted the demon as it sprang over the back of the sofa.

He rolled off the side of the sofa and landed on his hands and knees on the narrow stretch of floor beside the thrift store coffee table. Connor crawled around the short side of the coffee table as fast as he could. He was halfway to his feet when the demon kicked him in the ass. He went sprawling across the floor and fell against the entertainment center. The massive flat-screen television swayed precariously above him, and Connor protected his head with his forearms, expecting the fifty-inch screen to crash down on top of him. But the television stabilized, and Connor pushed up off the floor. He felt the air shift behind him. The demon grabbed a handful of his hair and knocked him back down to his knees. A chunk of his scalp ripped free, and he swatted at the fist holding him in place.

"I should have gotten rid of you weeks ago," it whispered in his ear. He barely heard it over the rising din of the sirens. Its hot breath sent shivers of revulsion through his body. Connor struggled against the fist holding him in place, twisting and slapping at it ineffectually. It yanked his head back, exposing his throat, and he felt his scalp begin to lift away from his skull. Its legs pressed against his side as it shifted its weight, and from the corner of his eye, Connor saw it draw its free hand back, curling its claws into deadly hooks. With nothing left to lose, he plunged the twelve-inch stainless steel prongs of the carving fork into the creature's foot. The demon roared in pain and surprise and released its hold on his hair.

Connor ripped the meat fork out of its foot and twisted around, so they were facing each other. He glimpsed a flicker of fear in its remaining eye.

"Fuck you!" he screamed and thrust the fork between the creature's ribs. The prongs met with resistance, but Connor threw his weight behind it, driving it deep into the creature's chest.

The demon shrieked in pain and stepped back uncertainly. Dark, frothy liquid erupted from between its needle teeth, spraying Connor's upturned face. Connor turned his face away with a disgusted grimace and violently twisted the carving fork to the left and then back to the right, shredding the creature's internal organs. The demon half-heartedly grabbed for him before a violent tremor tore through its body, and it collapsed, crushing Connor beneath it.

The police cruiser came to an abrupt stop outside the boarding house. Its front bumper barely missed the rickety picket fence. Bremner was following up on Anna's report, determined to track down the girl in question, when the dispatcher requested that all available units report to Webster's Boarding House. Some kid had called in a domestic disturbance but had been vague on details. It didn't matter. Bremner turned on the lights and sirens and jammed his foot down on the accelerator.

The backup vehicle pulled up alongside Bremner. Chandler and Phil hopped out, joining him and Joe at the front gate. All four drew their weapons when some kid came sprinting at them from behind a parked car a few houses down. When he saw them pull their guns, he skidded to a stop and threw his hands in the air.

"Don't shoot!" he cried out, his face pinched with fear. "I live there." He nodded at the boarding house. "I'm Nathan Webster. I was the one who called you."

Bremner waved at the others, motioning for everyone to lower their guns.

"What's going on in there?" Bremner asked Nathan. "Is Jim beating on your mom again?"

Nathan slowly lowered his hands to his sides and approached the cops. "I'm not sure. My brother busted into my room and made me climb out the window. He told me to call 911."

"You don't know why he asked you to call for assistance?"

Nathan shook his head. "No, sir. Connor told me to wait at Mrs. Chapman's place until you came. I stuck around for a minute or two and heard yelling and loud crashing sounds, but I don't know if that was Dad or maybe one of the residents flipping out."

"All right. You did the right thing by calling us. We're going to go in and find out what's going on. Do you know if your brother is still inside?"

"I haven't seen him come out. Do you think he's OK? I shouldn't have left him alone in there. I'm such a gutless prick." Nathan peered up at the house.

"Nathan, I need you to wait in the back of the cruiser for me while we go inside and check on your brother."

Nathan reluctantly walked over to the SUV and opened the back door on the passenger side. "Please don't hurt my brother," he begged as he slid into the back seat and pulled the door shut behind him.

Bremner led his men up the walk and paused at the bottom of the porch steps. He turned to his men and, in a low voice, said, "We need to proceed with extreme caution. Considering the highly violent nature of the homicides, we should be prepared for any outcome. It might turn out that this Ella girl has nothing to do with any of it, but until we know otherwise, let's assume she's armed and dangerous. And remember, it's a boarding house. We don't know how many other people are inside, so be alert and keep your wits about you."

Bremner looked long and hard at Joe, conflicted about whether he should take the inexperienced officer into such a volatile situation. He was tempted to order him to remain outside with Nathan Webster, but truthfully, he was afraid of what they were walking into. The more men he had on his side, the better. Hoping he was making the right decision, he quietly mounted the porch steps and indicated for the others to follow. He pushed the front door open and stepped inside.

They paused inside the entry, waiting for their eyes to adjust to the dimly lit interior before continuing into the house.

"Hello? Connor? It's Chief Bremner with the Taylor's End Police. Is everything OK?" His voice carried along the hallway and echoed throughout the house, but he received no response. The place was as quiet as a mausoleum. The tread of their boots, thudding against the floorboards, sounded like a herd of cattle stampeding down the hallway of this deathly silent house.

The smell hit them before they had even reached the door to Jim's office. Joe wrinkled his nose and turned his face away from the offensive odor.

"What the heck is that smell?" he asked.

Bremner frowned and shared a grave look with Phil and Chandler. "That smell is bad news."

"So is that," Phil added, pointing at the wrecked banister lying in a splintered jumble on the floor. Bremner's eyes fell on the figure lying at the base of the stairs. He rushed over and squatted beside Jim's body. Although it was obvious the man was dead, he went ahead and checked for a pulse anyway.

"Are those his guts strewn everywhere like silly string?" Joe asked. He clapped a hand over his mouth.

Bremner nodded slowly. "He's dead. I can't even begin to guess how this happened, but I think we need to assume that whoever is responsible could still be in the house."

There was a thump somewhere overhead. Chandler and Phil raised their weapons in unison and looked up at the second story landing for movement. It was difficult to see anything from their position on the ground floor. Bremner mounted the stairs, careful to skirt around the bloody trail of viscera.

When he reached the second floor, a timid voice called out. "Connor, is that you?"

"No. It's the police. Identify yourself." Bremner crossed the landing and gave the men's bathroom a cursory examination before stepping over to the closed door beside it.

"Are you really a police officer?"

"Yes. I'm Chief Bremner. I need to know who I'm talking to."

There was a brief pause. "My name is Thomas Wilson. I have a room here at the boarding house."

"OK, Thomas, do you have a weapon in there with you?"

"No, sir. I'm unarmed."

Bremner stepped back from the door and raised his weapon. "Thomas, I need you to open the door very slowly and step out of the bathroom with your hands raised."

The lock clicked, and Thomas opened the door. He squeezed through the narrow gap with a grimace. Bremner stepped over to the frightened man and checked that he wasn't concealing a weapon on his person. He discovered the bite on his back. The wound looked nasty, but the bleeding appeared to have slowed. It had to hurt like hell, but it was by no means life-threatening.

"Can you tell me what happened here? Who hurt you?"

With his hands still raised above his head, Thomas answered, "I don't know for sure. It looked a bit like the young girl staying in the room upstairs, but somehow all twisted and different. I can't explain it any better than that. It tried to kill me, but Connor distracted it. Have you seen Connor? Is he all right?"

"You can lower your hands now," Bremner told him, and Thomas winced as he dropped his arms to his sides.

"We haven't located Connor yet," Bremner said, waving Chandler over. Chandler joined them after hastily climbing the attic stairs to check Ella's room.

"She's not upstairs."

Bremner nodded. "Check the rooms down the hall, then escort Mr. Wilson downstairs." He turned to Thomas and said, "Mr. Wilson, Officer Chandler will take you outside to wait for the paramedics while we search the remainder of the property. Do you think you'll make it downstairs all right?"

"I'll make it."

"Good job." Bremner led him over to the staircase, where they waited for Chandler.

Downstairs, Joe stood with one hand resting on the butt of his gun. The idea of some drifter being responsible for the violence made sense. Still, Joe thought it was a bit of a stretch to think this Ella character was responsible for killing a group of people, some of whom outweighed her by at least fifty pounds, in some cases considerably more.

Listening to Bremner and Chandler moving around upstairs, Joe felt compelled to do something more meaningful than standing around guarding a body while the others did the real work. Although he was new to the force, he had earned his badge and was proficient with a firearm. Determined to prove his worth, Joe abandoned his post by Jim's body and went in search of Ella.

Phil cracked open the door to the basement and flipped the light switch before disappearing down the stairs. With Chandler and Chief Bremner upstairs and Phil checking out the basement, it was up to Joe to investigate the apartment at the rear of the house.

Before he could overthink the situation and wuss out, Joe turned the handle and let himself into the apartment. Broken glass crunched under his feet, and he raised his weapon in readiness as he stepped over the broken vase.

"Holy crap!" he yelled. His eyes fell on the vaguely human lump on the floor in front of the flat-screen television. As he inched closer to it, he was able to discern the outline of an arm, legs tangled together, and what appeared to be the back of a head, the hair long and matted with blood.

"Chief!" he called out. "You'd better come and see this!" Joe crouched down to get a better look. It was no good. He was unable to distinguish anything beyond the likelihood of one being male and the other female, and that was just an assumption based on their clothing.

He placed his gun in its hip holster and reached for the body on top. He knew he should wait for Bremner, but one of them might still be alive. Joe grabbed the body by the shoulders and tried to roll it over, but the dead weight refused to budge. He slipped in the blackish sludge coating the floor around the bodies. After adjusting his stance and anchoring his feet, he took hold under the armpits and managed to roll the body off the other and onto the floor beside him. As he did, it reached up and snatched a handful of his jacket.

Startled, Joe cried out. It pulled him closer to its distorted features. He struggled against the creature as it dragged him down but even injured as it was, Joe was no match for its strength. It spread its jaws wide open, and Joe braced himself for a savage mauling. Instead, a thick dark fog drifted from the demon's open mouth into his own. He gagged and clawed at his neck as his throat and nostrils filled with the strange substance. It felt like cotton candy was clogging his airways, and he thought he was going to suffocate right there in the Webster's crummy living room. Then, right when his vision began to fade into blackness, the demon's hands dropped away. The feverish light in its single hellish eye extinguished like a snuffed candle.

Joe took a couple of rasping breaths before slowly rising to his feet and straightening his uniform. He bent down to retrieve his hat, smoothed his hair back, and placed it on his head. He stood for a moment, appraising the bodies on the floor at his feet, a nasty smile twisting his mouth. With a dismissive shrug, he turned away from the bloody pair and headed for the door.

Bremner was on his way downstairs when he spotted Joe beating a hasty retreat from the boarding house.

"Hey, Joe. Is everything alright?" he called as he descended the stairs.

Joe continued down the hall toward the front door and raised his hand. "Yes, sir. Everything is just peachy, thank you."

Puzzled by Joe's odd behavior, Bremner considered going after him, but he was already severely lacking manpower. Hopefully, Chandler would calm the kid down if he was freaking out over seeing Jim Webster's guts strewn all over the stairs. He'd reached the threshold to the apartment when he heard the cruiser's engine roar to life, followed by the squeal of tires. What the hell was going on out there? Surely Chandler hadn't let the rookie drive off when they were right in the middle of a multi-homicide? He spotted the bodies on the living room floor and dismissed all thoughts about Joe. For now, he had more pressing matters to deal with.

He approached the two figures lying on the floor. One of them was Connor Webster. The other body wasn't so easy to identify. It wasn't until he crouched beside her that he decided it was probably the girl they had come to take in for questioning. As he examined her beaten body, the face cut and bruised and almost unrecognizable, it was difficult to reconcile the attractive, waifish young woman Anna had described with the weathered ruin of humanity lying dead at his feet.

With one eye cruelly gouged out and what appeared to be a large carving fork jutting from her chest, he wondered if such a frail and broken person could be responsible for the spate of murders in Taylor's End.

Unable to do anything for the dead girl, Bremner turned his attention to the boy lying beside her. Awash with guilt, he was excruciatingly aware that his failure to piece it together sooner had resulted in most of the Webster family being wiped out in a single murderous rampage. Before he had even reached out to check for a pulse, he saw Connor's eyeballs rolling around beneath the thin tissue of his closed eyelids. Bremner dropped to his knees beside the boy and gently nudged his shoulder. "Connor? Connor, can you hear me? It's Chief Bremner. Wake up. You're safe now."

Connor groaned, and his eyes fluttered open. "Am I dead?" he croaked uncertainly.

Bremner shook his head and smiled. "No, Connor. You're not dead."

Connor tried to sit up. He made it to his elbows and groaned. "Maybe that's not such a good idea. The room is starting to spin out of focus," he said and sank back down.

"Take it easy." Bremner placed a hand on his arm. "Just lie down until the paramedics arrive. They're not far away. Can you tell me what happened here?"

Connor glanced across at Ella, his body taut with anxiety. When he realized she was no longer a threat, he let out a loud sigh, all the tension draining from his body. "As long as you get the paramedics to give me the good stuff. I feel like I had the shit beaten out of me."

"You *look* like you had the shit beaten out of you," Bremner agreed. "What happened?"

"She went berserk and killed my mom. Then Jim went to find out what was going on, and she killed him too. I got my brother out of the house, and then I went upstairs to fuck her up. We fought, and she nearly ended me the way she ended Todd and my mom, but I guess I got her instead." He managed a small smile. "She is dead, isn't she?"

Approaching sirens wailed outside. "Yeah, the girl is dead. You did a good thing, protecting your brother the way you did." Bremner excused himself, walked over to the door to the apartment, and beckoned to a group of officers. They were followed shortly by the paramedics. "Wait with the boy and get someone to secure the scene while I step outside for a minute."

He joined Chandler beside the ambulance, where he was waiting with Thomas, who was sitting on a stretcher with a large square bandage on his back. They walked away from the ambulance so they couldn't be overheard, and Bremner asked, "What the hell happened to Joe? He up and left the house without so much as a backward glance."

Chandler frowned. "I have no idea what got into him. He asked for the keys to my patrol car, which I thought was kind of weird, but he told me you instructed him to go back to the station, so I handed them over. He had this strange expression on his face, now that I think about it. His eyes were all hard and angry. You know Joe; he's always smiling and happy. It seemed really out of character, even for someone who just walked into something as brutal as that."

"Yeah, that doesn't sound like Joe at all," Bremner agreed.

The paramedics came down the path, wheeling Connor out on a stretcher, and Nathan ran over to hug his brother.

"I thought you were dead," Nathan said, sobbing.

Connor grinned, reached out, and squeezed his brother's hand. "Fuck no. It takes more than some rabid nutcase to take me down."

ABOUT THE AUTHOR

Naomi H Brown is an Australian writer who lives in a crumbling cottage with a sprawling back garden. She is run ragged by three demanding cats and a fluffy black pom-pom that may or may not be a dog.

She enjoys curling up by the fire with a cup of Earl Grey tea, or if she is feeling naughty, a vodka lime and soda (easy on the lime and soda), Netflix binges, bumblebees and Josh Homme from QOTSA.

When she isn't working on her latest book, she can be found rescuing unwanted furniture from the side of the road and giving it a makeover with a little bit of imagination and lashings of paint.

Discover more at www.naomihbrown.com

ALSO BY

Reign of Flesh

Mechanical wasps have taken over the skies, reducing humans to fleshy confetti and buildings to smoldering rubble. Jess, a young woman burdened with the responsibility of raising her 12-year-old sister Sasha, is suddenly thrust into a brutal fight for survival as she attempts to flee the city.

Dodging killer drones and marauding gangs, Jess is forced to face her darker instincts while becoming a beacon of hope to a group of misfits she and her sister meet along the way.

The rules have changed. The old way of life is dead. Sometimes it's a choice of kill or be killed. Sometimes an unlikely hero emerges from amongst the carnage.